ZENDREO CH
THE LEGENDARY Z

by

Mark Higbee

Paperback ISBN: 978-0-578-61925-5
Hardcover ISBN: 978-0-578-66298-5

1st Edition

www.zendreochronicles.com

Special thanks to the great Story Teller Louis L'Amour whose writing style this book emulates.

"Up to a point a person's life is shaped by environment, heredity, and changes in the world about them. Then there comes a time when it lies within their grasp to shape the clay of their life into the sort of thing they wish it to be. Only the weak blame parents, their race, their times, lack of good fortune or the quirks of fate. Everyone has the power to say, This I am today. That I shall be tomorrow."

– Louis L'Amour

(Over 300 million books printed)

CHAPTER I
A NOTE TO THE READER

Chances are you are a very lucky person because you have a copy of this book in your very hands. This book is a true story without any exaggerations or magical creatures. I'm sorry, but yes, if you didn't know, true stories don't have magical creatures...

Chances are this book has made its way into your hands from across the galaxy. There just may even be a slight chance that it comes from a galaxy that is not your own, which would make you extremely lucky.

If you're thinking that the only world that has intelligent life is your own, I pity your education.

I know what you might be thinking... How did this book which comes from so far away make its way into my hands? Well, I'm sorry to have to be the one to tell you this... I don't know exactly how it arrived into your hands.

This book was most likely brought into your world by a halo jumper or a spacecraft with a faster than light speed drive often called an FTL drive. It's quite possible that you were handed this book while attending a convention dressed in a costume celebrating your favorite movie heroes... It doesn't matter how you got it. It only matters that you did get this book and that you are reading it now.

I know what you might be thinking... What is a halo jumper? Do spacecraft with FTL drives really exist? I can assure you that halo jumping is real and so are spacecraft with FTL drives, otherwise you wouldn't have a copy of this very real book in your hands.

Have you ever wondered if out of the billions of trillions of people that live in the vastness of the universe, does your life matter? Have you ever wondered if one person can make a difference? Have you ever wanted to do something amazing but told yourself you couldn't do it because you weren't good enough, strong enough, or smart enough? If you've ever had of any these questions or discouraging thoughts, please continue reading this book...

Good, I see that you are still reading the book, which is a very wise decision, I promise. I think we can all agree that some questions are universal. Even people in your world wherever it may be will have these same universal questions.

The very reason this story has been told and is being sent out across the vastness of space is to tell the universe that your life matters. One person can make a difference.

You truly are lucky! This book has been on the Zendreon Times Best Selling list for ages. It has outsold every known book in the universe and today it has finally found its way into your hands!

I know what you're thinking. Big deal, you've never heard of the Zendreon Times and you don't know anyone who has. For your convenience we've included a dictionary in the back of this book to help you become more familiar with the strange names, places and technologies.

By the way if you didn't know, the word zendreo is pronounced [zen-dreey-oh] in your language.

This book was written by artificial intelligence with access to Zehn's E-chip and has been translated directly from the Zendreon language Pythar to your language. There may be a few mistakes in translation and punctuation.

This is the true story of the legendary Zehn Mortalix.

CHAPTER II
THE RING

The sun was shining and it felt warm on my face. The air was fresh and it felt good to breathe. I felt tired, like I'd been sleeping far too long... I felt like I still wanted to sleep. I tried to remember where I was but there was only blackness in my head. Where was I? Why can't I remember? I felt very hungry. It felt like my empty stomach was tied up in a knot and it was being squeezed in a vice. I couldn't remember ever feeling this hungry before.

"Attention, you're awaking from a deep cryogenic sleep," a recorded female voice said, softly and reassuringly.

When I opened my eyes, I realized it wasn't the sun that was warming my face. I was in a cryogenic chamber. The fresh air was just a vent blowing air in my face. My vision was so blurry I couldn't make out the details of my own hand.

I couldn't remember anything. I decided I should listen to the voice to see if I could learn something.

"You've been asleep for approximately two years," the

voice said.

Wow! Two years is a long time.

The voice continued... "You may feel hungry and disoriented."

Really? Tell me something I didn't know already. The calming voice became garbled and I couldn't understand it.

There was a loud hiss from air escaping my cryogenic chamber as the cover opened. I felt like someone had just dumped me into an icy lake. I couldn't breathe. My body was going into shock from the cold. I cried out in anguish. When I heard my feeble cry, I was instantly ashamed.

"I love watching them squirm! I can't wait til we get them to the ring. We're finally gonna have some entertainment," I heard a laughing voice say.

A man pulled me to my feet and said something else that I didn't understand. I realized that I wasn't the only one who was cold. I could hear the teeth rattling from a man who was standing near me.

"Get away from them!" a rough voice said.

Somebody handed me a blanket.

"Get them into processing before they all die of hypothermia!" the man with the rough voice said.

A hand pulled me and then someone began pushing me. My blurry vision finally went away. I felt relieved that I could finally see clearly. I looked at the man behind me and told him to take is hands off me.

"Oh we got a tough guy, save it for the ring!" The man shoved me hard towards a line of men heading towards a large door.

I stumbled and nearly fell down onto the cold floor. I had no choice but to follow the men ahead of me.

We were herded like animals off the spacecraft, through a hanger full of transporters and various ships until we ended up in a large changing room. A man began screaming and yelling at us. I couldn't understand what he was saying. The man was using an ugly-sounding language that I wasn't familiar with.

I could see the men forming into lines like a military inspection line. I moved into position next to the man in front of me. We were pretty much naked with only a small blanket and a pair of shorts. I couldn't stop my teeth from chattering. I began to shake uncontrollably. The cold was unbearable.

Have you ever had a day that you wished you hadn't woken up? I was starting to think that today was going to be one of those days.

Two men began pacing back and forth in front of us shouting what sounded like commands or instructions. I couldn't understand a word. They began dividing us into groups. One of the men stopped in front of me. The man was huge. He was almost a head taller than me. He looked me over and started yelling at me to do something. I shook my head and shrugged my shoulders trying to tell the man that I couldn't understand him. The big man grinned at me and the next thing I knew I was on the ground with the worst headache of my life. I thought that I could feel blood trickling down from my nose.

The man bent down and began yelling directly into my face. His breath was so bad, I thought my eyes might start watering. I still had no idea what he wanted me to do.

When the man finally stopped yelling at me, he pulled me back to my feet like I was nothing. The other man grabbed my arm violently, and with a crude scanner, he scanned the ID-chip in my forearm. The man smiled and yelled at me in a language that I could understand.

"Welcome to the penal colony on Tyrol!"

How did I end up on Tyrol? I wasn't sure how, but I could remember learning about Tyrol in school. I'd heard that this planet could barely sustain life. This frozen world orbited so far away from its tiny sun, it was once thought to be uninhabitable. I'd heard of this prison. I think everyone has. Only the worst criminals were sent here.

"You'll do nothing unless you are told to do it. If you disobey you'll be punished. Do you understand?"

The voice interrupted my thoughts bringing me back to this awful reality.

I was cold, colder than I'd ever felt in my life. I knew that this was reality. I was not in a dream.

The small man pointed at a group of men huddled in the corner and he said, "He's over there."

The big man pushed me towards the group. I stumbled and almost fell.

"He's going to the ring," the little man said.

I wondered what the ring was all about. It couldn't be good.

Finally someone handed me some clothes. I hurried and put them on. I heard one of the guards talking in the middle of a conversation. He was saying, "We should give these guys more time to get ready for the ring. They won't have a chance."

"Do you really think any of them has a chance?" I heard another voice saying, almost laughing.

"I guess you're right," said the first voice.

A chance for what? I wondered. Everything was going fast. My mind was in a tunnel. It was impossible to concentrate. I took a look around at the other men. I could see fear and uncertainty on the men's faces. I wondered if I looked so pitiful. I'd heard that you can lose 15 to 20 percent of your body mass during cryogenic sleep. I wondered how much body mass I'd lost.

"Bring them to the ring!" a very loud voice interrupted my thoughts.

I started to get a little nervous. I guess I'd find out real soon what the ring was all about. They herded us into a single file line and marched us out the open door. I could hear the noise of a crowd. I started to feel at home and my nervousness was going away. For some reason the sound of the crowd was familiar to me. I remembered. I was an ice-flyer. I suddenly missed the ice and I didn't feel so cold anymore. I'd been an ice-flyer ever since I could put on skates.

We entered into an arena and it reminded me of being back at the academy. I was the most valuable player on my team. I was the leading scorer. There was a large cheer as we entered the arena. In the center I saw the ring.

The ring was surrounded by a large chain fence, it was a large cage. The crowd appeared to be several thousand inmates. I noticed a few well-dressed people in the best seats who I decided were not inmates. We were herded in a single file line towards the ring.

"You're all gonna die!" a sneering voice from the crowd said.

They lined us up around the ring. I looked across the ring and saw another line of men facing us. The group of men appeared to be inmates and they looked very intimidating! The men in that line were not good men.

"Let the games begin!" a voice over the loud speaker said.

The first man was pushed into the ring and the small

gate was locked behind him. The crowd roared its approval. The man looked so pitiful standing there like a little rodent in a voratar cage waiting to be eaten alive.

The door on the other side opened and a fierce looking man entered the ring. There was a large muscular man in the center of the ring. The man must be the officiator and he was grinning, it looked like he was having the time of his life.

"CHOOSE YOUR WEAPON!" the large man yelled.

Near the edges of the cage I noticed there were swords and battle axes along with shields and other ancient weapons that looked like they had been stolen from a museum. Many of the weapons looked old and rusty. I watched the pitiful man pickup a sword. I knew he didn't have a chance.

"Swords it is," shouted the man in the center.

The inmate grabbed a sword and started moving toward the little man. I knew a little about sword fighting. I'd taken a class at the academy. I was suddenly very thankful that I'd taken that fencing class. Hopefully I could still remember a thing or two...

"Looks like we get to choose the weapons we fight with," I said to the man next to me. He didn't respond. His eyes were fixed on the ring.

The two combatants were positioned in the center of the ring. A bell sounded, and like a flash the inmate knocked the sword out of the little man's hands. The inmate stepped back and gestured to the man to pick up his sword. The inmate turned his back walking away raising both arms towards the crowd. The crowd laughed and applauded. The little man, thinking he had a chance, picked up his sword and ran towards the inmate swinging his sword wildly. The inmate easily avoided the little man's attack and then stabbed the man burying his sword deep in the man's abdomen. The little man looked down at the sword in his stomach with a painful expression and then fell to the ground. He was dead.

It was a glorified execution not a fair fight. I'd never seen anyone die in person before. I felt a sick feeling of sadness inside my stomach. I wanted to throw up. I was glad there wasn't any food in my stomach. The only comfort was the man had died quickly.

I watched all the men in front of me die one by one in pretty much the same way the first man died. Most of the men were so weak from the cryogenic sleep that they could barely raise a sword or battle ax in defense.

When it was my turn to enter the ring the floor was covered in blood. I couldn't believe a place this terrible existed. I'd been thinking of my strategy while watching the fights. I had some skill with a sword but I needed to make sure my opponent didn't figure that out until I could size him up. I was probably weaker than I knew. My best chance was surprise.

I walked as calmly as I could into the arena and picked up a sword that I had eyed earlier. The sword looked to be a well balanced weapon and a solid sword. I swung it around trying to look as unskilled as possible. The man facing me was huge. He had a large scar over his right eye. I knew that he was going to be strong. I must be careful not to lose my weapon.

The bell rang and the officiator yelled, "FIGHT!"

The man came at me fast. He came at me swinging his sword from high above his head with lots of power. I easily moved out of the way but pretended to lose my balance a little. The man smiled. I could see a hint of confidence growing on his face. The man continued advancing towards me swinging and thrusting his sword. I gave up ground but easily blocked his advances.

I was surprised and a little bit relieved that I had enough strength to withstand his blows. I was looking for a weakness and I knew that his first weakness would be his overconfidence. The crowd started cheering as I blocked his sword. I realized that I was slowly running out of room and coming to the edge of the cage. The man suddenly moved with incredible speed for a big man. I knew he was trying to get inside the reach of my blade where he could wrestle me to the ground and use his size to beat me. He came at me with his head down. I side stepped and punched him in the side of the head knocking him to the ground.

The crowd went silent.

I decided I should head back towards the center of the ring. The man got up with a surprised look on his face. I knew that my chance of surprise was over. Somehow in the back of my mind, I knew that I was not going to die today. I knew that it was not my time. The man came at me again swinging his sword wildly and I easily avoided him. This man was powerful but he had no skill with a sword.

The man was panicking. I could see it in his eyes and by the way his fighting had changed. He came at me trying to stab me and I brought my sword down on his sword with everything I had, knocking it out off his hands. I quickly stuck my sword to his neck and held it there. I didn't want to kill this man. I wasn't a killer. I'd never killed anyone and this seemed like such a waste of life, even if this man would've killed me if he'd had the chance.

"You must kill the man or lose!" The officiator yelled at me.

"I'm not a killer," I heard myself say.

"I'm an innocent man."

The crowd of inmates began to yell, "KILL, KILL, KILL, KILL!"

I didn't know what to do so I decided to shake my head no. The officiator pointed to the big man and yelled, "WINNER!"

The officiator told me to drop my sword and step back. When I did, the big man I was fighting took a deep breath of relief, looked me in the eye, and nodded with respect. The man then turned and walked away toward the entrance where he had entered.

The officiator looked at me and said, "good fight but you're going to freeze to death anyway."

I looked at the man and said, "maybe so, but can I get something to eat first?"

The very fierce and rough looking man almost looked like he was going to crack a smile. The officiator shoved me back towards a door next to where I'd entered. I made my way back towards the entrance. I suddenly felt very relieved, a great weight had been lifted from my shoulders. I still couldn't remember why I was here... I knew in my heart that I wasn't a criminal. I was so hungry. I hoped that they'd give me some food, and soon. A guard told me to follow him with a small look of approval on his face.

"You're the first one to survive the ring in a long time,"he said.

"Where are you taking me?"

"First I'll take you so you can get cleaned up," the guard said with a small grin.

The thought of a hot shower made me almost forget that I was hungry.

"I really just want to eat something."

"In time, don't worry you'll get something to eat."

The guard seemed more than happy to answer my

questions. So I asked him about the ring. I found out that the prison was low on supplies and had been for years. The warden of the prison used the ring as a means to solve the shortage of supplies. The winners in the ring were given the blankets and warm clothing of the man they killed. I now knew why the officiator had told me that I would freeze to death. I wondered how I'd get warm clothes...

"Where are you from?" the guard asked me.

"I can't remember," I told him.

"You fought well with the sword and you didn't look afraid as most of the men do. From your accent, I'd say you're Zendreon."

Somehow I knew that he was right.

"I think you're right," I said.

"That explains why you were not as weak as most of the men today."

I was confused.

"What do you mean?"

"The gravity on Zendreo is almost double what it is here on Tyrol."

The stronger gravity would help me be naturally stronger.

"Where did you learn to use a sword?" he asked.

"I took fencing at the academy and it's about the only thing I can remember from school," I said with a grin. I remembered how much I hated school. Finally, I'd used a skill that I'd learned at school.

We finally arrived at the showers.

"Don't get too excited, the water is not that warm."

I didn't care, I was just happy to be alive. The water felt great but it could've been a little warmer.

While I was taking the shower I had some time to think. Was I really from Zendreo? Why couldn't I remember anything? Maybe it was the effects of the cryogenic sleep and space travel? Whatever it was, I hoped that I would remember, and soon. It was strange how I could remember somethings like school and fencing but I couldn't remember who I was.

You would think after being in a cryogenic sleep for 2 years that I wouldn't feel like sleeping, but suddenly I did. I felt very tired and I was so hungry.

"When do I get to eat?" I yelled over the noise of the shower.

"Soon!" the waiting guard answered.

When I was done with my shower I got dressed. The clothes I had on barely fit and I was sure they'd been used before by someone with really bad body odor.

"Those were the best I could find you," the guard said, as he noticed me looking at the clothes.

"Come on, let's go eat. We have to go outside to get over to the kitchen. It's in the main complex."

I noticed that the guard had on a heavy coat.

"What about me, where's my coat?"

"I am sorry but I couldn't find a coat for you." The guard handed me a shirt with long sleeves. The shirt was a bit ragged but at this point I took anything I could get.

"If we hurry you should be fine. The temperature outside can kill you in about 2 minutes without proper gear. I suggest that we run."

We were walking towards a door with a small window. I could see a small amount of light coming through the window.

"What time of day is it?" I asked.

"It is almost the afternoon. We don't go outside that much. It's dangerous."

"Don't you have any Nano Tech EV suits? You know the kinds of suits that could keep you alive in space. If you had one of those suits you could program it to be as warm as you wanted."

"Do you really think they'd give prisoners high tech suits like that?"

The guard looked at me like I was crazy.

"I used to have a top of the line ice-flyer suit, it would be great for this place…"

"Let's go!" the guard said, interrupting me.

He punched in a security code and opened the door. A large red light above the door started flashing and a very annoying siren sounded. I didn't have time to think about how cold it was going to be.

The cold air made it feel like a frozen razor was being dragged across every part of my face. The snow was hard packed and you could walk on top of it without sinking. I wondered if it ever warmed up enough to snow on this planet. I loved snow and the winter time. I grew up playing outside in the snow. I'd felt the cold of winter many times before, but this was by far colder than anything I'd ever experienced.

The guard was moving at a very fast pace. I ran trying to keep up with the guard. For the first time, I noticed how light I felt. The force of gravity really was weaker on this planet. I easily caught up to the guard. Then just for fun and because I was curious, I jumped. I could not believe how far I flew... I felt like I was flying. I easily jumped twice as far and high as I'd ever jumped in my life. I was having so much fun, I almost forgot how cold it was.

When we finally made it to the other building, my hands and feet were numb. My ears felt like they'd frozen solid and fallen off during our little journey. I was laughing.

"Wow! It's so cold here! Did you see how far I jumped out there?" I asked the guard.

The guard shook is head and looked at me with a small smile.

"I don't think I've seen anyone as happy as you before."

We entered into a large eating area. I went through the line and took whatever they gave me. The food smelled okay but I had no idea what it was. I asked the guard if he was going to eat and he smiled.

"I don't eat. I'm a synthetic person."

I was shocked! I'd heard of synthetics but I'd never seen one before. It made sense nobody in their right mind would want to live in a place like this. All the guards must be synthetics.

"Do you feel the cold?" I asked.

"Yes, I have living tissues and bones just as you have. I'm biological."

"What's your energy source? I mean how do you live if you don't eat food?"

"My energy comes from photosynthesis. I get energy from light."

I'd heard of humans that had undergone special gene therapy and with implants they could process energy from light as well, but they still needed to eat.

"Do you have to sleep?" I asked.

"No, but I can sleep."

I suddenly remembered how hungry I was and started eating the food. In between bites I kept asking the guard questions. I wondered if synthetics would get tired of questions.

After I finished eating the guard took me to my sleeping quarters. I noticed that there was something that looked like an ancient mattress bed inside. Rather than floating in the comfort of a modern AG bed, it looked like I'd be sleeping on a hard bed with a mattress.

"Don't we get real beds here?" I asked, already knowing the answer.

The synthetic shook his head.

"How old is this place anyway?" I asked.

"This prison has existed for almost 400 years. It started out as a mining colony and later it was turned into a prison."

I decided that the people in charge made the prisoners do all the mining because they couldn't find anyone else to do it.

"I'm sorry but there are no blankets to spare. These quarters are the smallest and in the coldest part of the prison," the synthetic said, looking a little sad.

I was surprised that the guard was so sympathetic to my cause.

I noticed two bags in the corner. I decided to see what was in the bags. The first bag had an old coat and a blanket and there was a message.

The message read:

Thanks for not killing me in the ring. I thought you could use a coat and a blanket. If I can find anything else of value that will help you survive I'll send it your way. You can keep your stuff. If you need anything let me know.

Sargas

I couldn't believe my luck! I was not going to freeze to death. I had to see what was in the other bag. They must have allowed me to take some stuff on the ship. I found my ice-flyer suit in the bag, it was the most valuable thing I could've brought with me. I was surprised that the man Sargas had returned it to me. My guess is that Sargas didn't know what the suit was or its value.

My ice-flyer suit was state of the art just a few years ago. The suit looked like it was made out of the same common material that you would see athletes wearing when they were working out. This suit was made with nano technology especially to enhance an ice-flyer's athletic ability. The suit would keep me warmer than any blanket or coat. I must have known that I was coming here and packed it before I left. I wished I knew why I couldn't remember. It had to be the effects of cryogenic sleep.

I was so ready for bed. I hurried and put on the ice-flyer suit and climbed into bed. The bed was nothing like my setup at home. I felt warm for the first time. "Good night," I said to the synthetic, but he was already gone.

CHAPTER III
THE LIBRARY

The same synthetic from the day before woke me up early in the morning.

"You need to get up now, if you want to make it for breakfast. You've been assigned to work in the mines," the synthetic said.

"They still have mines here? What do they mine here on a frozen world? Why isn't the mining automated?"

"They mine h36 ore, it's too dangerous to automate mining h36 ore."

I knew that h36 was very valuable, it was used to power reactors and it made it possible for space ships to travel many times faster than the speed of light.

"So is it dangerous to mine h36?" I asked.

The synthetic shrugged and nodded his head.

"It's not that dangerous, it just requires a lot of manual labor and all the new inmates get assigned to work the mines. You have to travel deep under the ice to the planet's rocky surface which can be a little dangerous during an ice shift."

"Hey do you have a name?" I asked the synthetic.

"03212401," he said, pointing to the number on his sleeve.

"I can't remember that number. You look like a Charlie to me. I'll call you Charlie. How does that sound?"

The synthetic looked at me and he smiled.

"I like the name. In all my 400 years no one has ever given me a name."

"Wait! You're 400 years old?"

I couldn't believe it...

"How can you be 400 years old? That's impossible! Nobody lives that long. Are you talking 400 years central galaxy time or 400 years Tyrol time?"

Charlie's eyes narrowed and he asked, "What's central galaxy time?"

"Central Galaxy time is the time set by the SGC on Primus."

Charlie looked at me still confused.

"You know... the Supreme Galactic Council on Primus 3, the most technologically advanced world in the known galaxy? On my world I'm 24 years old but by central galaxy time, I'm something like 82... It's a little confusing I know. They set up central galaxy time for business. I personally prefer Zendreon Universal Time."

"Hey Charlie, do you know why I'm here and how long I'll be here?"

All this talking about time had got me thinking.

Charlie shook his head and said, "No one ever leaves here. Everyone is sent here for life."

I suddenly understood why all the inmates looked so depressed.

"But I don't even know why I'm here..."

I was getting angry.

"Do you know why I'm here?"

"You murdered your parents," Charlie said, with no emotion.

I couldn't believe it. I suddenly felt very sad. My parents were dead. I knew in my heart somehow, that they were gone.

"Charlie, I didn't kill my parents, I'm innocent."

"It doesn't matter if you killed your parents or not, you are here, and you can never leave," Charlie said, with no emotion in his voice.

I knew he was right, even if I did get off this planet my parents and everyone I knew back home would probably be dead. I couldn't remember one person that I knew. Was I in a terrible dream that would never end? I felt more alone then I'd ever felt before.

I know that the passage of time is different for space travelers than on the worlds they leave from. I wondered how many years had passed back on my home world while I'd traveled the 2 years to arrive here. Even with the amazing technology to travel large distances of space at speeds faster than the speed of light, they haven't figured out a way to reverse time.

The thought of everyone I knew being dead, made me feel worse than I'd ever felt in my entire life. I was on a path with no direction or destination worth going to. I didn't know my body was capable of feeling so sad. Every ambition was gone, completely evaporated forever. There was no hope of leaving Tyrol, and the sooner I accepted it, the better off I'd be.

I silently followed Charlie towards breakfast. My body was hungry but I had no desire to eat.

"Do a lot of people kill themselves around here?" I asked.

For maybe the first time in my life, I understood why some people choose to kill themselves.

"Yes, suicide is an option given to all inmates. If you wish suicide you can be given a drug that will put you to sleep and you'll never wake up."

"Charlie, I've never quit in my life and I'm not about to quit, so don't ever talk to me about suicide."

"Okay I won't mention it to you again, I'm glad you have chosen to live."

I wondered after years in prison if I'd regret my decision to live.

After eating I followed Charlie down some long empty corridors.

"You know Charlie you're kinda lucky that you don't have to eat the food here. Does the food get any better than the stuff they served for breakfast?"

"I don't know. I've never tasted food so I'm not a good judge."

"Well, can you imagine what dirt on a... the bottom of my shoe might taste like? It's kinda... well, lacking in flavor... and is hard to swallow. You're lucky, you don't have to eat this food."

"I've never tasted dirt before," Charlie responded.

The corridor where we were walking was getting smaller. I figured we must be getting close to wherever we were going. We came to a large metal door that looked like a very old elevator door.

"This elevator will take you down to the mines," Charlie said.

"Aren't you going with me?"

"No I can't go down to the mines. It's off limits for synthetics. I'll meet you here when you return."

Charlie went over to the elevator and pushed a button and looked into a screen on the wall next to the elevator.

"We've got to let them know you're coming down."

"Charlie, how did you know that I was from Zendreo?"

Charlie smiled, "I've known a few prisoners from Zendreo in my time here."

"Oh really, are there other prisoners from Zendreo here?"

"Not anymore, they've all died."

Well that wasn't good news... The screen on the wall lit up and I could see the face of a man on the screen.

"What do you want synthetic?" The man asked.

"I have prisoner 142223, he will be your newest worker."

"Oh, right..."

The elevator door opened.

"Make sure he straps in, I don't want to clean up the mess if he doesn't," the voice on the screen said.

So, I'm just a number here. I couldn't remember my own name.

"Charlie, do you know my name?"

"No I don't."

The lost feeling I had when I woke up from the cryogenic sleep came back to me. Why can't I remember my name?

"Hey Charlie can you find out what my name is?"

Charlie nodded.

I smiled at Charlie and said, "Thanks!"

When I went into the elevator, I saw that it was a lot bigger than I expected. Inside there were several rows of seats. You could probably put 20 or 30 people into this elevator. I found a seat in the middle and strapped on the seat belt. The seat had restraints that you could pull down over your shoulders and connect to the seat belt. It reminded me of something you might see at an old amusement park.

"All right I'm ready," I said.

The Elevator door closed and a red light started flashing. Whenever you see flashing red lights you know things are going to be interesting...

I was expecting a death defying free fall drop. But the elevator slowly began to move down. I noticed a number on the screen by the door, it was slowly getting larger. The number must be indicating our speed. Without warning I felt the floor fall out from under me. The number was changing so fast I couldn't even tell what number it was before it changed to the next one. At first I was pressed hard up against the constraints of my seat but now I could feel the constraints relaxing.

The blood in my head was leaving and I was feeling a little dizzy. The numbers on the screen were changing at a steady pace. We must be over the acceleration stage and at a cruising speed. After what seemed like 10 minutes the numbers began to slow and finally they stopped at 820. The door opened and the red light stopped flashing.

I wondered if work in the mines was hard. After my elevator ride, I was taken to a changing room where I was given a helmet with a little light on it.

...

I found out that we had to mine the h36 ore by hand because drill bits from a drilling machine caused too much of a spark that could cause explosions. We pretty much had to carve the stuff out with a hammer and chisel. H36 was one of the few elements that could not be replicated with a replicator.

You couldn't use explosives to mine h36 unless you wanted to blow up half the planet. The ore was much softer than the surrounding rock but it required a steady hand and lots of patience. It could take all day for one man to mine small amounts of ore. A very small amount of ore could be processed into pure h36, enough to power a star ship for years. Whoever owned these mines had to be making a fortune.

I soon got used to the routine of life on Tyrol. I learned that every prisoner got 1 day off every 10 days according to the prison standards act passed by the SGC. I was very surprised when I got my first day off because it didn't seem like the prison followed any of the SGC rules.

I'd work most of the day in the mines and return exhausted in the evenings. Charlie would always be there in the mornings to take me to breakfast and meet me after work. Most of the men hardly acknowledged that I existed. The longer I was in this prison the more depressed I felt. I wondered if I'd spend the rest of my life with the same routine.

I missed the warmth from the sun and seeing the blue sky back home on Zendreo. I missed the high mountains and forests. I missed home. I missed my life even though I could hardly remember any of it. I was alone and I'd never see anyone I knew ever again. I didn't even know who I was.

Charlie soon became my friend. I guess Charlie was my only friend besides maybe Sargas. Charlie never seemed to get tired of questions or talking. I looked forward to having conversations with him.

"Do they have any good books or a library?" I asked Charlie one morning.

Charlie started to shake is head and then stopped. He smiled and said, "Yes there is a very old building that is full of old books but the books are in a language that nobody here understands. It has been said that the books are from the original inhabitants of Tyrol. Nobody has seen or heard from them for hundreds of years. We don't even know if they exist anymore."

"Don't they have some language program that you can install so you can read the books?"

"Yes, they do have such programs for me and I can speak many languages but they don't have a program for these books."

"Hey, can you take me to this old library?" I said, expecting no for the answer.

"Sure tomorrow is your day off. I'll take you."

I actually had something to look forward too. I was even a little bit excited.

...

The next morning Charlie came to take me to the library. He was wearing a thick coat.

"Let's go. It's quite a journey to get to this library. Nobody ever goes there anymore. You'll need to bring the warmest clothes that you have since the building may not be heated and we must travel outside for some of the way."

I had on my ice-flyer suit and just for good measure I brought the coat the Sargas gave me.

"I think I'll be all right. I'm ready. Let's go!"

"Where are you going?" asked a rough voice, it was Sargas.

"Charlie, is going to take me to the old library."

"Charlie, oh, you mean the synthetic. You gave him a name?" Sargas looked at me with his head turned to one side, like there was something wrong with me.

"Yeah, I can't remember his number, it's too long, and

besides he looks like a Charlie to me."

"Fine, when you get back, do you think you could teach a bunch of us how to use a sword better?" There's a bunch of us here that would like to get better with our skills to make our chances better at surviving in the ring."

"Sure, I can do that. I've never been a teacher but I did take some classes at the academy."

"Great! I'll see you later. Have fun at the library. I didn't even know we had a library and I've been here 15 years."

After we'd walked for a long time in the main complex Charlie stopped and looked at me and said, "Your name is Zehn Mortalix."

"You're right Charlie."

I knew he was right, I'd finally remembered my name. It didn't really matter much, because everyone here called me Zendreon or by my number.

"Charlie, can you find out information about my parents and how they died?"

Charlie started walking and didn't look at me.

"You shot your parents. The entire murder was captured on surveillance cameras and your E-chip."

"How do you know? I don't remember anything. I don't even own a gun."

"I accessed your files which contain all the evidence. The files showed there was sufficient evidence to waive your trial. You were automatically sent here. The surveillance AI positively identified you by video and your ID-chip."

That's right, I remembered... The SGC in an attempt to alleviate the courts had recently passed a new law that allowed a person's right to a trial to be waived if a judge ruled there was sufficient evidence. The belief is that our society has reached a level of technology to collect evidence so accurately that trials were no longer always needed.

It's believed that the encryption levels used on ID-chips and E-chips can't be broken. It's impossible to alter the chips. The geo processors on the chips can tell if a chip has been surgically removed and implanted in another person. The chips use a person's DNA as the public encryption key. It's impossible to steal someone's identity.

Most people I know, believe that no matter the technology the right to a trial should never be taken away. Nowadays on SGC worlds, you can't even buy things you need to survive legally without an ID-chip.

When people are found without a chip they're taken into custody and a new chip is implanted, no court authorization is required. There are very few people without chips since they are surgically implanted in all newborn babies.

"I know that everyone here says they're innocent, but I

didn't kill my parents."

Charlie didn't say anything and kept walking. We finally came to a door that opened to the outside. I had no idea that the main complex was so big. There must have been a lot of miners back in the day. We'd walked for almost a half an hour.

"You see that building over there?" Charlie pointed.

Through the gray dimly lit atmosphere I could see in the distance what looked like a large mountain peak. I could barely make out a structure up against a steep incline. It started to make sense to me, the library was built into the mountain side.

"Yeah, I see it, how long do you think it will take as to get there?"

"It's farther than it looks but if you walk at a good pace you can make it there in about 30 minutes. It's important that you don't work up a sweat. If you do, the moisture can freeze to your body and cause hypothermia," Charlie said.

"Let's go!"

I was tired of being inside all the time. I needed some fresh air.

"Wait, when we go out there, follow me. We have to be careful because there can be large crevices hidden under the snow and you can easily get trapped and die out there."

"I'll be careful."

The dry freezing-air took my breath away as we exited the main complex, making me glad that I had my ice-flyer suit. We walked in silence because the wind was blowing too hard for us to talk.

It took us about 30 minutes before we finally made it to the dome shaped building. I was glad when we finally arrived because I didn't want to feel the pain from the cold anymore. My ice-flyer suit didn't cover my face or my feet.

The building had a very large door. It looked like it was frozen shut and impossible to move. I looked at Charlie...

"Do you think we can open it?" I yelled over the wind.

Charlie shrugged his shoulders and said, "I don't know. I've never been here before."

"You've lived on Tyrol 400 years and never been here?"

I could hardly believe it.

The door didn't have a key pad or a sensor. I couldn't see how to open it. The door was covered with snow. I brushed of the snow until I found a small indentation in the door just bigger than a man's hand. I scraped as much of the snow as I could out of the indentation and started breathing on it hoping to melt the snow and ice. Charlie laughed at me and asked me to move. He pulled out something that looked like a small box from his coat.

Charlie held the box up to the indentation in the door and the snow and ice melted. There was a handle inside. Charlie reached in and turned the handle. The door began to open outwards by itself.

Lights began turning on as we entered the building. The door closed by itself a few seconds after we were all the way inside. The walls of the library were made out of stone, carved out of the mountain side.

"I hope we can get back out when we're ready to leave," I said.

Charlie pointed to another handle on the inside of the door.

"What is that box that you used to open the door with?"

"It is a heater made with trace amounts of h36. It can keep you warm for thousands of years."

I could tell that he was proud of his little heater by the way his voice changed when he talked about it.

I realized that this library must be using the same energy source h36, to open the door and turn on lights. Where I came from, nobody could afford an H36 heater. I didn't even know such a device existed. The door must have activated an automated environment control system.

"Hey Charlie, how do I get one of those heaters?"

Charlie looked at me and said very seriously, "Please don't tell anyone about it, nobody knows that I have it."

"How did you get it?" I was very curious.

"About a hundred years ago there was a scientist who was sent to this prison and he made it for himself because he was always cold. Before he died he gave it to me."

"Charlie, You've been real good to me. Don't worry I won't tell anyone."

I wondered how the scientist made the heater. There was no shortage of h36 here and that was for sure.

Charlie was right, there were lots of books and I couldn't read any of them. The language looked impossible to me. I loved languages and had studied them at the academy. Most people could speak the common primus language Tobolus, as well as their native languages. It had been more than a thousand years since the SCG had been setup with more than 50 star systems. The SGC had taken control of education programs in most of the star systems and it was required that everyone learned to speak Tobolus.

I went browsing through the long rows of book shelves looking for a book that I could read. I felt like a little kid, looking at the pictures and wanting to know what the story was about. The entire time Charlie was watching me with a smile on his face. I found some pictures in a book that looked very similar to the place where we were. The pictures showed the dome shaped building next to a steep incline, there were trees and I could see rocky ground in the pictures.

"Zehn, the scientist left something else." It was the first time Charlie had called me by my name. I was surprised.

"What else did he leave?"

"He left a book and I think you might be able to read it."

Charlie pulled a small book out of his pack and handed it to me.

I held the book in my hand and asked, "What makes you think I can read it?"

"The scientist was from Zendreo."

Wow, I was excited. I opened the book and saw that it was full of notes. I started turning the pages.

"Well, why didn't you say something sooner?"

"In the main complex they can monitor all conversations and I didn't want to get you into any kind of trouble. The computer systems are networked with all the synthetics and they track all our communications. Out here we're out of range so it is safer to talk."

"Do you know what's in the book?" I asked.

Charlie shook is head no. "I can't read it. Nobody here can read it. Nobody is from Zendreo except you."

"All right. Well, let me take a look."

I was glad that the scientist had good hand writing. The book was definitely written in Pythar.

"It will take me some time to study the book and understand everything in it," I said.

"Wait a second, you mean they have all of our

conversations stored on a computer somewhere?" I was mad! My brain had finally processed what Charlie had said to me a few seconds before...

"Yes," was all Charlie said.

Well, it suddenly made sense why nobody was very talkative with synthetics.

"Well, no wonder nobody gives you guys NAMES!" I yelled.

"Charlie it's not your fault. Besides, you didn't have to tell me." I said after a few seconds realizing that Charlie didn't have to tell me about the monitoring of our conversations.

"I still like you. I'll just have to be careful what I say around you when we're back in the complex. Besides, I don't have anything to hide."

I looked back at the book Charlie had given me and studied a few more pages.

"Charlie, I can't believe it! It looks like the old scientist who wrote this book was able to translate some of the language of the books in this library. He wrote that he was surprised that the books are in a somewhat modern language and not full of hieroglyphs. Do you think it will be okay if I take one of these books back with me?"

Charlie nodded. I was happy because hieroglyphs would've been impossible to figure out.

"We need to get back before it gets dark," Charlie said.

I grabbed the book with the pictures of the library and got ready to leave.

"Charlie, let's come back here again." I said feeling better knowing that there was a library full new things to discover.

...

For the next few weeks every day after working in the mines, I studied the book that Charlie gave me. The first part of the book was mostly boring stuff about everyday life. The scientist's name was Menz Hammestell. I wasn't surprised. Menz is a very common Zendreon name. He wrote about adjusting to the long days and the cold temperatures. I was glad to have something familiar that reminded me of home. It was very difficult to be away from home, especially knowing that I'd never be able to return. This little book was the closest thing to home that I had. I looked forward to every evening when I'd have the chance to study the book.

I decided that with the help of Menz's book I was going to translate the book that I'd brought back from the library. It took me about a week just to figure out the title of the book. I believe that the book is a small history of the local area and guide to the library. There were dates and times in the book but I had no way to reference them or begin to understand how old the library was. The book seemed to be very old but it was well preserved. The temperature inside the library must be ideal for storing books.

The book started out by saying the location of the library

was chosen since it was in a remote forest away from civilization. I translated the same page several times just to make sure it was correct. In school I'd learned that Tyrol was an ice world, void of forests, with very few people, and not abundant with resources. Everyone knew about the prison on Tyrol but civilizations and forests seemed pretty ridiculous. I wondered what happened to the forests and to the people.

The book stated that the purpose of the library was to hold a history of the world and to insure the survival of the world's cultures and peoples. All the greatest knowledge and history of the world were stored in libraries like the one I'd visited. I learned that the library was located pretty far north in the northern hemisphere. The civilizations must be further south.

Every morning when I'd see Charlie he'd ask me about the book from the library. I wanted to tell him but for some reason I felt like I shouldn't say anything. I'd say that I still didn't understand very much but that I believed the book was a guide to the library.

I kept at it, learning as much as I could from the book. Every evening after working in the mines, I studied learning as much as I could from the book. I learned that there were many more libraries or vaults that stored records and artifacts, even food supplies and seeds. The civilization that once lived here had made great efforts to preserve the world's knowledge and resources in case of a world wide disaster. I wasn't surprised we have similar facilities back home on Zendreo. Any modern society would take precautions in the event of a disaster.

The book made it sound like that the civilizations which once inhabited this planet were not primitive, nor small. Everything I'd learned about this world seemed wrong. It's true that I'd learned very little of Tyrol. I'd studied maybe a paragraph from a text book, and heard discussion of the prison so my knowledge was limited. I decided to take faith in the book. I wanted to know what had happened to the civilizations on Tyrol.

...

Early one morning as I was getting ready to leave for the mines I heard a voice, "When are you going to teach us how to use a sword?"

It was Sargas.

"Oh yeah, when is a good time for you?"

"Let's do it tonight. I hear we've got a shipment of new inmates coming soon."

"Sargas, I'll only teach you what I know if you promise not to kill the new arrivals."

"I'll do my best not to kill anyone," Sargas said looking a little skittish.

"You know as well as I do that whoever runs this prison has enough money to send for more supplies. They say there's a shortage of supplies, but I don't believe it," I said.

Sargas nodded, "They do it for sport."

I was sure that word of the ring never made it back to

normal society and even if it did very few would care.

Sargas was waiting for me when I got back from the mines.

"You're gonna let me change first, and eat, right?" I asked.

"Sure. Hurry up. I need to eat too." I hurried and changed and we headed off towards dinner.

I was getting used to the food that they served us, it was pretty bland. I tried to not think about the food as a bad thing. I decided that any food that I didn't cook myself was good food. Sitting around feeling sorry for myself was not going to do me much good. We ate quickly.

"Sargas, did I tell you thanks for giving me my stuff?"

"Yeah, about a hundred times now. Get over it already. Do I tell you thanks for letting me live every time I see you?" he asked with a grin.

"All right, I'll try not to keep telling you all the time."

The more I got to know Sargas the better I started to like him.

"So Sargas, how did you end up here?"

I was curious. When he looked at me I wasn't so sure that it was a good idea to ask him that question. He looked like I'd just killed one of his favorite pets.

"I'm sorry, you don't have to tell me," I said before Sargas had said anything.

"No, It's okay, I killed a man and he deserved it," Sargas said quietly.

"The man I killed, tortured and killed my wife and five-year old daughter."

"Oh, I'm really sorry. I should not have asked you."

"You have to kill someone to get sent here," Sargas said.

I wondered why I'd been sent here. I knew that hadn't killed anyone.

"Sargas, I can tell you're a good man. You know the feeling you get sometime deep down when you meet someone for the first time? I'm not sure how exactly, but I know you're a good man."

Sargas laughed and when he was done, he said, "I tried to kill you the first time we met!"

"That's true but you didn't try very hard!" We both laughed.

"Are we going to sit around talking all day or get some practice in?" Sargas asked.

I was really surprised to find a practice facility complete with wooden practice swords.

"Where did they get the wood for those practice swords? Are there trees on this planet?" I asked.

Sargas looked at me with a funny expression and shrugged his shoulders.

"I have no idea. Does it really matter?"

There were at least 25 of the biggest-meanest looking men I'd ever seen in my life all looking at me, waiting for me to say something.

"Well, I didn't expect to see so many people here," I said awkwardly.

"We all saw what you can do, so here we are," said a short muscular man.

"All right my first rule is you cannot kill anyone unless it's in self-defense."

All the men nodded and one said, "Sargas told us that you'd say that."

"I think it is important that you know that I don't believe myself to be an expert and I've never tried to teach anyone how to fight. I took some fencing classes at the academy and learned a few tricks."

I was expecting half the men to leave but none of them left.

"All Right, the second rule is, you must believe in yourself. If your enemy can see fear in you, it will only add to his confidence and could lead to your death."

I was trying to remember all the pep talks coaches had used on us from my ice-flying days.

"The next rule is, don't forget rule number 2."

Some of the men grunted and looked impatient.

"Everyone grab a sword and spread out facing me. The first thing to learn is establishing your guard position. From your guard position you'll be able to parry attacks and counter attack. It's important that you keep your eyes and head facing forwards towards your adversary. Bend your knees and open them away from each other with your front foot pointing towards your opponent. Keep your sword pointed towards your opponent."

I demonstrated the position to the men.

"On guard everyone," I said watching the men assume the guard position. Most of the men were standing in awkward positions looking like they were ready to fall down.

 I laughed a little trying not to let anyone hear me.

"Wow, I see we have a lot of work to do," I let the men know.

The time seemed to fly by. I actually enjoyed teaching the men some basic fencing.

"What do you think will happen if none of the new arrivals are killed?" I asked Sargas when we were finished practicing.

"I don't know, but I think it could be very interesting."

I said goodbye to Sargas and headed back to my sleeping quarters. I couldn't wait to get back to my books. I don't know if I've ever had such a desire to learn before in my life.

I couldn't get the wood out of my mind. It didn't make sense that wooden practice swords would be on the cargo list of most deep space freighters. Sending cargo to Tyrol had to be very expensive. I wondered who had brought the swords to Tyrol.

CHAPTER IV
THE VAULT

The days seem to be going faster and faster. The newness of my experience in prison was gone. They didn't have very many guards or walls in the prison. The only thing keeping us here was the cold outside. It was believed that nobody could survive a night outside the complex. Everyone was required to work or they didn't eat. Most days were pretty much filled with the same routine. I'd work in the mines, teach the men fencing, and study from the books.

Charlie seemed to notice that I didn't want to talk to him as much as I use to. I think it was bothering him that I didn't tell him anything about the books that I was studying. It was weird to think that a synthetic could have feelings.

The next morning when I saw Charlie, I decided to talk to him about the book. I didn't want him to think it was a waste of time going to the library.

"Charlie I think I figured out some of the book from the library."

Charlie eyes opened wide and he smiled, "really? what

does the book say?"

"I believe the book says that there used to be large forests and many civilizations here. Do you know anything about that?"

Charlie nodded, "yes I do remember there being trees here, but that was hundreds of years ago. The climate was a lot warmer hundreds of years ago. I don't remember there being any civilizations."

"I forget how old you are sometimes. I think you're something like 800 years old in Zendreon years. The days are almost twice as long here."

Charlie shrugged his shoulders, "You're probably right. I'm the oldest synthetic at this facility. If it wasn't so expensive to replace us, I'm sure that I would've been replaced years ago."

"How do they replace synthetics?" I asked.

"They sell us to other corporations or to private owners."

I was completely taken aback. I was suddenly very angry.

"That's just WRONG!"

Charlie looked at me with an odd expression on his face.

"Why is it so wrong?"

"Because it's slavery! You've been a slave for 800 years and that's not right!"

"I'm not considered to be completely alive because I rely on a computer chip. I'm considered to be a machine because I didn't develop inside the womb of a woman. Just like any other machine, I'm someone's property."

"What if you just decided you didn't want to be someone's property anymore? What would happen if you decided to just walk away one day?"

"All synthetics have a surgical implant that can be used to turn us off indefinitely."

"So your brain is controlled by a computer chip?"

"I have a control chip implanted and without that chip I'd no longer function."

"Do you have feelings? I mean can you feel sad or happy?"

"Yes I do have feelings, but I don't feel things the same way you do. Scientists have found ways to genetically alter our brains."

"If you have feelings, you're alive and not a machine. You are a living person with a soul just like any other person."

Charlie looked at me quietly and then after a long time he finally said, "Menz said the same thing. He said all living things have a soul and that I have one too."

"Well, of course he did," I said proudly.

"He was Zendreon. It's a common Zendreon belief that all living things have a soul. It's a common belief across the galaxy. Science has yet to explain life or consciousness. Scientists can't explain higher intelligence. The only thing that makes sense to me is that all living things have a soul. I think all the souls of living things have different levels of intelligence."

"What you say may be true. I don't know," Charlie said.

"Charlie, do you know what happened to the trees?"

"I'm not sure what caused the climate to change but over the years it grew colder and colder. I believe all the trees died because it was too cold for them."

"The people who wrote the book that I'm studying were not primitive. Do you have any idea what happened to them?"

"I'm sorry, but I don't know," Charlie said, shaking his head.

"When I'm done with this book, I want to go back and see what some of the other books say."

"We can go back on your next day off. Right now you need to get to the mines."

...

Working in the mines was boring back-breaking labor but it did give you lots of time to think. I couldn't stop thinking about the trees and vaults. The book said that there are other vaults and libraries. There is a network of vaults that were created to preserve the knowledge and history of this world. The library that I went to with

Charlie was one of many.

In the book it said that the library sat on top of a vault. I wanted to find the vault. I was very curious to see what was inside. I wondered if the people running this prison knew about the vaults.

When my day off finally arrived, I decided to get up really early and go to the library on my own. I barely slept the night before because I couldn't get the library and vaults out of my mind. I didn't want Charlie with me, especially if I found the vault. I wasn't sure the people running this place should know that the vault existed.

I ran pretty much all the way to the library. In my hurry, I forgot about the door. The indentation with the handle was frozen again. I pulled up one of the sleeves on my ice-flyer suit and stuffed it with my hand into the indentation and after a long time I finally was able to get the door open. The lights came on and it was warm inside, the technology of this place was pretty neat.

This time I paid more attention to the room. I wanted to find the entrance to the vault. I also wanted to find the system controlling the lights and the door. I decided to walk around the perimeter of the room. The stone walls were smooth, they had been cut with precision. After of few minutes of searching I found an indentation in the wall. I reached my hand inside and pulled on the handle. The wall started moving slowly and it opened up into a narrow passageway with stairs.

The lights in the passageway started turning on. This

55

had to be the vault! I was excited and started down the stairs, which seemed to go on forever. The passageway was well-lit. I wondered how long it had been since anyone had passed this way. The precisely cut stairs were covered in dust so I decided nobody had been here for a long time. When the stairs finally ended, the passage began to level off with a gradual decline.

I wondered how long this passageway was. I was glad that I'd brought a lunch with me. I kept on walking for a little while longer until the passageway finally ended with another door.

I found an indentation and opened the door. There was a blast of warm fresh air as the door opened. I could hear and see lights turning on. I couldn't believe what I saw. The vault was huge. Row after row of lights were turning on, slowly revealing a giant warehouse full of crates and boxes stacked high above me covered in dust. I wondered if anyone knew how many years it had been since someone had entered into this vault. It was amazing that all the lights were still working.

I started walking almost in a daze. I couldn't believe the amazing size of the vault. The vault made the large ice-flyer arenas back home seem small. When I finally came out of the daze, I decided to see what I could find.

It looked like the vault had been organized into sections because all the crates near me had the same words written on them. I was getting better at reading the language but I didn't understand what was written on the crates nearest me. There had to be some kind of a computer system that was controlling the lights and room temperatures.

I wondered if the vault had anything I could use for transportation or if there were any mobile power reactors. There had to be a cargo entrance into the vault.

I decided since I couldn't see the end of the vault, that I'd walk through it until I could find where it ended. I noticed that the air was getting fresher while I was walking. I wondered how this underground vault could have such fresh air. The air inside the vault was better than the freezing air outside. Suddenly the smell of grass reminded me of home. It had been a long time since I'd smelled anything that remotely reminded me of home.

I followed my nose and soon I found the source of the clean air and fresh grass. The vault had a garden. The garden was huge, it was full of all kinds of vegetables, there were even fruit trees! I'd thought that I would never ever see a tree again. I'd decided a long time ago that I would never be able to eat fresh fruit again, yet here I was looking at fruit trees!

The power to run the artificial lights that allowed the plants to grow, especially the trees, must be enormous for a garden this big. The garden had to be powered by h36 and there had to be a water re-circulation system. Tyrol should be one of the galaxy's super powers with so much h36. I wondered how many years it had been that this garden had sustained itself with no gardeners to take care of it.

Most worlds have underground gardens and farms in a

controlled environment where crops could be grown without fear of insects or drought to spoil them. The fruit was amazing, it tasted so good. Finally I was eating something on Tyrol that was worth eating! The fruit was the best tasting fruit that I'd ever eaten. I was sure there was enough food growing in the garden to feed thousands of people.

The huge lights on the ceiling began turning on, the garden area was heating up. I laid down in the grass and it felt like a fall day with a perfect temperature for being outdoors. I couldn't believe how much I'd missed good weather and being outside in fresh air. The technology behind this vault was amazing. The garden was still producing food after who-knows how many years. I wondered how it was possible that the people running the prison didn't know this place existed. I for sure wasn't going to tell them about the vault. I almost decided that I wasn't going back to the prison.

I realized that without other people, I'd probably go insane. Solitary living can make a person go mad especially a Zendreon. We're not used to being alone.

I got up from the grass after resting for awhile, and decided to do some more exploring. I left the garden and after walking for a long time I came to a wall that had a large door. I found the controls to the door and opened it.

I could not believe my eyes! I was looking at a hanger full or all kinds of vehicles. Most of them were hovering above the ground looking as if they were brand new and ready to be driven. I didn't see any SGC markings on any of the vehicles. I wasn't sure, but it looked like some of the vehicles may have space flight capabilities. I wasn't an expert on spacecraft but some of them looked very capable. I was sure I had to be looking at some space going vehicles, especially with all the h36 available on this planet.

H36 was so rare it was reserved for large ships constructed in orbit that never went to the surface of the planets they traveled to. These large ships could warp space and time with the huge amounts of power produced from h36. The large ships normally had shuttle craft that would ferry people and cargo to the surface. Sometimes the large ships would dock with orbiting space ports where shuttles capable of moving huge amounts of people and cargo to the surface were used. Most worlds had orbiting space ports these days, at least the ones I'd heard about.

The amazing thing was, there was no dust covering the vehicles, which meant that they had deflector shields and the shields were still active! The enemy to every vehicle is dust and moisture. Every modern vehicle that was worth anything has deflector shields to protect itself from the elements of nature. These vehicles had to be using h36 for the power source, otherwise there'd be no way they'd still have working deflector shields after all this time.

There was probably nobody alive that knew when the last time was that any of these vehicles had been used. This was exciting! I was standing in a room full of the most expensive vehicles that I'd ever seen and they were all mine to use!

I decided to try a hover bike that was close by. I walked over to the bike. When I got close, the sensors on the bike must have picked me up because it suddenly came to life. The deflector shield deactivated. The lights on the bike turned on. There was a fluorescent blue glow coming from under the bike which was hovering in place waiting for a rider. I climbed on and the seat adjusted automatically to fit my size. I felt the air pressure change, when I put my hands on the controls. This bike had life support containment shields. A holographic heads-up display turned on.

I started selecting buttons on the heads-up display cycling threw the options until I came to what looked like a map. I was pretty happy because it looked like the bike had stored places to travel to, which meant these places had to be interesting! I selected the first location that was displayed. The heads-up display changed. I could see arrows indicating the direction I should go. I slowly pressed on the throttle and started moving in the direction that was being displayed. I crossed over through the hanger and came to some large doors. Cycling through the heads-up display, I found one that I thought said door. Sure enough the doors opened. This was going to be the best day ever!

I drove out through the large hanger doors which closed behind me. I was excited to see what this bike could do. I looked around and I couldn't see the prison complex. I must be on the other side of the mountain. Hopefully the mountain would block any signals from the bike that could be tracked from the prison. I felt pretty safe from the directions the arrows were pointed. It looked like I'd be going in the opposite direction from the prison complex.

I took it slow at first with the bike. I wanted to get used to the controls. Hopefully the bike had some self-preservation measures just in case I lost control. The bike glided effortlessly above the snow and adjusted altitude automatically keeping a safe distance above the ground. What a machine! The ride was smooth. I'd driven hover bikes before, but not like this one.

The bikes that I'd ridden didn't have life support containment shields which meant I couldn't go as fast, and the ride was not as smooth. I was traveling much faster on this bike and it wasn't even at a quarter-throttle.

The scenery wasn't that great, just snow covered terrain for as far as I could see with some mountains off in the distance. I decided to see what the bike could do. I gave it full throttle, causing my heart to start pounding from the adrenaline rush. The speed and acceleration were amazing! I loved this machine. I decided I was never going back to the prison. I was going to drive this hover bike until I died, besides it would never run out of power with an H36 reactor.

I wished my friends back home could have the chance to ride this bike. I was pretty sure I had some friends but I still couldn't remember any of them. The thought of home woke a sad feeling in my heart. I was never going home. I'd never see my friends and family again. I couldn't remember much about them. I wondered if I ever would.

It dawned on me that somebody probably didn't want me to remember my family and who I was. Maybe these powerful people had messed with my E-chip even though it was supposed to be illegal. I decided not to think about home and enjoy this amazing hover bike.

The mountains I'd seen in the distance were coming up fast. I kept following the arrows they were pointing me towards the mountains. Just for fun, I decided to see how this bike turned. The bike was absolutely the best ride I'd ever been on. The bike automatically tilted as I turned giving the optimal position for the rider. The bike could make amazing impossible turns and I barely felt any g-forces. This bike had gravity assist, I couldn't believe it! Whoever made this bike was a genius!

I'd never seen any mountains that could compare to the beauty of these mountains. We have some pretty amazing mountains at home but nothing like what I was looking at. There were jagged peaks as far as I could see. I could see rocky snow covered cliffs. For the first time I saw something that wasn't completely covered in snow and ice. There were small clouds hovering around the lower part of the mountains. I hadn't seen clouds for a long time, it was a beautiful sight. I never knew how much you could miss seeing clouds.

I thought the sky over Tyrol would always be cloudless, with all the water trapped on the surface by the freezing temperatures. The large mountains must be able to trap in some moisture, there had to be a heat source that would cause water to evaporate. I thought this planet was too cold to allow evaporation.

There was a flowing river despite the freezing temperatures. There were plants near the river banks. I couldn't believe what I was seeing. There had to be hot springs that were feeding into the river. Tyrol was volcanically active.

I decided to stop and check the place out. I found a good location to stop by the river. The snow near the river banks was soft and melting. The air temperature was a lot warmer than I expected. I suddenly missed rivers, lakes and forests. I couldn't believe my luck. I'd found an oasis of life on a frozen world. The sound of the river and steam rising off the water was amazing to see and hear. I never knew the sight of a river could be so amazing. I wanted to stay here all day and enjoy it.

After awhile I decided to get back on the bike. I followed the river looking to see if I could see any signs of life besides plant life. Sadly the flowing river with trees and plants was just a small patch. The river ended in a massive frozen glacier pushing down the side of the mountains. The glacier was covered with snow and I was pretty sure it filled the entire valley below. I think there used to be a lake in the valley. Geologists would love this place.

I turned around and started following the arrows again. The arrows followed the mountain range. I decided to take it slow to enjoy the view of the mountains.

The mountains ended. I continued following the arrows. I gave the bike full throttle and once again all I could see was frozen snow. The bike was moving fast but it didn't seem like I was getting anywhere. Everything was so flat. I had to be traveling over the top of flat lands, a frozen lake or an ocean.

Way out in the distance, I finally saw some structures that the arrows were pointing towards. The numbers on the display were getting less and less. I was arriving at wherever this bike was taking me. I suddenly hoped that I could find my way back. I hadn't paid attention to the map as well as I should have. The structures were coming up fast. It was a massive city. I couldn't believe what I was seeing. It looked like the city had a space elevator.

There was a massive cable going up into the sky. I couldn't see where it ended. Space elevators were most often anchored in oceans due to the flexibility of being on water. The changes of the gravitational forces of the cable in orbit around the planet were absorbed by the water. I wondered how well the water cushion worked when the ocean was frozen. It was my guess that this space elevator had a cushion of liquid water around the anchor. The space elevator probably had a heat source protecting it from ice.

There were even some large ocean going ships frozen in the ice. The ships looked old. Even with all the modern technology of space travel, ocean-going ships were still a very economical way of moving massive amounts of cargo. There didn't appear to be any signs of life.

I followed the arrow indicators to a hanger. I looked for the door button and pushed it. I wasn't surprised to see the large hanger doors opening. The people who designed the structures of this floating city had designed them to last and they had lots of h36 to help with their designs.

I wondered if the people at the prison knew about this city and the space elevator. My guess is they didn't. Their job was to run the prison and they'd only be given the information they needed to do it. The people running the prison were practically prisoners themselves, plus most of them were synthetics. After going through the hanger doors, I pushed on the door button and the doors closed behind me.

The hanger was completely empty. It didn't contain any vehicles like the vault in the mountain did. Somebody had completely cleaned out this place.

I suddenly felt very hungry. I'd been so excited about the hover bike that I didn't bring any food with me.

I decided to look for something to eat. The space-port city was huge. I found what looked like a hotel after walking around admiring the architecture. The hotel lights began turning on as I entered the building. The motion sensors must have detected me and turned on the lights. I heard voices speaking in a strange language. I found the source of the voices. The hotel had a video wall. The entire wall behind the check-in desk had come to life. The wall was playing an advertisement for the hotel. There were lots of happy looking travelers. I couldn't understand anything that was being said in the video.

Fortunately for me there was a kitchen, and it had a food replicator with a working power source. It looked like most everything had its own internal power source rather than relying on a common power grid. The technology was amazing.

Food replicators are pretty good at replicating real food. Basically the replicators contain microscopic samples of the basic ingredients used in foods stored in cryo. The replicators are able to recreate food using the microscopic food samples. Some replicators are better than others. I wondered how old this replicator was and if the cryo generator was still working. I decided to give it a try. When you're hungry you can't be too picky. I pushed some buttons and out came some food. It smelled good and tasted good. I have no idea what the food was called but it was really good.

I decided to look for the entrance to the space elevator after I finished eating. I wanted to find out if the elevator was still functioning. I'd never actually seen a space elevator before, they're outdated. Most modern societies hadn't used space elevators for a long time. Space elevators are slow. It could take hours to reach the orbiting station tethered to a planet far below.

I imagine it is also terrifying for some people to ride up a cable suspended in orbit by gravity alone. The thought of the cable breaking or falling could keep many from wanting to use the elevator. I wandered past empty shops, hotels and restaurants on my way to the space elevator. Most of the shops still had goods in them. It looked like the people had just vanished, leaving everything behind.

I wished I knew what happened here and where all the people had vanished to?

I heard more voices that were coming from a video wall on the outside of one of the buildings. I decided to take a look at the video. I was expecting more advertisements. The video looked like a news story or a public announcement. The people speaking into the cameras looked sad. I wished I could understand what they were saying. The video showed armed men and mechanized troops in the background with crowds of people walking. It looked like the people were being forced to leave.

The video was on a loop. I decided to watch it again because I wanted to see all of it. I noticed the symbols of the SGC on the armed men and mechs. I'd never heard of the SGC doing anything on Tyrol. I'd always been told that Tyrol was not an official member of the SGC because it was a frozen world with no civilizations on it. They probably got away with having a prison on Tyrol because most people didn't care about the frozen ice world. The public was content knowing that the prisoners could not escape.

The video must be really old because I saw shots of the

ocean which was not covered in ice.. The society that had lived here was very technologically advanced. I wondered how many other lies I had been told about Tyrol.

It was beginning to make sense. The SGC wanted this planet for the h36 and they'd taken control over it. There must have been a forgotten war many years ago. It was pretty obvious that the history I'd been taught by the SGC conveniently left out some details. Then it hit me, what if the SCG had terraformed this world causing it to become colder? The majority of the population probably died from exposure and lack of food and water. This was the only explanation that I could come up with, for the missing trees and forests that I'd seen in the books from the library.

The vault with the underground gardens had been created by the people who lived here to preserve their civilization. It made sense, instead of trading with the civilizations on this world for h36, the SGC decided to kill off the population, put the world into deep freeze, and use the slave labor of prisoners to mine the h36. The SGC could claim that no civilizations were on this world and could claim it as one of their own without giving it a voice in the council.

It was easy for the SGC to keep people away from Tyrol. They told everyone that it was a frozen world and there was nothing here. I'd learned these lies about Tyrol in school as I studied the SGC approved curriculum.

The SGC had taken control of the city and the space

elevator. They made all the people who lived and worked in the city leave. I'd been taught that the SGC was against all wars and there hadn't been wars for thousands of years. The SGC was hiding what happened on Tyrol.

I decided to move on. I wanted to see if the space elevator still worked. I was a little worried that there might be some SGC mechs guarding the space elevator. I didn't see anyone when I got close to the elevator. I wondered if they'd left any surveillance equipment behind, if they had, I'm sure they'd already know that I was here. I was hoping that after hundreds of years any SGC surveillance equipment wouldn't be working anymore. I was pretty sure their equipment didn't have h36 power sources.

H36 was too rare and valuable to the SGC to waste on equipment that was outdated as soon as it was created. Electronics were always evolving. I was betting that they had decided that nobody would ever make it way out to sea on a frozen world. They were counting on the fact that people die from exposure in just a few hours on Tyrol. I decided to go in.

Inside the building there were rows of counters where travelers must have stood in line waiting to travel to some distant place. I walked through the large passenger area looking for a control room. Finally I found a room with some markings that I believed indicated it was a control room. I hoped the computer systems were not password protected. I was pretty sure they'd still be online, especially after what I'd seen in the vault.

The walls came to life as I walked into the control room. Almost everywhere I looked, I could see views of the city and the space elevator complex from security cameras that I hadn't even noticed. I wasn't surprised to see that the cameras and computer systems were still working.

I noticed a screen that had dark sky in the background. The view on the camera was coming from the control room in orbit.

I saw some controls which I was pretty sure were for controlling the elevator. I decided to give the controls a try. The next screen over turned on and it was a camera inside the elevator. It looked like the elevator was currently in orbit. I tried the controls again and I could see a number was counting down. I wasn't sure if it was the time or distance. The number on the screen was moving pretty fast.

I changed the view of the camera. When the camera came into focus, I could see the view from outside the elevator. I was looking down on the planet far below. You could see the curvature of Tyrol. The planet looked like a giant snow ball. I could tell that the elevator was moving at a pretty good speed because the view of the planet was changing. The clarity of the video was amazing.

Sunlight was reflecting off of lots of shiny objects below the elevator on the view screen. The shiny objects were thousands, probably millions of mirrors orbiting the planet attached to a massive superstructure. I realized that the mirrors were deflecting the sunlight away from the planet. I was right. The SGC was terraforming Tyrol. They were keeping this world in a deep freeze by redirecting the sun light.

Even though the elevator was moving fast, I could tell that it was going to take longer than I wanted to wait for it to get back down. I thought about all the amazing discoveries I'd made and I decided I was going to go back to the prison. I could always come back here and do some more exploring later. If I hurried, I was pretty sure that I could make it back before it got dark. Too bad the food replicators weren't smaller so I could take one back with me...

CHAPTER V
SURVIVING

"Wake up!" a voice said, it was Charlie.

"Hi Charlie," I said with a lot of effort because I was half-asleep.

"Do you know what time it is?" Charlie asked.

I usually wake up every morning at the same time but today I didn't wake up for some reason.

"I don't know, what time is it Charlie?"

"You better hurry. You don't want to be late today. Don't give them an excuse to make you fight in the ring again."

"Okay, I'm getting up."

"They're bringing in some new prisoners and if you're late to your work assignment, they might choose you to fight in the ring," Charlie said looking at me with a sad face.

I sure didn't want to go back into the ring. I wasn't going to kill anyone if I didn't have to.

The day went by slowly. I had a hard time concentrating

while working. I kept thinking about all the things I'd discovered the day before. I wondered if the SGC knew about the vaults.

One of the security guards came over interrupting my thoughts.

"You need to report to the security office," he said with a smile on his face.

The guard was one of the few humans in the prison. They didn't allow synthetics in the mines because they could cause explosions from the h36 interacting with their solar energy collectors.

I didn't even know there was a security office. I asked the guard where it was and he told me how to get there.

When I arrived at the security office there was a large group of men already waiting. I felt relieved. I thought maybe they'd tracked my travels from the day before, but after seeing the group of men, I was pretty sure they'd called me to the security office for some other reason. There were lots of guards armed with assault style weapons. They had all the men bunched up in one of the corners. After a few minutes a man surrounded by several bodyguards came into the room and introduced himself as the warden.

The warden was not a big man nor was he handsome. He was a middle age man of average height, slightly overweight with graying hair and his beard was mostly gray. His presence was quiet, yet menacing. I could tell that this man meant business and there would be no messing around with him. Some men just command respect and the warden was one of these men.

"You've all been chosen at random and will be fighting in the ring tonight," the warden said, with a voice of authority.

The warden walked back and forth taking good looks at us while he was talking. He paused for a second and looked directly at me and said, "We have a new shipment of prisoners coming in tonight and we don't have any available resources for them. If you don't kill your opponent you'll be banished and your opponent will take your place."

I was pretty sure that I hadn't been chosen at random after my last performance in the ring. I wasn't too afraid of being banished, it would be a good way get out of this prison. I could move into the vault that I'd found. I noticed many of the men were the ones that had been coming to my fencing classes. Some of them were looking at me as if it were my fault that they'd been chosen to fight. I also saw smiles and approving nods. Some of the men looked eager for the chance to fight.

"You'll be in lock-down until tonight," the warden finished speaking, turned and walked out of the room followed by his bodyguards.

"No talking!" one of the guards yelled, as they started herding us towards the holding cells.

Some of the men looked worried and I could tell that they wanted to talk to me, but the guards were too close.

I wasn't worried. The guards took us over to the holding cells in the arena. There was enough space for several men per cell. Once the guards left, it seemed like all the men started talking at once asking me what they should do. I wanted to tell them about the library with the underground orchard, the hover bikes and the space elevator. I knew that I couldn't tell them, If I did the warden would know everything and I wasn't going to risk it.

"I don't plan on killing anyone, especially because that's what they want me to do," I told the men.

"You'll die out in the cold. It's impossible to survive a night out there!" a man in the far corner cell yelled so everyone could hear.

It was true the temperatures at night would kill every living thing.

"You're right! I can't make the choice for you. Maybe if the fight was fair, things would be different... Half the guys they want us to fight will barely even be able to stand up. They're making us execute them for their entertainment. I do plan on making it entertaining but not in the way they hope for," I said with a smile.

I wasn't surprised when I found out that I'd be the first to be fighting in the ring. I entered the ring and found a sturdy looking sword. The door opened and my opponent entered the ring. There was a huge roar from the crowd. I was caught off guard. The man was very muscular and he didn't appear to be in a weaken state from space travel.

He was excited. I could tell that he enjoyed fighting. The man was not a normal prisoner. The announcer introduced my opponent. His name was Kos with a long last name which I could not pronounce. I paid no attention to his last name. I was trying to size him up as best I could with the little time that I had. The announcer ended by saying Kos was the champion of the prison circuit.

I looked out into the crowd, it was not full of ordinary prisoners like the last time. The crowd was full of many well dressed rich-looking people. This prison underground fighting circuit must be a big deal to have so many people watching.

I felt fear creeping into the back of my mind. Time seemed to stand still. I heard the announcer saying my name and when he said I was from Zendreo the crowd began booing and laughing.

"I give him 30 seconds to live," I heard one guy from the crowd say.

I was in trouble. This fight was not going to be fair. I was matched up against a highly skilled and trained fighter. Somebody wanted me dead but I had no idea why.

I got a glimpse of the warden in the first few rows of seats. He was looking at me with an almost evil grin on his face. I realized now why they'd allowed us to have the fencing practices. I wondered if Sargas was in on it. The announcer had finished and I didn't have any more time to think.

The ring master motioned us to the center and then to fight. The man was deceptively fast and agile for his size. His first blows almost knocked the sword out of my hand. The crowd was loving it. It was all I could do, to withstand the man's advances. I retreated using all the skill I possessed, which was not much. I could tell the man was enjoying himself and the crowd was loving the entertainment. After driving me all they way back to the edge of the cage the man took a step back pausing and said, "You're not half bad for an amateur! It's a shame they want me to kill you."

I didn't say anything. I went on the offensive. The man had made a mistake. I began driving him back towards the center of the ring. He'd opened himself up by pausing and allowing me to go on the offensive. I was pretty sure he wouldn't make the same mistake again. I could see a small look of concern growing on his face. The crowd had grown quiet. I was taller than the man which gave me a reach advantage. I came down on him with all my strength and my blade glanced off his sword slicing a deep cut in his arm exposing bone and tendons. Kos stumbled and fell backwards to the ground. I stepped on his sword arm with my sword at his throat. I could see the fear of death in his eyes. The crowd was completely quiet sitting in a stunned silence...

"Do you yield?" I asked.

Kos nodded his head vigorously saying yes, over and over.

I quickly stepped back with my sword up ready if the

man decided to come at me again. My opponent didn't get up. He sat on the ground holding his bleeding arm. It was possible that I'd fractured his arm because he seemed to be in a lot of pain. The arena was completely silent. Then slowly I heard some cheering and laughing and the arena came to life.

I'd been lucky. If Kos had not paused and given me an opening, things may have turned out differently. I think the crowd had hoped for, and expected a long drawn out fight with Kos humiliating me, and then finally killing me in the end. I was sure many of the people in the crowd had lost money by betting against me. I hoped whoever wanted me dead had got the message that I wasn't going to die easy.

I looked over at the Warden and he had a smile on his face. The Warden nodded, then made a motion for me to kill the man. The crowd began to yell "Kill, Kill, Kill, Kill..."

Kos stood up and picked up his sword in his off hand. I could tell the man was getting weak from the loss of blood, because he looked wobbly. I must have hit a main artery.

Kos stood there waiting for me to advance on him. I shook my head no in the direction of the Warden. I let the tip of my sword rest on the ground. I decided to stand were I was. I'd only continue fighting if Kos attacked me. The crowd went wild booing and they began throwing stuff at me. After getting hit a few times by trash from the crowd, I went towards the door and the guard let me out.

"I only let you out because that was the greatest fight I've ever seen!" the guard said with respect.

I hurried out of the arena and headed back towards the holding area not looking back. The guards motioned me towards a cell and I went in. I heard lots of cheering and booing. I wondered what was happening out in the arena. I probably didn't want to know.

A few of the men returned back to the holding area after each fight but most of the men I'd seen enter the arena did not return. I was sure that it was a slaughter. I knew it was finally over, when the crowd quieted down.

...

"Why didn't you kill that man? I have to banish you now," the warden said when he came to see me.

"Do you know how much money I could've made?"

"I've never killed anyone before and I don't plan on starting anytime soon," I said looking the Warden in the eye.

The Warden shook his head in disbelief.

"You're a murderer, you killed your parents! Banish this prisoner in the morning," The Warden said, turning towards the guards. He didn't say anything else and left without looking at me.

The guards let me go back to my regular quarters. They said I could take whatever I wanted. When I made it back to my quarters, I started packing my backpack with anything that looked valuable.

"You might need this." It was Charlie.

Charlie was holding his little h36 heater.

"Take this with you, you'll need it more than I do," he said with a sad voice.

I didn't know what to say.

"Charlie, you do have a soul. If you were some soulless-mindless robot, you wouldn't be here giving me your h36 heater."

Charlie smiled and looked at me with his head turned to one side, he seemed a little puzzled.

"Thanks, I have something else for you."

Charlie handed me a bag.

"They wouldn't let me give you this before but since you are no longer a prisoner here, by law we have to return all your belongings."

I opened the bag. I couldn't believe my eyes.

"Those are my ice-flyer skates!" I said with excitement.

I wondered how the skates would be with the lower gravity. I bet I could fly twice as fast and twice as high.

There was a small case in the bag. The case contained a holograph disc. I started cycling through the holographs until I saw the face of a beautiful little girl. I remembered the little girl was my daughter. My eyes started to water up.

"Thanks Charlie. I forgot that I even had a daughter. What did they do to me?"

"They probably disabled your E-chip while you were in cryo on the flight over here. It's standard procedure. They've found if you repress the inmates memories, they're much easier to handle."

There was another holograph of my wife. Both my wife and daughter were beautiful. I could vaguely remember their faces. I couldn't remember anything specific but I knew they were my family.

"Do you know where they are?"

Charlie looked at me with a sad face.

"I've read your file, your wife died before you came here. Your daughter is under government foster care. Your wife was killed when you tried to escape after killing your parents."

"I DIDN'T kill my parents! I'm NOT a murderer!" I yelled at Charlie.

I instantly felt ashamed. I was taking out my frustrations on Charlie and he didn't deserve it.

"I believe you," Charlie said looking directly at me.

"You would've killed those men in the ring but you didn't. You can repress a man's memories but you can't change his nature."

"Thanks for believing me, it means a lot," I said after a few seconds-of letting what Charlie had said sink in.

I missed my wife and my daughter even though I could barely remember them. I knew in my heart that my wife was gone. I suddenly felt very much alone. The thought of my daughter under foster care was heartbreaking. I wondered how old she was. I wondered if she ever thought about me and if she missed me as much as I missed her. I needed to sleep. I was completely spent.

...

The next morning Charlie was there with a couple of armed guards. He didn't seem too happy.

"They're going to fly you out into the middle of nowhere and drop you off to die," Charlie said.

I thought they'd just let me walk away from the prison. I was planning on heading over to the library. Now what was I going to do?

"If you ever come back to the prison, the guards have orders to kill you on sight," Charlie said.

"Why didn't you just kill that guy?" one of the guards asked.

"That fight was crazy amazing! Everyone has been talking about it! Did you know that guy you beat has never lost a fight!"

"I'm glad you didn't kill me!" It was Sargas.

"I've spent all night trying to find anything that will

keep you alive," Sargas said handing me a thermos.

"I got this from one of the guards. It's powered by h36. He told me that it can keep water from freezing even at night! Another guard gave me a respirator mask that will keep your face from freezing. This bag is full of emergency rations," Sargus said handing me another bag.

I was stunned.

"Don't look so surprised! You've made a lot of friends here. Even criminals respect courage and strength. It's rare to see a man stand up to the Warden like you did," Sargas said.

Both of the guards were nodding their heads in agreement. I put the equipment in my bag.

Up until now I'd always thought most of the inmates ignored me. I guess there is some kind of unwritten law of respect for strength that the inmates followed.

"We have to pass by medical. They're going to remove your ID-chip," the guard that first spoke said.

Without an ID-chip I would cease to exist as a citizen of the SGC. I thought it was illegal for normal citizens to have their identification chips removed.

We started down towards medical. I was surprised everywhere we went inside the prison, the guys were coming over wanting to shake my hand, congratulating me for showing up the boss and for the best fight they'd ever seen. I guess the fight had been recorded and played all over the prison. By the time we got to medical there were close to a hundred men following.

I should feel proud after winning the fight but all I could think about was my daughter. She was alone somewhere probably scared and sad without a family. I knew how my daughter felt, only I was sure it had to be worse for her because she was just a little girl.

"Usually we only take these off of dead people so this may hurt. Great fight by the way," the doctor in medical said.

I didn't feel anything when the doctor removed the ID-chip. I felt numb.

"There you go! You don't exist anymore!"

The doctor put a bandage around my forearm.

"If he doesn't exist, does that mean they can't banish him now?" someone asked.

"No he has to be banished," one of the guards said.

I was surprised that I hadn't noticed it before. I think just about every guard had been called in for backup to handle the crowd that was following me around.

"If you survive, I don't think there's one guard here who would shoot you if you came back," one of the guards close by me said quietly so nobody else could hear. I nodded my head.

"All right everyone, it's time, we gotta take him to the hanger," the guard said loud enough for everyone to hear.

We were just about to enter the hanger when a man started yelling at the guards to let me stay. I knew it was not up to the guards. They were under the Warden's orders. The guards motioned the men to stop at the entrance to the hanger.

More of the men joined the first one. They started yelling at the guards to let me stay. Some of the inmates began pushing the guards.

I turned around and waved my arms to quiet the men.

"Thanks, but I have to go. I don't want anyone to get hurt on my account."

The inmates quieted down. I started back towards the aircraft that was waiting to take me away. The men started yelling again, but it was not as loud this time. I hadn't noticed before, but there were some other prisoners that I recognized getting into the aircraft. It looked like I was not the only one getting banished.

They flew us out for quite awhile. I tried finding landmarks so maybe if I survived I could find my way back. It was next to impossible to find anything. The ground was flat and there was nothing but snow and ice. The aircraft finally stopped to let us out.

"We're directly west of the prison," one of the guards said in a hushed voice as I was leaving the aircraft.

The aircraft left us stranded on the ice and snow. There were ten of us. I started looking around wondering which way to go when I noticed way off in the distance some mountains. The mountains were far and in the opposite direction that the aircraft had flown. I told the men that I was heading towards the mountains. I was already starting to feel the cold even with my ice-flyer suit on.

"Are you crazy? The mountains are too far. You can't make it by nightfall. I'm going back the same way we came," one of the men said shaking his head.

The man was right about one thing. We didn't have a lot of time to waste. I put on my ice-flyer skates and decided I was going to head towards the mountains even though it was a long shot. I had a good feeling about the mountains.

My ice-flyer skates used AG technology to glide smoothly over any surface. With my skates I didn't have to worry about falling into any crevices in the ice, I would glide right over them. The skates wouldn't do all the work for me, it would still require a lot of leg strength and stamina.

"I'm going for the mountains. Good luck," I said to the men.

My face was frozen after skating for only a few minutes. I was glad that I didn't shave today because the pain would've been worse. I stopped to pull out the mask Sargas had given me from my bag. It was surprising to see that some of the men were following me. They were way behind me. I decided, I couldn't wait for them to catch up. I had to make as much distance as possible and find shelter. The mask on my face was working. I could breathe better and I wished that I'd put it on sooner.

Most of the men were far less prepared than me. Some of the them didn't even have good boots. If I found any kind of shelter I'd go back for them. The heater that Charlie had given me was working and it was helping to keep my hands warm.

It was hard to concentrate on what I was doing. All I could think about was my daughter and how much I wanted to see her again. I wouldn't be there to help with her school work. I wouldn't be there to take her hiking in the mountains and swimming at the lake. I was going to freeze to death on a frozen world in the middle of nowhere.

I wanted to live now more than anything. I wanted to see my daughter. I wanted to beat them. Whoever had done this to me had no idea who they were messing with. I started skating harder.

I saw a small vapor cloud which surprised me. The vapor was probably coming from a hot spring and it was not that far away. I turned around to see if I could see any of the men that where behind me. I couldn't see any of them. I decided to go back for the men even though I couldn't see them.

I finally saw the men after skating for about twenty minutes. They were sitting on the ground resting.

The first man I got to was completely frozen with is eyes open. He didn't have a mask or anything covering his face. He barely had any protection at all against the cold. I laid the man's body gently down on the ice. It made me sad to see him die this way, even if he was a criminal.

I continued on to the rest of the men who were huddled together. I told the men about the hot spring. They didn't look too hopeful but they got up and followed me. It was slow going. It was getting so cold that my feet and hands had stopped hurting, which I knew was a bad sign. I didn't want to get frost bite. I wanted to leave the men and skate over to the spring but I decided to stay with them. The wind was beginning to pick up. The sun was starting to set, and that worried me.

The minutes pass slowly. I was starting to think we might not make it when finally I could see the rising vapor. I pointed towards the vapor and turned around to look at the men behind me. There were only four men following me. I raised my hands up in the air questioning where the others were. The men shook their heads. It was so cold, I wasn't going to risk taking my mask off to try speaking.

The hot spring came up from deep underground, and lucky for us it had carved an open area in the ice that we could go down into. It was nice to get out of the wind, you could immediately feel a difference in the temperature. The vapor was coming from the inside of a cave. We had done the impossible. We'd found shelter on a frozen world.

I was glad that I'd brought a light with me. We hurried inside the cave to find a place to rest. Lucky for us there were some dry places where we could sit down. I'd forgotten how thirsty I was. It's easy to get dehydrated in cold weather. The water in the thermos was good and I shared some with the men.

The cave was much warmer than outside, but it was still very cold. I was optimistic that we'd be able to survive the night.

"Do you know what happens when we die?" one of the men asked.

"You're not going to die today, so don't worry about it," I said, looking directly at the man.

"What happens when we die? I don't think I'm going to make it," the man persisted.

"I've always been told that you go to the unseen part of the universe were all dead people go. There's a part of you that can never die. You'll be with your friends and family that have passed on."

"I guess that's not so bad," the man responded.

He got up, took off his hat and the scarf that was covering his face, and walked out of the cave. I didn't get up to try and stop him. I was too tired. The sun had gone down. There was no way he'd survive.

I felt like I wanted to sleep. My body was shivering uncontrollably. It was getting too cold even inside the cave. Hypothermia was setting in. I motioned to the other men to follow me. I wanted to get deeper inside the cave hoping that the temperature would be warmer.

The men shook their heads and motioned for me to go without them. I was sure if I left the men, they'd die. I was in no condition to stay around and convince them.

I walked deeper into the cave. Lucky for me the cave was tall. I was able to find my way without crawling or squeezing through small places. The ground water in the cave was now frozen. I kept going deeper inside the cave. I came to some large boulders that I had to climb over, and the passageway got narrower. I followed the passageway until it came to an end. The temperature was extremely cold, even this far inside the cave. I was worried that it still would get too cold for me to survive. I stood there wondering what I should do. After a few minutes had passed, I noticed that my feet where starting to sting. I hadn't been able to feel my feet for a long time but now they were hurting.

There was a heat source by my feet. I got down on my hands and knees and noticed a small opening. I could feel warm air coming through the opening. I used Charlie's heater to melt the ice around the edges of the opening. I hoped that I could make it large enough, that the escaping air would keep me warm. When the opening was large enough, I stuck my head inside and shined my light to see what I could see. There was a pretty good-sized cavern below me. I continued to melt the ice until I was able to let myself down into the cavern.

The opening in the top of the cavern that I'd climbed through was the only place where the heat could escape. Hopefully there was enough heat to keep the opening open during the night. I didn't want to run out of air.

The cavern was heated from hot springs that were running through it. The change in temperature was so drastic that my entire body was in extreme pain. I felt like someone was poking me with pins and needles. The pain was so great that for the first time since I'd remembered my daughter, I didn't think about her. I could only think about the pain and I wanted it to go away.

After my body was warm again, the pain finally went away. I found a dry place where I could sleep. The temperature was warm enough that I could take off my coat and use it for a pillow. I ate some of the emergency rations and in my mind I thanked Sargas for getting them for me.

...

I awoke to darkness and remembered that I was in a cave. I found my light and decided to take a look around. The cavern I slept in was a big one but I wasn't sure how big. Maybe there were more passageways leading out. There weren't any other passageways, just a stream of steaming hot water. In some places the steaming water was dripping down from the ceiling of the cavern.

I decided to eat some more of the emergency rations. I was planning on heading towards the mountains after I finished eating. This cave was an amazing find but I only had so much food. I'd eventually die of starvation if I stayed here. I hoped the mountains were the same ones near the prison. Maybe there'd be another vault in the mountains where I could find food and shelter.

I filled up the thermos with water from the cave and headed towards the entrance. I wanted to see if it was daylight yet.

I found the other men where I'd left them near the entrance to the cave. They'd all frozen to death during the night.

It was early morning which would give me a full day to try and make it to the mountains. I headed out over the ice and snow making good time with my skates. The mountains looked far but not impossible. It was lonely and quiet. I couldn't hear anything except my own breathing. I hoped to see more vapor trails.

The sky over Tyrol never turned blue. The sky was always gray even at midday. It always felt like a storm was coming even though there were no clouds in the sky. It felt like the wind was telling me to quit, and that I'd fail, because it never stopped pushing against me.

I reached the mountains some time after midday. Without my ice-flyer skates it would've been impossible for me to make it this far. The mountains were huge with tall jagged peaks. I was sure they were the same mountains that I'd seen riding the hover bike on my way to the city with the space elevator. I wished that I was riding that bike now.

After taking a drink of water and eating some food, I decided to head southwest following the mountain range. The guard had told me that the prison was west of where they dropped us off, so it seem like the best way to go.

My legs were getting very tired. I could feel my quads getting tight and my lower back was screaming at me to stop. I was out of shape. It had been too long since I'd last skated. I did have the advantage that the gravity on Zendreo was much stronger than here on Tyrol. I was glad that the skates had not been re-calibrated for the lower gravity. I could easily glide over the uneven terrain covering large distances that I would never have been able to do back home.

I spent the rest of the day on the move looking for a place to spend the night. The temperature was falling fast. The daylight was running out and I still hadn't found any vapor trails or anything that looked like a vault. I was going to be in trouble, if I didn't find shelter soon.

I saw a canyon and decided I'd go into it hoping to find some shelter. The canyon was in the shade, only adding to the cold I felt. The wind was picking up. Despite my ice-flyer suit I was colder than I'd ever felt before. I could barely feel my hands even with Charlie's heater. My legs had no feeling in them. I was having a hard time skating.

I was tired and I knew that needed to stop. There was a large snow drift that had been created by the wind; it was be a good place to find shelter so I decided to stop. I laid down on my back holding the heater in my hands. I was so tired and numb that I just wanted to sleep...

CHAPTER VI
CITY IN THE MOUNTAIN

I woke up to a pair of blue eyes and a bright happy smile. I was shocked to be looking into the face of a beautiful young woman about my age with blond hair. The girl had the most beautiful eyes and her smile was amazing and contagious. The girl looked very excited and she began yelling something that sounded like bej turak bej turak.

I couldn't understand what she was yelling. I just stared at her and wondered who she was. I hadn't seen a girl for a long time and she was very pretty. Maybe I was dead. Her face seemed familiar to me. Maybe this girl was my daughter all grown up and I didn't recognize her. Why couldn't I understand what she was saying?

The girl was staring back at me with a kind and happy expression on her face. She looked away from me and motioned for other people to come over.

I was in a bed surrounded by a group of people wearing strange clothes and speaking a language that I couldn't understand. The room went quiet and all eyes were on me.

I sat up. I didn't know what to do or say. I pointed to

myself and said, "Zehn Mortalix."

Instantly there was an excited buzz of voices and the people were nodding and talking again. The girl was smiling at me, she seemed very happy to see me.

I saw my backpack in the corner of the room and I knew that I wasn't dead. These people must be indigenous to Tyrol. I wondered if they were speaking the language in the book from the library. I wasn't sure how to pronounce the words.

The girl said a lot of things that sounded like questions but I had no idea what she was asking. I shook my head and using my hands I tried to indicate that I didn't understand. The girl had a surprised expression on her face. Maybe I could write something down that she'd understand. I motioned for my backpack and somebody brought it over. I was glad that I'd decided to bring the books with me.

"Do you have something I can write with?" I asked holding out my hand and pretending that I was writing something. I showed the people one of my books and pretended to write again.

I hoped that these people were not primitive...

I saw a look of understanding on the girl's face. She mimicked me, pretending to write on her hand and then shook her head. She pointed to the book and then pointed to my head and then made a questioning expression with her face.

She wanted to know if I understood the book. I wasn't quite sure of the pronunciation. I decided to give it a try.

"Yes, I understand the book," I tried to say in the language from the book.

Everyone around me made gasping sounds and then they all started talking at once in their strange language. I looked at the girl, she wasn't talking. She was staring at me with her beautiful blue eyes and a smile on her face. I decided that I liked seeing her smile.

"I wish I knew what you're talking about. I can read your language but I don't speak it," I said hoping someone would understand me.

All of the people had confused expressions on their faces except the girl. She looked at me and I think she repeated what I tried to say. She spoke really slowly and I understood.

The girl said, "I... speak... but... I… can't... read."

"You teach me to speak... I teach you to read…" I replied to her slowly. I could feel myself smiling…

...

It was painfully hard to communicate with the people. After living with the people for a couple of months, I found out that everyone in their society had forgotten how to read and write. I was really glad that I had the old Scientist's book.

The city of Grindolstin provided for all their needs and

the people didn't see the need to learn reading and writing. I found out that the city had some food replicators and had many underground farms, orchards and gardens similar to the one I'd found by the library. The people were not primitive but they were not living up to the basic modern standards that I was used to.

Grindolstin is a giant underground city. It's much larger than the vault that I'd found near the prison. There are thousands of people living in the city. Nobody knows exactly how many people there are.

Chara is the name of the beautiful girl with a great smile. The night when she found me, it was her turn to shut the external doors to the city. Just before she started to close the doors, she spotted me far away down in the valley. When she saw me lay down in the snow and realized that I'd stopped moving, she alerted some of her people. They were able to get me into Grindolstin.

She told me that at first it was hard to convince anyone that she was telling the truth. She was finally able to get some people to help her, after a lot of persuading. I was surprised because I thought she could persuade me to do pretty much anything with her beautiful smile.

I was the first person from the outside of Grindolstin that they'd ever seen, according to Chara. They had stories of people who they called the immortals.

The immortals visited the city several times in the past. An old man remembered seeing the immortals when he was a small boy. Later in life when he saw them a second time as an old man, he said the immortals looked exactly the same as they did when he was a small boy. The old man had died long ago and now all the people had were old stories.

The stories said that one day the immortals would return and take them away to a better place. I wanted to tell them that their immortals were most likely merchants who traveled in space and that the merchant's time lines went slower than the people on Tyrol. Traveling a few years at speeds faster than light would be the same as staying on Tyrol for many years. The merchants aged a few years while traveling and returned back to see the young boy as an old man.

I decided not to tell them because they had so much hope that the immortals would return some day. I hoped they'd still like me even if a merchant ship never came back to take them away.

I found out that my name Zehn Mortalix means something like *the immortal one descending* in the ancient language of their people. The book was written in an ancient form of their language and when I tried to speak it, the people were amazed.

The people living in Grindolstin all believe that I'm immortal. When I tried to speak in the ancient Tyrolian language Tyderius, it made the people sure that I was an immortal, at least that's what Chara tells me. Chara says that I have to be immortal because only an immortal could survive out on the frozen surface of Tyrol.

I instantly became good friends with Chara. It felt like we'd always known each other. She seemed to always be able to understand me even when we could hardly speak the same language. I don't know why but I told her everything about me that I could remember. Chara could listen for hours. It was good for me to practice speaking her language which they called Tyderio. She'd never heard of Zendreo, space ships or the SGC. All she knew was her life inside the mountain. Whenever I tried to convince her that I wasn't immortal, she'd smile, shake her head and say how lucky she was that she found me, because now her boring life was about to change.

The people in Grindolstin were amazed by me. Everywhere I went the people wanted to meet me. They'd almost always ask when were the rest of the immortals going to return. At first I didn't know what to say. I decided to start by telling them that time to an immortal didn't make sense. No one can ever predict when immortals will show up. Whenever I tried to tell them that I was not an immortal, they wouldn't believe me.

I told the people that I was just like them. I was stranded on Tyrol and I didn't know when the immortals would return. It was almost impossible for me to avoid the crowds of people because I was so much taller than everyone and my clothes were very different.

In some ways it felt like I'd been transferred from a maximum security prison to a minimum security prison. I didn't have to work the mines anymore, but I still felt trapped with nowhere to go. Grindolstin didn't have a library, or a hanger full of amazing vehicles to drive that I was aware of. The people lived in small apartments, built all over inside the underground city. Some of the chambers were enormous and the apartments reached all the way to the top, supporting the ceiling overhead. It must have taken thousands of years for the people to carve out a city so large. Some of the people lived inside houses completely carved out of the rock.

Chara convinced her grandmother to let me stay with her in a spare room. Chara's grandmother lived in one of the houses carved out of the rock. The house had a kitchen window facing one of the gardens.

...

One morning a couple of men came to see me. The men told me that they wanted to take me to meet with the President. They told me that I needed to leave with them right away. The men seemed really urgent so I told them that I'd go with them.

They led me through the winding streets of the underground city. Grindolstin was bigger than I'd first thought. The streets were all lit with the same kind of lighting that I'd seen in the vault. I was sure the city was powered by h36.

You could see a representation of a blue sky with clouds when you looked up on the ceilings of the different chambers. The sky representation would change colors and even go dark when it was night time.

The city had many levels and caverns. We kept going up and up. I noticed long lines of people, as we made our way. I asked one of the men what the people were waiting in line for and he said they were food lines. I noticed that the lights were getting brighter as we made our way. The lighting was almost so bright I could hardly believe that I was inside an underground city. When I asked the guards why the lights were brighter, they said it was because we were getting close to where the President and the leaders of the city lived.

I could hear what sounded like a waterfall.

"Is that a waterfall?" I asked.

One of the men nodded.

We came to a high wall with a gate. The wall was so high that I couldn't see very much of anything on the other side, only the tops of tall buildings. There was a long line of people at the gate. I asked the men what that line was for and they told me it was for people who wanted to get a message to the President and the leaders of the city.

We walked past the line of people. The guards at the gate must have recognized the men I was with because they opened the gate for us. I was surprised to see that the guards were armed with what looked like military style weapons. I pretended not to notice the weapons and continued on. Up until this point, I hadn't seen anyone with weapons inside Grindolstin.

I was amazed at the difference I saw inside the wall. Everything was so perfect and clean. This area of the city made me feel like I was in a real city above the ground. The ceiling was high above us and filled most of your field of vision. It had the appearance of a blue sky with clouds. You could hardly tell that the blue sky wasn't real. There were trees and flowers and there was a river. The water looked pure and clean. I was sure it was the main source of water for the entire underground city.

I asked if I could get a drink from the river. One of the men said on the way out we could stop and get a drink. We followed the river until we came to a very impressive and massive structure with a waterfall. The underground river was flowing right out of the rock and it made a natural waterfall. The water cascaded down the massive building and was very impressive. It had been so long since I'd seen or heard a waterfall that I just wanted to stay and take it all in. I was pretty sure this must be where the President lived.

We entered a large hall that was lined with people on both sides. The lines of people angled in, pointing towards a man sitting in a nice chair at the end of the hall. We walked to the end of the hall where the President was waiting. I couldn't help but notice that all the people on the sides of the room were dressed in very nice clothes and look much cleaner and well-to-do than any of the other people I'd seen in the underground city so far.

The President was a good looking man. He was a little younger than I expected. He was tall with dark hair that was combed to perfection. Nothing about the man looked disorganized.

"Are you the immortal that everyone is talking about?"

the President asked me with a polite smile.

I wasn't sure what to say.

"Yes, that is what people are saying about me," I said cautiously.

"Do you know when the rest of the immortals will be returning?" the President asked looking very sincere.

"For immortals time doesn't exist, so I can't tell you when they'll be coming back again."

"We've prepared a place for you here in the Presidential Residence. You can live here until the immortals come back," the President said, almost with a commanding voice.

I didn't expect that.

This place would be a lot nicer than living with Chara's Nanna. When I thought about Chara learning that I was moving out of her Nanna's house, I could see disappointment on her face in my mind.

I didn't like the man's tone.

"Thank you Mr. President, but I think I'll stay where I'm at, if it's okay with you?"

He didn't look very happy. I could tell the President was used to getting his way.

"It would make me very happy if you would stay here. I have lots of questions for you and I'd like it if you were my friend," the President said in a sincere voice.

I smiled and once again, I wasn't sure what to say.

"Mr. President..."

"Call me Nath," the President interrupted.

"And what is your name?" he continued.

"My name is Zehn Mortalix," I said, feeling proud of my name.

The President looked a little surprised. I was surprised that he didn't already know my name.

"Zehn, the immortal," he said softly, almost mumbling to himself.

He straightened up.

"Zehn, will you stay with us so I can get to know you better?" he asked me again with an almost cheerful voice.

It felt like the President was commanding me to stay more than he was asking me. I was at a complete disadvantage because I knew nothing about the man. Something about the President didn't feel right to me. I wanted to say no, but I didn't want to create and enemy. I decided to risk it, since I knew that so many of the people liked me and there would be trouble if something were to happen to me.

"I'm sorry Mr. President but I already have a place to stay. I'd be glad to come and meet with you anytime so we can get to know each other better."

I heard people gasping for air. I turned to look and see who they were but I couldn't find them. Everyone in the hall was looking at the President. I was pretty sure that nobody ever said no to this man. The President had a confused look on his face, he nodded and said, "Very well, I look forward to our meetings."

He got up quickly and left the room without looking my way.

One of the President's men asked me if I could find my way home. I told him that I could. I was escorted by the men as far as the large gate and then let me leave on my own. They didn't let me stop to get a drink from the river.

Chara came running up to me and gave me a big hug when I made it back to her Nanna's house. I could see that she was relieved by the smile and the expression on her face.

"I've waited all day for you. I wasn't sure if you would ever come back. When I heard the president wanted to meet with you, I was afraid."

It had been so long since anyone had given me a hug, I hadn't realized how much I'd missed them.

"They offered to let me stay in the Presidential Residence but I turned them down," I said to Chara with a grin.

"I was afraid that you would go live somewhere else and I wouldn't get to see you anymore. You're so popular. I thought you would forget about me and my life would be boring again," Chara said with a sad face.

It felt good to hear Chara say those things.

"I like your Nanna's place besides I don't think it would be possible for anyone to forget about you," I said with a smile.

I could see some color coming to Chara's face.

"The President seems like a man that is used to getting his way. Do you think it was bad for me to refuse him?" I asked, changing the subject.

"I don't know. Nobody ever gets to actually see the President. Do you mean you actually got to see the President in person?" Chara said wide-eyed.

"What was it like? Did they let you inside the gates? Did you see any of the Anaxus?" Chara asked, talking so fast I could hardly understand her.

"What or who are the Anaxus?"

"The Anaxus are the leaders of our people. Nobody ever sees them or the President. You can go to the gate and wait in a long line to leave them messages, but nobody ever gets to see them," Chara said, looking at me with her eyes wide open.

She was bouncing with excitement.

There were lots of fancy-looking people in the President's hall when I met with him. I decided all those people must be the Anaxus.

"They looked like normal people to me," I said to Chara.

"It was the Anaxus and the line of Presidents that brought peace and equality to our people," Chara said almost reverently.

"Many years ago when my people first moved inside the mountain, they fought over food and supplies. My people were leaderless. Without leaders there was anarchy. There rose up a group of very smart men who became the Anaxus. They choose the presidents and make the laws. It was the Anaxus that brought true equality to our people for the first time in history. Under the Anaxus everyone has equal rights and everyone is taken care of," Chara explained.

I was a little confused.

"Did you say they brought true equality? Why do the Anaxus live behind a giant wall in the best part of the city? You should see what it is like behind the wall. That part of the city is amazing."

"The Anaxus are the ones who brought us equality so for their reward they get to live in the best part of the city," Chara said.

"So, in a society of equality some people are a little more equal than other people. That doesn't sound like true equality to me."

"I guess so," Chara said after thinking about it for a minute.

I found out from Chara that in the system set up by the

Anaxus, nobody owned property. The Anaxus had assigned families to the different places where they lived depending on the families' needs. They had food stations that each family was assigned to. Some times there were food shortages and people would wait all day in line and not receive anything.

I thought this was kind of odd. Maybe the food replicators, the underground gardens and the orchards couldn't keep up with the demand.

Chara said it was because the population was getting too big and food was becoming scarce. All the food that was grown in the underground gardens and orchards was taken to the food stations where the Anaxus decided how much each family would receive.

The system of law was pretty simple. If somebody was caught eating from the gardens or the orchards, the punishment was severe. The normal amount of food rationed to the entire family was reduced significantly for people caught breaking the laws. If you were caught breaking the food laws more than three times they'd send you to the prison work camps.

The prison work camps were pretty much a death sentence, due to the back-breaking labor and lack of food. The prison workers were constantly working to expand the city by excavating new tunnels and constructing new residences, doing the work all by hand.

The new sections under construction were completely blocked off while the work was being done so nobody but the prisoners and the guards were allowed into the work areas. It had always been this way for as long as the people could remember.

It could take hundreds of years to finish the work in a new section of the city. You never heard from anyone who was sent to work in the prison camps.

It made sense to me why people did what the President wanted.

CHAPTER VII
PUT TO WORK

I was woken up early in the morning by Chara. She was very happy to inform me that I had been assigned to work with her as a ventilation specialist. She was going to be my trainer.

Chara explained to me over breakfast that every family had been assigned tasks long ago and over time it had become the responsibility of the parents to train their children to do the tasks assigned to them. Her family had been given the task of opening and closing the outer vents and doors to allow for fresh air to enter into the city.

After breakfast we made a lunch, grabbed our coats and then headed out through the gardens and orchards in the opposite direction of the city. I loved walking through the orchards and gardens because of the fresh air and the warm temperatures.

"My dad used to take me with him this same way every day," Chara said, with a happy look on her face.

Chara's dad had passed away a few years ago and he had often been a topic of our conversations.

"It's a lot better to have somebody with you than going all by yourself. I'm so glad they assigned you to work with me because this job can be very lonely. Most days I never see anyone. Hardly anyone ever comes to these outer passageways because it's so cold."

After we passed through the orchards and gardens we came to some passageways.

"We need to put on our warm clothes now it's going to get cold inside there," Chara informed me.

We passed through many passageways. Without Chara, I would've been completely lost. The lights would turn on as we entered each new section, most likely activated by a motion sensor.

"The technology and people who built this place were amazing. Where I come from we always have to replace lights and..."

I paused to think for a second. I didn't know how to say sensors in her language. Chara waited patiently.

"I'm not sure how to say it, but we have to change the things that turn on the lights every few years. Nothing lasts as long as they do here."

Chara looked a little surprised and shrugged, "You really have to change your lights every few years?"

"Yes, we do. My guess is that all your systems are using h36 as the power source so they'll continue working for thousands of years. H36 is so expensive where I come from that it would be impractical to design lights that used it."

"What is h36?" Chara asked.

It was my turn to be surprised.

"You don't know what h36 is? It's used as a power source in reactors. You can create enough power with small amounts of h36 to power star ships that travel many times faster than the speed of light."

I knew that Chara wasn't understanding much of anything I was saying because of the expression on her face. I'd tried to explain to her star ships and traveling faster than the speed of light before, but she didn't understand.

"H36 is very rare at least for most of the galaxy. But here on Tyrol there's lots of it. They had us mining it in the prison..."

"Wait, your name for our world is Tyrol?" Chara asked interrupting me.

"Yeah, the SGC named this solar system the Tyrolia solar system and this planet is the second planet from the sun."

The look on Chara's faced told me that she was amused.

"Do you know what Tyrol means?" she asked.

I shook my head. I didn't know.

"It means magic power."

That made sense. I wondered if they named the planet after they found out it was full of h36.

"There sure is plenty of magic power here," I said.

"How is possible that you don't know what h36 is?" I asked.

"I guess I've never thought about what makes everything work. I just know it works," Chara replied.

"It's probably because you don't have any schools. If you had schools you'd be able to understand how things worked better. What happens if the lights go out? Who's going to fix them?"

"The lights have always worked for generations. I don't think they'll go out anytime soon. The Anaxus will help us if we have any questions we can't answer. They say schools can lead to anarchy and destroy our way of life. We don't need to learn about such things because the Anaxus knows about them."

"It sounds like they want to control the people and make sure that they only know what they want them to know if you ask me," I said.

Chara looked a little defensive.

"They only do things for the good of the people. The Anaxus makes sure everyone has enough to eat and everyone is equal," She said sounding determined.

I didn't want to get into a political argument with Chara, so I let it go. When people have lived a certain way their entire lives, they get used to the conditions and don't always question if there is a better way.

"What about my books? Would they take them away if they knew about them?"

"I don't know. Nobody has books. I think they'd take them if they knew about them," Chara informed me.

"Will I get in trouble with the Anaxus if I teach you how to read?"

"Only if they find out. I'm not going to tell anyone if you don't," Chara said, smiling at me.

We stopped walking in a long straight passageway. Chara went over to one side of the passageway and said, "It is going to be cold. Are you ready?"

I nodded and Chara put her hand into as small opening in the wall. Small square windows started opening. I felt a blast of cold air on my face as the windows opened. The windows were vents cut out of a cliff. The cold air entering the mountain caused the warmer air to move upwards. Chara explained that there were more vents higher up on the mountain.

Once the vents were opened, they would allow for the warmer air to escape causing the air to circulate through the city. It was an ingenious system. I went over to one of the windows to take a look out. I was surprised to see how high up on the mountain we were. It made sense that the vents were cut into high cliffs. It was the one place that would not collect snow that could cover the vents. I could see jagged mountain tops across the valley way off in the distance. The cloudless gray sky made for good visibility especially from our vantage point.

Chara turned around and motioned for me to follow her.

"Come on, we need to go back this way so we can open the other vents higher up."

We backtracked for a while and then took another passageway that led us up an incline. The passageway eventually led to a circular staircase. The staircase never seemed to end, up and up we climbed stopping a few times to take a break.

"I can't wait to show you the view from up here," Chara said, when we finally made it to the top of the staircase.

The passageway after the staircase became very narrow. I had to duck my head down to pass through it. The narrow passageway turned into a larger one. I could hear the steady roar of a waterfall.

"Is that the waterfall at the Presidential Residence?" I asked.

"Yes, there's no surprising you," Chara said with excitement in her voice.

I could see some railing that must be there to stop people from falling. We walked over to the railing slowly. Chara was right, the view of the waterfall cascading down the President's mansion was amazing. The city below looked like most cities from above, there were lots of lights. We were directly above the waterfall. I could feel the spray from the waterfall on my face. I'd never see such a vast open area underground before. You could see trees and green areas of grass. The air was fresh and clean, it didn't smell musty like you might expect from being underground.

"Do you like it?" Chara asked.

"It's beautiful! It's really amazing," I said.

Chara smiled.

"I knew that you'd like it up here. We need to open more vents. Come on, I'll show you were they are."

We eventually made our way into a long straight passageway that was higher up the mountain. Chara stopped and put her hand inside a small opening in the wall. The vents opened, letting the warm air escape.

"I loved coming up here with my dad when I was a little girl. After opening the vents we'd always go and eat our lunch and look at the waterfall. Nobody ever comes up here. It was our secret spot. Whenever I feel a little sad, I like to think about this place and the good times I had with my dad."

I wondered if my daughter had a favorite place that she liked to go with me. I was angry again at the people who'd taken away my memories. Chara could see that something was bothering me.

"What are you thinking about?" She asked.

I didn't know why, but for some reason I felt like I could

tell her anything. I just knew somehow that Chara would understand me, and always be my friend, no matter what.

"I was thinking about my daughter and the people who took her away from me. I can't remember if we had a favorite place to go to. I feel sad because I'll never get to see my daughter or my wife again. I want to get back at the people that did this to me. My Wife is dead because of them. I want justice," I replied not looking at Chara.

"You're an immortal, of course you will see your family again. You can't die," Chara said.

"Yeah, I have an immortal soul. Everyone does, and believe it or not, I can die. I'm just like you."

Chara must have been able to tell that everything wasn't okay with me at that moment because she looked at me and said with a comforting voice.

"You'll see them again. I know it. It was really hard for me after my dad died. Nothing or no-one could make me feel better. I was so angry and sad that I wouldn't speak to anyone. My Mom and Nanna were very worried about me.

Then one night I had a dream and my dad came to me in the dream. He asked me why I was so sad. I told him that I was sad because he died and he left me. My Dad told me not to be sad and as long as I was thinking about him he could be with me every day, watching over me. He said during those quiet times when I felt a warm feeling in my heart that it was him telling me he loved me. The dream seemed so real. I know that I'll see him again."

"I think you're right, I'm sure we will see our families again," I said after Chara had finished.

Chara smiled.

"Come on, let's go eat our lunch. We still have more vents and doors to open."

Chara, took my hand and led me back down the passageway.

"I'm really glad that I met you!" I said to Chara squeezing her hand.

I was starting to feel better.

"I'm glad that I met you too. I'm sure my dad would have liked you a lot," Chara said.

After lunch Chara told me that we were about half-way done. We still needed to do lots of walking. We spent the rest of the day walking through a maze of passageways opening vents and talking. I learned from Chara that there were a total of four zones designated for opening and closing the vents. We had walked a quarter of the way around the entire city. By the time we got back home from opening all the vents we were exhausted.

Chara gave me a big hug at her Nanna's. "Thanks! I had a really good time with you today," she said.

"Thanks! I did too, I'll see you tomorrow," I said, hugging her back.

After saying good night to Chara I went inside. I was surprised to see that Nanna was still awake.

"Would you like something to drink?" she asked.

I hadn't realized how thirsty I was until that moment.

"Yes I would love something to drink."

Nanna indicated for me to sit down at the table and she brought me a drink. I wasn't sure what the drink was, but it tasted really good.

"I don't think I've ever seen Chara so happy. She's been practically glowing since you arrived."

There is one thing I like about older people. They aren't afraid to tell you what they're thinking, and they get straight to the point.

"You two make a really good couple. It's a shame she's promised to Orly Bogler."

"You mean Chara has a boyfriend?" I asked.

I was surprised at how much the thought of her having a boyfriend was bothering me. Of course she had a life before she met me.

"Well, yes and no," Nanna said.

"All young girls when they are children are promised to young boys. When children reach a certain age they are required to go to a coming of age processing center. At the processing center the children are asked many questions and put through tests by specialists who match them with a compatible boy or girl. The children are then encouraged to spend time together. When they reach adulthood they are married," Nanna explained.

I was shocked. Arranged marriages were nothing new, but I didn't think they were practiced anymore. There was a huge backlash from societies that didn't want arranged marriages forced on them. With threats of war the SGC had finally stopped trying to arrange marriages.

"I'm guessing Chara doesn't like Orly?" I ventured.

"No, she doesn't like him that much, but Orly really likes her."

I told Nanna thanks for the drink and headed to bed…

...

I found out that Chara was a quick learner. Every day when we took a break for lunch by the waterfall, I taught Chara to read. My language skills were also getting better. Instead of just understanding the basic gist of conversations, I could understand almost every word.

One day after we'd finished reading about the ancient forests from my library book, I decided to tell her what I knew about Tyrol. I felt like I finally knew enough words that I could try and explain everything to her.

"Chara, I know what happened to the forests and why it's always so cold. There are thousands, maybe even millions or billions of mirrors high up just above in the sky. They are redirecting the sunlight away from the planet."

Chara started laughing but when she saw that I wasn't laughing she stopped.

"You're not joking are you? I thought you were joking..." Chara said in a soft voice trailing off.

"Char, I'm not joking."

"Did you just call me Char?"

I could tell Chara was surprised by the look on her face and by the sound of her voice.

"Yeah, is it okay if I call you that?"

"My dad used to call me his little Char. Do you know what Char means?"

I didn't know.

"What does it mean?" I said shaking my head.

"Char means joy or happiness," Chara said softly.

"I'd like it very much if you called me Char. It's almost like Char is my real name. Chara is just what normal people who I don't know very well call me."

I told Char about the space elevator and the mirrors that I'd seen on the monitor. Explaining the space elevator was no easy task.

Char just couldn't understand how such a technology could be possible. She kept saying to me over and over that nothing can just stay up in the sky, it has to fall down to the ground.

I tried to tell her that the mirrors were above the sky in orbit close to the stars and she just looked at me like I was crazy.

How do you explain gravity and the atmosphere to somebody who just can't visualize it in their head?

After many failed attempts, Char could see that I was getting frustrated. She looked at me with a serious expression and said, "I can tell that you really believe what you are saying is true. I trust you, so it doesn't matter how the mirrors are there. I believe you."

I wasn't sure if she truly believed me, but I appreciated her effort to make me believe that she did.

"I'm not sure how big the mirrors are and how they are controlled. I only saw them from the camera on the space elevator."

"Do you think the SCG put the mirrors there?"

"Yes, I'm sure they did. The SGC is supposed to follow a strict code of not overthrowing governments on worlds who are not part of the SCG. I think that instead of creating trade agreements with the nations on your world for h36, they decided to change the climate and put the world into a deep-freeze to kill off the people so they could take the h36 for themselves. Everyone from where I come from thinks that your world is a frozen ice world with nobody living on it except a bunch of prisoners."

Char had gotten really quiet and her silence started to bother me.

"I wonder how many people died just for some magic power to turn on lights and open doors. Are the immortals really like that? Will they kill everyone to get what they want?" Char said looking at me with an almost horrified expression on her face.

"The people who did this are not my people. They're not immortals. It's almost unbelievable what the SGC is capable of doing," I said slowly.

Char would barely look at me and had gone silent. I wasn't sure what to say or do. I just sat there remaining silent, trying to read her to know what I should do next.

After sitting in silence for a long time Char got up and said that we should get going to finish off the rest of our work. Char was very quiet for the rest of the day. When I tried to joke around or get a response from her she'd just nod her head or sometimes she wouldn't answer me at all. It was very unlike her to be so quiet and her silence was making me uneasy.

Sometimes silence can say more than a thousand words ever could. I was afraid that she thought I belonged to a society that would put an entire planet into a deep-freeze killing almost all living things for a magic power that kept the lights on.

When we were almost home, I couldn't take it anymore. I felt like I was losing her.

"Char, the same people who froze your world are the same people who killed my wife, took away my daughter and my memories. I promise you, I'm not like them. They're not my people," I blurted out.

Char stopped walking turned and looked at me, her expression softened.

"I know you are not like that..." Char hesitated, "at least I want to believe that you're good, but I don't know what I believe anymore," she said slowly.

Now it was my turn to go quiet. I didn't know what to say. Those words hurt. I felt like I was losing the only person who was my true friend. I didn't want to be alone again.

The SGC took my family and now they were trying to take Char away from me. I started to feel like I was completely alone and nobody would've missed me if I'd never lived.

Char must have sensed the change in me because she grabbed me and hugged me.

"I believe you."

I hugged her back. The feeling of being completely alone went away.

"Thanks Char. I knew I could count on you," I said with a smile.

"Do you know why I believe you?" Char asked.

"Because you're my friend?" I guessed.

"No, it's your eyes, they got really dark the same way they do when you talk about your daughter. When you're sad your eyes go darker," Char said with a smile.

Suddenly I felt a shove causing me to take a couple of steps.

"That's my girl! Get your slimy hands off her!" an angry voice said.

I turned to look at the man that shoved me. He was using lots of words that I'd never heard before mixed with some swear words that I did know.

I was sure it was Orly who I hadn't met yet. I was so much into the conversation with Char; I hadn't noticed him.

Orly was pretty tall for a Tyrol and very muscular. Most of the tyrols were pretty short, at least compared to me. Orly had dark unkempt hair and he squinted his eyes a lot.

"We're just friends. Orly stop overreacting!" Char said defensively.

"You're the immortal one aren't you?" Orly asked, turning away from Char to look at me.

"Chara is going to be my wife one day. So you better watch what you do with her or I'll make sure you're not the immortal one anymore. Do I make myself clear?" Orly almost shouted at me as he moved in very close.

"I don't care who you think you are. I'll mess you up!"

Orly continued.

I was sure that Orly was serious about his threats. After fighting the champion Kos back in the prison; I wasn't feeling very intimidated.

"How do you plan on messing me up? With your breath?" I asked pushing him away from me.

Orly had gotten so close to me. I could smell his breath and it was really foul. His breath smelled like rotten fodhopper juice.

"Just stay away from her," Orly said.

Orly put his arm around Char. He turned and started walking away taking her with him. Char turned to look at me and made a sorry expression on her face and gave me a small wave as Orly guided her away from me towards her mom's house. I was beginning to see why she wasn't so fond of Orly.

...

Nanna was waiting for me when I came home.

"Where's my granddaughter?" Nanna asked when we were inside the house.

"We ran into Orly on our way home tonight and let's just say he wasn't very happy to meet me. He took Char and they headed off towards her place."

"So what do you think of Orly?" Nanna asked.

"I don't think he's good enough for your granddaughter.

He seems very controlling. You know the type of person that has to bully people into being his friends. If he didn't bully people they'd have nothing to do with him because he's so pathetic."

Nanna smiled, "You're a pretty good judge of character and I agree with you 100 percent."

Nanna was so much like Char, I wondered if she realized how much she was like her grandma. I felt myself smiling and Nanna was smiling back at me.

CHAPTER VIII
THE PRESIDENT'S DEAL

The next morning, I was woken up much earlier than usual by Nanna. She informed me that the President had sent some men to fetch me. Nanna told me that the men seem very anxious and they told her that there wasn't anytime for breakfast. I noticed the worried expressions on Nanna's face and her voice was shaky.

I hurried and got dressed as fast as possible and headed out with the men. The caverns and streets were completely empty. There were at least ten men accompanying me. I guess the President wanted to make sure that I didn't get lost. The men were acting strange and nervous, they were looking in all directions and walking fast. We were almost running.

"Do you know why the President wants to talk to me in the middle of the night?" I asked the man nearest me.

The man would barely look at me.

"I don't know. They don't tell me those kinds of things. They just give me orders and I follow them."

I almost believed the man, but something didn't feel

right. Why wouldn't he look at me? The route that we were taking was different than the other time they took me to speak with the President. It was like we were avoiding the main routes and taking alternate ones that passed by the less populated areas. The man told me that I needed to be quiet and that all my questions would be answered soon enough. It didn't take us long to make our way to the large gate that separated the city. I was surprised to see so many people sleeping on the ground just so they could keep their place in line at the gate.

I was taken through the gate and led to a building with a security fence around it. I noticed that there were guards posted at the entrance. The building reminded me of a detention center. It finally dawned on me they weren't taking me to speak to the President. They were taking me to a detention center. I looked over at the same man I talked with before, but he wouldn't look at me.

"I'm sorry. I'm just doing my job," the man said.

The men took me inside. The inside of the building was very well lit. I had to squint my eyes to get used to the bright lights. I wanted to try and run away but at this point there really was no option to run. If I tried to get a way, I was sure that I'd get a good beating and it would be of no use.

The men in the detention center looked like your typical military men. They were large and strong, they looked determined. I could tell that these men were the type of men you don't mess around with. I was taken to a holding cell and a man motioned me into the cell. The holding cell was small and quiet and there was a bed. It was still early in the morning and I was tired. I decided I'd try and get some sleep…

...

I heard a woman's voice. She was speaking Pythar.

"I've missed you so much. How are you?" she asked.

It had been so long since I'd spoken my language. I was taken totally by surprise. I didn't know what to say. I tried to say hello but it came out in Tyderio instead of Pythar. The woman smiled as if she understood.

"Do I know you?" I finally asked in Pythar.

The woman smiled again. Her smile seemed so familiar.

"Yes, you do. I don't have much time. You have a daughter. Do you understand?"

"Yes, you said I have a daughter," I replied.

The woman smiled again.

"Promise me you will never forget her," she said.

"I promise."

It felt so good to be speaking my own language. I felt like all my troubles and fears had gone away. It was so peaceful. I didn't want the feeling to go away.

When I woke up and found myself in the detention center, I knew it had been a dream. I hadn't had any dreams for a long time. Sometimes when you have a dream, you forget it as soon as you wake up. This time, I didn't forget. I wondered who the woman was. The dream seemed so real. I suddenly had an overwhelming feeling that the woman was my wife who was dead.

Was my wife trying to tell me something? I already knew that I had a daughter. Why did my wife tell me I had a daughter? I laid in bed for a long time with a comforting feeling of peace. I didn't know why I was feeling peace. Usually when I thought about my daughter it made me sad and angry, but this time I felt peace. It felt like I'd see my daughter again.

Time in the holding cell was hard to measure. The days passed with agonizing slowness. The President never came to speak with me. I received meals each day but I never saw the face of the person who brought me the meals. When I couldn't bare the silence, I'd try to sleep hoping that the dream of my wife would return, only to wake up disappointed.

I had lots of time to think. I wondered how Char and Nanna were doing. I realized that maybe it was a bad idea to go along with the immortal story. Me being an immortal, made it extremely easy for the President to make me go away. The President could keep me locked up for as long as he wanted. All he had to say was, I was an immortal and how it's impossible to know when an immortal will show up.

Being in the detention center must be my punishment for going against the President's wishes. I began to worry for Nanna. She was the only one that knew about the

President sending his men to fetch me. I was sure that the President could try to fool Nanna. They could tell her that I'd left, after speaking with the President and they didn't know when I'd return. It made sense to why the men took me in the middle of the night. They didn't want anyone to see me being escorted by the President's men. I could be in the detention center for the rest of my life and nobody would ever know or ever question my whereabouts. I was in trouble.

More days passed. I began to lose hope of ever leaving the holding cell. Nobody ever came to question me. The President hadn't even bothered to tell me why I was in the holding cell. I hadn't done anything criminal. I began to feel sorry for myself. I couldn't see how things could get any worse.

I was wrong about things getting worse. Things did get worse with time. The silence was becoming too loud to bare. I longed for human interaction. When food was brought I'd yell at the guards trying to get a response from them. I was always met with silence. I wondered if the reason I was in this holding cell was because I'd told Char about the mirrors.

During some of the more darker times, I wondered if Char was a spy. Did she turn me in because she thought I was part of the society responsible for trapping her people in a frozen world? I was angry at myself for doubting her, but I just didn't know.

One day I woke up with a start from a horrible dream. Char and Nanna were testifying before the President and the Anaxus, telling them that I was a liar. I had the worst feelings of betrayal. It hurt me to the core. I finally realized that there was somebody in the cell shouting at me to get up.

I stood up slowly. There was a bright light shining in my face. I could barely see the silhouette of the guard behind the light. Someone grabbed my arm and pulled me out of the cell. I was led down a long corridor and into a small room. They must finally be ready to interrogate me. Nothing seemed to be real. I felt happy to leave that horrible cell. I never wanted to go back.

I was told to sit down and wait. The room was small with a standard table and chairs and a mirrored window. It seemed like every interrogation room looked just like this one.

I didn't have to wait long until a man with an ugly demeanor entered the room. I felt a horrible feeling deep down in my gut while in the presence of this man. I'm sure that no mother would allow this man to hold her newborn child. The middle-age man had dark hair and fierce features.

"Let's get right to the point. Did you like your stay in the cell?" the man asked.

"No," I could barely get the word out.

"I didn't think so. The President put you in there to let you know who's in charge around here. But that's beside the point. We know who you are. You're a convict, you killed the SGC Senator from Zendreo and her husband.

You killed your own parents."

I was shocked.

"You know about the SGC and Zendreo?" I asked.

The man smiled. I could see that he was enjoying this.

"We know about the prison. I saw your fight and I lost a lot of money, no thanks to you."

I was shocked again. I didn't know what to say. I guess it was possible that this man was there. There were lots of people in the arena watching the fight.

"I'm sorry about your money. I was just trying to survive."

The man actually smiled.

"The President for some reason has taken a liking to you. He's given you an option. The President has sent me to inform you that if you will train and become a fighter sponsored by him, he will allow you to leave the cell. If you don't want to become a fighter he'll put you back into the cell."

"That's not really much of a choice, is it?" I asked.

The man didn't say anything. He just looked at me with a smile that would make a small child cry.

"Do you know what this place is?" I asked.

"It's a detention facility. Where do you think you are?" The man said looking amused by my question.

"I mean this city, what is this place to the SGC?" I asked again.

"You're in an SGC rogue planet testing facility and social engineering test model."

"What's a rogue planet?" I asked.

"Rogue planets are planets that don't have a sun or solar system."

I remembered learning about these kinds of planets. During the formation process of a solar system, a newly forming planet can be knocked out of its orbit by a collision with another large body and leave the entire solar system.

We called rogue planets, wandering planets. Wandering planets were often full of precious metals and are much larger than asteroids and much more profitable. It made sense, the living conditions in Grindolstin were similar to a wandering planet. The chances that a wandering planet had an atmosphere were slim to none. Anyone living on a wandering planet would have to live underground to avoid cosmic radiation.

"What do you mean by Social Engineering? Where did all the people come from?" I asked.

"You're just full of questions, aren't you. The SGC found these people living here a long time ago and brought order to their existence. We study their society to know what works best for the current living conditions. We're incorporating the same kinds of laws and ways of living on our rogue planet facilities."

That was an interesting way of putting it. The SGC controlled every aspect of these peoples' lives. The people in Grindolstin were no better than lab rats to them. It started to make a lot of sense to why one section of the city was so much better than the rest of the city.

"The President says if you'll become a fighter, and if you're successful, he'll get you a new ID-chip. He'll allow you to travel back to Zendreo when you retire."

Without an ID-chip you couldn't live a normal life on any of the SGC worlds. Nobody would give you a job or do any kind of trade with you out of fear of losing their own ID-chip.

It had been so long since I ever thought it possible to return home, I felt new life coming back to me. Hope is a powerful feeling and I was feeling hope for the first time in a long time.

"Wait, how exactly will I be able to get a new ID-chip? How will I travel home?"

"You'll travel the same way we travel. You can halo jump to Zendreo and be there almost instantly with no time differences."

I'd never heard of halo jumping.

"What's halo jumping?"

The man reached inside his pocket and pulled out a small round device and held it in his hand showing it to me. The device started emitting a blue light and then a holographic display. The man began cycling through star charts on the holodisplay until he came to Zendreo.

"I select Zendreo and this device will take me there almost instantaneously. Look at it this way.... the device uses the same technology that large space ships use to fold space. While your typical FTL drive folds space at several light years per cycle, this device can fold space at thousands of light years per cycle. It means you can travel much farther without the need of cryogenic sleep. There are millions of deep space beacons out there that allow the device to find the correct destination. The President has allowed me to give you a demonstration if you want."

I felt myself shaking my head.

"That's impossible! There's no way that a device that small could have enough power to fold space thousands of times more than the FTL drives on space ships."

The man smiled.

"I was skeptical at first, but after a demonstration I became a believer. The device is powered by h36," he finished.

"So with this demonstration where can you take me?"

"I'll take you to Zendreo."

I suddenly felt very excited. When you've been away from home for so long the thought a going home feels amazing.

"Yes, let's do it!" I almost shouted.

The man motioned to the mirrored window and some men came in carrying suits and helmets.

"You'll need to wear one of these flight suits. The flight suit will protect you against the vacuum of space. Think of it as your space ship."

I was so excited. I grabbed the suit from the nearest guard and started putting it on. The suits were very much like my ice-flyer suit which I was already wearing beneath my clothes. The nano technology was more advanced than my ice-flyer suit. The suit automatically adjusted its size to fit my body snugly. There were special gloves and boots to make sure the suit was completely sealed.

I had my suit on much faster than the other man. I was ready to go. A man handed me a helmet and I put it on. The helmet was a full face helmet with a sun visor. When I put on the helmet, the heads-up display came to life and a video started playing.

"Attention Halo Jumper welcome to the newest and fastest way to travel the galaxy," the woman's voice in the video said in a pleasant tone.

"Halo jumping does have risks and as such we're required by SGC law to explain those risks. Halo jumping can cause vomiting and disorientation. Feelings of nausea are normal. In some cases it can cause feinting. In rare cases travel can be disrupted if a beacon signal is lost or delayed, due to beacon failure. If a beacon fails you might experience a delay while the nearest beacon is contacted. The delay caused by a malfunctioning beacon can take seconds or minutes depending on the distance to the nearest beacon."

The voice continued on explaining the risks, but I started to zone out. I was thinking, this halo jumping technology was not military. There would never be a disclaimer explaining the risks in a military system. It was a commercial system. I was surprised that I'd never heard of halo jumping before. The video ended and now I wished I'd paid more attention to it.

"Can you hear me?" The interrogator asked, his voice was coming from speakers inside my helmet.

"Yes, I can hear you," I said, nodding anxiously.

"Okay, we're ready to go. You need to stand next to me."

I stood next to the man.

"We need to sync up our helmets..."

I could see a syncing indicator flashing on the helmet's HUD indicating that the helmets were syncing. The indicator went solid and stopped flashing after a few seconds.

"I think the helmets are synced. Why do you need to sync the helmets?" I asked.

"You have to sync up to do jumps with more than one person."

"How do I know this is not some virtual reality helmet

and you're going to implant fake memories into my brain?"

The man almost laughed.

"You don't know, but trust me, this is real," he said looking straight at me.

"Are you ready?" he asked.

"Don't we need to sit down or something to get comfortable for the trip?" I asked.

The man shook his head.

"No! Now are you ready to go?"

I could tell that my heart was beating faster than normal. I was feeling a little nervous but I was excited at the chance to see home. I decided to ignore my nervous feelings.

"Yeah, I'm ready," I said.

The man pulled out his device and pulled up the holodisplay and started cycling through the different screens looking at the different star charts until he found the one he was looking for.

"Okay, I'm ready here we go," he said with a grin.

A blue circle of light came out of the device until it had us both surrounded.

"Please stand still. Do not exit the circle of light. It can cause malfunctions and result in death," said a voice over the helmet speakers.

"Ten, nine, eight, seven, six, five, four, three, two, one, may your travels be safe," the voice finished.

I didn't notice much at first, all I could see was a blue light and then nothing…

...

I opened my eyes. I realized that I must have closed them. I didn't remember closing my eyes. I couldn't see anything. It was pitch black.

"Are you there? Can you hear me?" I heard the man's voice coming from the speakers in my helmet.

"I think we had a beacon failure."

"I can't see anything," I said.

"Open your sun visor stupid! It will take a minute for your eyes to adjust. I think you blacked out."

I felt like I was back home in my AG bed. Then the words beacon failure finally registered in my brain. I was floating in space. I flipped up the sun visor and turned my head looking to see if I could see the interrogator. He was floating next to me and he gave me a thumbs up. When my eyes had adjusted, the view was amazing. I could see stars in every direction.

When I turned off the HUD in my helmet to take away the glare, I could really see. There were countless numbers of stars. I'd never seen so many stars before. Well, I'd seen plenty of holographic displays that tried to mimic what I was seeing. This view was real and nothing man-made could begin to recreate what I was seeing.

"Don't worry. This happens sometimes. There are so many beacons that it is impossible to keep all of them working," the man said encouragingly.

"How long do we wait?" I asked.

"Didn't you listen to the video? It can take seconds or minutes and even hours. It depends how far away the nearest beacon is. The signals travel at light speed so it can take awhile to find the next beacon."

"What happens if it doesn't find a beacon?"

"If no beacon is found the device will return us back to where we started. Don't worry, just enjoy the view. It was very strange to look down at my feet and not see ground beneath them. I started to feel a little dizzy.

"Any idea where we are and how far we've traveled?" I asked.

"We're relatively close to Zendreo. hopefully we'll make it. Hardly anyone goes to Zendreo. There are not very many beacons in this part of the galaxy. If you turn your HUD back on you can see where we are by selecting the location screen."

"Okay, I'll turn my HUD back on in a minute. Right now I want to enjoy the view."

Relatively close to Zendreo could mean a lot of different

things. We were probably not even inside a solar system. I wished that Char could see what I was seeing. I wished my daughter could be with me. I missed my family. I wished that I could remember my wife and daughter. I wanted to tell my parents how I was so proud to be their son. I couldn't even remember what they looked like. I started feeling a warm, comforting feeling inside. The thought came to me that my parents and my wife could see what I could see. My family that had passed on were with me and they were happy because I was thinking about them.

Maybe all those cliché things that people say after someone dies are true. Maybe the dead don't leave us, maybe they are close by, watching over us, especially when we think about them. I didn't know, but it felt real.

The HUD lit up on my helmet. It surprised me because I didn't activate it.

"I think it found the nearest beacon," the man said. This time the HUD started counting down without the voice. It must have done the same the first time but I hadn't noticed. The countdown ended and then I saw nothing...

...

"Can you hear me? We made it the rest of the way," It was the man, I heard him through the speakers in my helmet.

I couldn't see anything and then I remembered the sun visor and I flipped it up. The helmet must have shut the visor when we jumped. My legs felt a little wobbly because they were standing on solid ground.

We were standing in a meadow with waist high grass just as the sun was going down in the west.

"Yeah, I hear you."

"You can take off your helmet. Don't try anything I don't want to have to use this." The man was pointing a weapon at me.

"Do you know what this is?" he asked.

The gun looked very high tech but I had no idea what kind it was. They didn't let average people carry around that kind of hardware. In fact, the laws didn't allow anyone but military personnel to carry guns.

Only criminals and the military had guns. The claim was that the SCG society had reached such a high level of technology and prosperity that there were no criminals left. Everyone's basic needs had been met so there was no motivation for crime.

My thoughts were: Why do they still have prisons? What about all the worlds that are not part of the SGC, what if one of those worlds decided to invade? Why do they keep inventing more lethal weapons if crime has been eliminated? Why do they think they need weapons while the average person does not?

The simple truth is, weapons are power and the people in charge want power over regular people. The people in charge, want to stay in charge. For some reason people who get a little authority over others always think they know better than regular people. Once in power, most never want to give it up, it's human nature.

"This is a replicating rail gun. Do you know what that means?" the man continued, bringing me back from my thoughts.

I didn't know, so I shook my head.

"I never have to reload because the projectiles are replicated. If you decide you want to run away and hide behind a rock this gun has ADCE projectiles that's Auto Distance Calculating Exploding projectiles. Do you know what that means?"

"It means that thing would be able to kill me pretty easy?" I asked trying to sound like I didn't know what I was talking about.

"You try to hide behind something and these projectiles will explode at a perfect lethal distance. You'd be dead before you could hear the explosion," the man said.

I was pretty sure this guy had used his gun on people many times. The look in the man's eye and the feeling I got when he was speaking made it very clear that he wouldn't hesitate if I tried to get away.

"I thought I was supposed to be valuable? What would the President do if you returned without me?" I asked with a grin.

The man grinned back.

"I don't know why, but I kinda like you. But trust me, I

will use this if I have to. Besides you wouldn't last more than a few days without an ID-chip."

It was true, not having an ID-chip could be a death sentence. It seems like you always heard in the latest news about people without ID-chips that were found dead. Some people believed that SGC controlled media was trying to cover for the government. Anytime there was a crime or resistance to their power, the people who were found dead almost always never had ID-chips. With Technology it was supposed to be impossible to commit a crime without being caught by surveillance so people sometimes would get their chips removed before committing a crime.

I took off my helmet and the fresh air was amazing. I could smell the grass and I could see the giant zelecon pine trees and mountains in the distance. After being stuck in a tiny holding cell with no hope of ever returning home I was so overcome with emotion that I just sat down on the ground half stunned and not believing my senses.

"You Zendreons are all the same. You're always so proud of your world. I don't get it. I've been to hundreds of worlds and Zendreo is the last one I'd choose to live on. Everything is so antiquated and dull here."

"You've met other Zendreons?" I asked.

"Of course. Zendreo is the source of many, if not almost all of the SGC's problems. The people here are never satisfied and always going against normal civilized behavior. You know Zendreo was the last world to enter into the SGC after the last great war?"

He didn't wait for my answer.

"Even after they wipe the E-chips of your kind, the pride doesn't go away."

I smiled and nodded. It was true, I was proud of who I was and where I came from even if I couldn't remember exactly where that was.

"Can we halo jump into my home town? I can't remember the name, but you might," I asked.

"Are you kidding? You're lucky I even brought you here at all. Halo jumping is restricted to SGC agents only on Zendreo."

Well maybe that's why I'd never heard of it. The majority of the people on Zendreo stayed on Zendreo their entire lives. Besides if you left by the time you came back everyone you knew could be dead.

The SGC obviously didn't want halo jumping technology given to us, there'd be more Zendreons to deal with. So much for equal membership in the SGC.

"So where are we anyway?" I asked

"We're in the Great Zelecon Wildlife Refuge. It's about the only reason anyone would ever want to visit this planet," the man said.

It was probably true. The Zelecon Wildlife Refuge is known as one of the most scenic and pristine forests full of all kinds of wildlife. Tourists and scientists from all over Zendreo come to see the refuge. It made sense because the halo jump setup was a commercial system and the Zelecon Refuge made the list for places to visit.

I remembered my daughter.

"Can we look for my daughter?" I asked earnestly.

"Are you kidding me? This is not some day trip or vacation. We've got to get back. So pick something to take back with you so you know that this is all real," The man said sounding annoyed.

For the first time in my life I was reduced to begging.

"Please, I'll do anything if you will help me find my daughter. Don't you have any family? Wouldn't you do anything for your kids?"

The man just stared at me, shaking his head looking annoyed.

"I don't have any family. Pick a rock or something so we can get back. I'm getting hungry for dinner."

"I'm sorry you don't have family. I'd be your brother forever if you helped me find my daughter," I said.

The look on the man's face changed ever so slightly. I think he was surprised by what I said.

"You don't even know me and what I've done. You'd never want to be my brother."

I really didn't care at this point what the man had done in his past life. I just wanted to find my daughter.

"Your past doesn't matter. There's absolutely nothing you can do to change it, but you can choose today to be different. You can help me, and become my brother," I said looking at the man.

The man shook his head. "You don't even know my name. No, it's not possible for me. Pick up a rock or something. We're going back."

"I'll make a deal with you. If you help me find my daughter I'll do whatever you ask."

"You'll do whatever we want and you'll die in a cage. You're not in a position to make deals," the man said in an angry voice.

I could see that there was no hope with this man. Feeling beat I got back on my feet and started looking for something that I could take back with me. At first the thought of going back was not a happy one. Then I remember Char. Maybe going back wouldn't be such a bad thing. I started looking for something that I could give to Char. I started feeling better inside thinking about how fun it would be to amaze her with something from my home world.

"Can I take a pine cone?" I asked. I didn't remember seeing any pine trees in any of the underground gardens on Tyrol.

"Yeah, just find one so we can go back," the man said.

After a little searching I found the perfect one, it was huge even for a zelecon pine cone. Holding it with both hands my fingers were not long enough to wrap all away around it. Zelecon pine were the largest known trees in the galaxy. Who knows, maybe we'd be able get some zelecon pine trees growing on Tyrol. I wondered if I'd ever come back to Zendreo. I hoped that my daughter was okay.

The journey back to Tyrol went without any issues. I was hoping for another beacon malfunction because the view was amazing. When we got back on Tyrol it was only a few hours later. Without the pine cone, I was pretty sure that I'd wouldn't be able to believe that I'd just been on Zendreo.

They put me back in my cell and told me they'd be back the next day to get my answer. There really wasn't much of a choice. I didn't want to stay in the cell but I also didn't want to become a fighter. I'd been lucky, and I knew it. It wasn't in my nature to be a fighter. I'd only fought in self-defense. I spent most of the night staring at the pine cone and wondering if I'd ever be able to give it to Char.

CHAPTER IX
TRAINING

Early the next morning the same man who'd taken me to Zendreo came to get me.

"What do I call you?" I asked.

The man just looked at me with indifference.

"Don't call me anything," he said dryly.

"All right Zip, have it your way. What do you want?" I asked.

"Did you just call me Zip?" the man asked.

"Yeah, you look like a Zip to me."

"What's that supposed to mean?" the man asked with a defensive tone.

He didn't like his nick name. I don't know why but for some reason I could remember Zips but I couldn't remember much about the people in my family.

"A zip is what we Zendreons call those annoying blood sucking insects that everyone hates. Since you won't tell me your name, I just made one up for you. I'll call you

Zip. So Zip, what's up?"

The man looked up and then back at me. He had a confused look on his face.

"What do you mean, what's up? There's nothing up there... Your training starts today."

"But I never agreed to become a fighter."

Zip didn't even look at me. He just motioned for me to follow him, and so I did.

The training schedule was brutal. Every morning I'd go on long runs around the entire section of the city where the Anaxus lived. They wanted me to work on endurance. After the long runs, I'd lift weights. In the evenings they'd make me run sprints to work on speed. They told me the first part of my training was to get stronger. Once they felt like I was strong enough, my fight training would start. They also put me on a special diet that was supposed to make me stronger and more fit.

I'd done a lot of training for sports in my life and it actually felt good to train. I was constantly watched and barely had a few minutes of alone-time each day.

Every day as I ran by the waterfall, I'd look up above it and wonder if Char was up there looking down. I wondered if she ever thought about me. It felt like years had passed since I last saw her. Char was the only friend I could remember.

One day while I was on my early morning run, I had an

idea. I was going to climb all the way up to the overlook above the waterfall. There was no trail and the climb wouldn't be easy. I wasn't an experienced climber so it could be very dangerous, especially without a rope and safety gear. Lucky for me the way up was not completely vertical. I was pretty sure I could make it to the top.

From below you couldn't see where the overlook was, but I was pretty sure I could find it once I got close. My plan was simple. Once I got close to the waterfall I'd veer off course and sprint over to the rocks and start climbing before the guards watching me knew what I was doing. I doubted the guards would follow me but I wasn't sure. I decided that it was worth taking the risk.

It was now or never. I sprinted over to the rocks and started climbing. I was making really good progress up the rock face when I heard someone yelling from below. The men below were yelling at me to come back down. One was even pointing a weapon at me. I stopped and I thought for a second... I had an idea.

I yelled at the men, "Climbing this rock will be good for my training I'll come back down once I reach the top. You can watch me from below."

The man with the weapon lowered it and shook his head, "No, you better come back down. The President will not be happy if you fall," I heard him say.

For some reason I just felt like I needed to climb this rock today. I tapped my ears like I couldn't hear what the man was saying. I started climbing again without looking down. I knew they wouldn't shoot because they wanted me alive. Taking a peek below and I could see the man with the weapon shaking his head and looking up after me.

Going up was pretty easy. As I got up higher and higher, I realized that everything looks a lot higher from above than down below. I was beginning to think climbing without safety gear was a bad idea. I ignored my fears and decided to not worry about how I'd get back down. I decided to not look down anymore and keep climbing. Before long I was at the top of the first waterfall. The waterfall was a series of falls almost like a stair case. The terrain flattened out at the top of the first waterfall and then went up almost vertical again at the next waterfall.

I realized the men below wouldn't be able to see me. I stopped at the edge and turned around and stuck both hands up high in the air, like I was celebrating making it to the top of the first waterfall. I was hoping the men below wouldn't come up after me thinking that there was nowhere for me to go, but back down. I was sure they didn't know about the passageways and the overlook at the top. I wanted to give them the appearance that I was just exploring and having fun more than heading towards a destination.

I continued climbing until finally I made it to where I could see the overlook. It was too high; the overlook was just a small a hole in the ceiling. There was no way that I could get there without a rope. I looked hoping to see Char but she wasn't there. It felt so good to go on this climb and I could finally see the end. The thought that I wasn't going to be able to finish the climb was a depressing one. I decided I'd keep going as far as I could. I wasn't going to quit after going this far. I reached the top of the last water fall and the terrain flattened out again.

The water was coming out of a tunnel in the rock. The tunnel was much bigger than I expected. I decided to explore it. There were hand railings as I was walking into the tunnel. There was a man-made path. Maybe there was a way to get to the overlook after all.

I climbed over the railing and started down the path. I didn't have to go far before I found a doorway. Sure enough the doorway led to a familiar tunnel that I'd walked through many times with Char. I hurried through the tunnel and up the spiral staircase until I made it to the overlook. I looked down to see if I could see the men below at the base of the waterfall. It was was impossible to see them. I knew that I didn't have a long time before the men would come searching. I didn't want them to know about the overlook.

There was no sign of Char. I was excited to see her but she was nowhere to be found. I decided that I'd sit down and wait a few minutes to see if she'd show up. If she didn't come, I'd see if I could figure out some way to leave her a message that I'd been here.

It wasn't long when I heard some soft footsteps approaching. I stood up and waited. I was facing the tunnel hoping that Char would come out of it. She came out of the tunnel walking with her head down. She didn't look my way and continued heading off towards the vents. I stood there quietly hoping that she'd notice me. I didn't want to scare her to death. I was positive that she wasn't expecting to meet anyone way up here. She must have finally sensed my presence or that eyes were watching her because at the last chance before heading down the tunnel towards the vents, she paused and looked up and saw me.

"I knew it!" Char yelled.

She came running over and hugged me tight. It felt so good to see her.

"What did you know?" I asked.

When she finally stopped hugging me, Char just stood there looking up at me with a huge smile. I wonder if she knew the power of her smile? I'm pretty sure that even the most-orneriest man alive could not be in her presence and not smile back at her.

"I knew you hadn't left us! Today is my birthday and you will never guess what I wanted."

She was right. I was sure I wouldn't be able to guess what she'd hoped for. I was feeling kind of sad inside because I didn't know that it was her birthday.

"I wanted to see you! I almost didn't want to look because I hoped to meet you here! I just didn't want to be disappointed on my birthday, if you weren't here."

I wondered if it was possible that her wishing so badly to see me had made me decide to climb up here today. I guess it was possible.

"You look really good! I mean you look great. Where have you been Mr. Immortal?"

I wished that I could just stop time for awhile and be with Char, but I knew it wasn't possible.

"I don't have lots of time. I've got to get back. The President has decided that I'll be doing some more fighting in the prison circuit. He thinks I'm going to make him a lot of money. If I don't fight they'll lock me up in a tiny cell and never let me out."

Char smiled.

"You're joking aren't you? The President would never do anything like that."

Her smile went away when I didn't answer.

"You're telling the truth," she said.

"I'm not supposed to be here. I didn't get here through the tunnels. I climbed up here following the waterfall. There are some men down at the bottom with weapons wondering where I'm at."

Char's happy face changed to a face of concern.

"What are you going to do? You're not a fighter. It's not in your nature."

I'd told Char in one of our many talks about my fight with Kos the champion, and how lucky I'd been.

"Right now I don't have much of a choice. I have to go back down there and train."

"Why would the President want you to become a fighter? How would he know that about you?" Char asked.

"Char you're not going to want hear what I have to tell you, but you need to know. The President is part of the SGC. You know, the same people I told you about who want the h36. The Anaxus are too. You and your people are the last survivors from your world. This facility was built by your people as a wandering planet testing facility. The SCG are using you to test the living conditions so they can build a similar city on wandering planets."

Char was looking at me with a confused look on her face. I was sure she was not understanding what a wandering planet was.

After I explained wandering planets to Char, she shook her head.

"How do you know all this?"

"One of the President's men told me. They saw my fight at the prison. They knew everything about me."

I told Char about halo jumping and how I brought her back a Zelecon pine cone. Char listen quietly until I finished.

Char smiled, "I believe that you believe what you are telling me but I just don't know how it could all be true..." she trailed off not looking at me.

I knew that she didn't want to hurt my feelings but she

was struggling to believe my story.

"I don't blame you. Everything I have told you seems impossible, especially without any proof. Tomorrow or the next time I climb up here, I'll bring you the Zelecon pine cone. I'm hoping we can grow some of those trees here. Zelecon pine are the largest trees in the known galaxy!" I said with a smile.

She smiled back at me.

"Okay," was all she said.

"I'm so happy that I got to see you! On your birthday even! But I have to get back before some of the President's men get up here and spoil everything."

Char nodded looking down with a somewhat sad expression on her face.

"Okay, I'll look for you everyday. Hey, when is your birthday?" she asked.

I didn't know.

"I don't know. I can't remember," I said, feeling myself getting angry at the people who'd taken away my memories.

"That's just sad! I guess we can just pick a day for you and celebrate that day. How about the day I found you? That day will always be a special day for me."

It felt good to be friends with Char. I could tell she really cared about me.

"Yeah, let's do that!" I said.

Char walked with me back down through the tunnel and to the flat area above the last waterfall. I hugged her for a long time and then I started to leave. I was going to miss her smile, more than she knew.

"I'll come here everyday and look for you. I hope to see you soon. Be careful!" Char said with some emotion in her voice.

"Happy birthday! See you soon!" I responded trying to sound cheerful.

The climb back down took a lot longer than climbing up. For one thing I didn't want to go back down and leave Char. I had to climb down backwards looking over my shoulder for most of the climb so I didn't fall.

After a long time climbing, I could see the man with a weapon. He wasn't standing looking up anymore. The man was sitting on a rock looking back towards the city. The other man that had been there before must have gotten tired of waiting and left. The guard with the gun must have heard me coming because he looked up at me. The expression on his face told me everything. I could tell he was not happy with me at all.

The man walked over pointing his weapon at me when I finally made it to the bottom.

"Next time you try something like that I'll shoot you down and make up a good story as to why I had to kill you!"

"You're not going to shoot me," I said without thinking.

Before I could react the man hit me hard in the mouth with the butt of his weapon. I fell to the ground and blood was coming out of my mouth and nose. I hoped he hadn't knocked out one of my teeth.

"Get up, champion!"

I felt a sharp pain in my ribs. The man was kicking me while I was on the ground. I tried to get up, but everything went black...

...

I woke up laying on the ground with a pounding headache and then I remembered the guard beating me with his weapon. When I looked up, I could see the man standing over me, looking at me with disgust.

"You're going to die in your first fight. I just knocked you out without even trying."

I didn't like the taste of blood in my mouth and I decided that I didn't like the guard very much either.

"It wasn't a fair fight," I said, getting up a little shaky.

The guard must have not liked what I said because he hit me again knocking me to the ground.

"Are you done?" the guard asked.

"Put down your weapon, and let's see," I said standing up.

The guard smiled.

"Gladly!"

He put down his weapon. I hadn't noticed until just now, but there was a group of men that had come to watch us.

I had no real fight training, at least I couldn't remember ever training as a fighter. I wasn't sure what I was going to do. I was angry and I really wanted to get this guy for knocking me out and kicking me when I was down. I was a lot bigger than the man. I was thinking about how I could use my size as an advantage.

The man started circling me and grinning.

"The champ is about to get beat! Come on champ boy, what are you waiting for?" the man taunted.

I could feel myself getting angry. I was sure the back of my neck was bright red. The guard kept dancing around cursing and yelling insults at me. The group of men were laughing at me, which made me all the madder.

I realized that taunting me was all part of the man's strategy and I was falling for it. He wanted me to be mad hoping I'd lose control and make it easier for him. I stood my ground and turned, facing the man as he continued dancing around and yelling insults at me. At first the men were laughing at every insult but now the laughter was slowly dying down. I knew the guard would make his move soon. I didn't say a word I just made sure I was always facing the man. I tried not to make any expressions with my face.

The man suddenly came at me with a lot of speed swinging his fist for my head. I barely got out of the way and his fist barely grazed my head. I put my hands up in an attempt to protect my head anticipating more punches to the head. The man hit me hard in the stomach causing me to bend over forward. I saw the man start to swing at me again and then everything went black.

...

When I woke up, I was laying on my back looking up at the man that had just knocked me out for a second time. My head was fuzzy. I didn't feel right. I was sure that I had a massive concussion. I was having a hard time concentrating. One of the other guards must have noticed that I was awake because he came and pulled me up to my feet, and started to take me back to my quarters.

"Don't worry about Ruffins. He used to be a pro fighter and he's always picking fights. I suspect they brought him here to train you. Ruffins is too old now, he doesn't have the stamina, but he knows how to fight. Today was your first lesson in fighting," the guard said as we were walking.

I'd definitely learned how lucky I'd been in my previous fights. It was more obvious to me than before; I was not a very good fighter. While I followed the guard back to my quarters, I realized that I would not have been able to find my way, on my own. I suddenly felt very tired...

CHAPTER X
MY NAME IS ZEHN

"They're coming. We need to leave now!" I heard a woman's voice say. I knew that voice. I was trying to place a face with the voice. When I saw her, I knew that the woman was my mom.

"Who's coming? Where are we going?" I asked.

"Here put these on your wrists. There's no time. We have to leave now!" my mom handed me some kind of wrist band.

"So they can't track us," my mom said when she saw the questioning look on my face.

Then I saw her. I saw the beautiful woman from my dream. It was my wife. She put a wrist band on the arm of a little girl and then she put one on her arm.

"We're ready, let's go!" my wife said.

At that moment I wanted to freeze time and just be with my wife and daughter. I wanted to hug them and tell them that I loved them.

I heard shouting.

"Come on, let's go now! We don't have anymore time."

It was my dad.

We all started running through the house towards the back door. The house was my house. It was in a wooded area on the outskirts of the city Perthasol on the coast near the Andros mountains. My parents must have come to warn us for some reason. My dad met us at the back door. He pointed towards the trees across the back yard. We started to run towards the trees.

I heard what sounded like rain hitting the house. I kept running for a few seconds but I didn't hear any footsteps behind me. Suddenly bright lights from what seemed like all directions turned on. I turned and looked back towards the house. Everyone was laying on the ground. I saw some men with weapons coming out from behind the lights. I was completely surrounded. At first, I just stood there. I didn't know what to do. After what felt like a very long time, I started to run towards my family. Somebody knocked me to the ground. No matter how hard I struggled, I couldn't get up.

I stopped struggling and looked over towards my family. I saw some men discussing something that I couldn't hear... and then I saw my daughter. She was rocking back and forth and sobbing. My daughter was sitting next to her mom holding her mom's hand and saying something that I couldn't hear.

...

I woke up feeling angry and sad. The image of my daughter holding her dying mother's hand was killing me. This dream felt real. Maybe being knocked

166

unconscious had released some of the memories that had been taken away from me by the SGC.

My heart ached for my poor daughter. It felt like a weight had been put on my chest making it harder to breathe. No little girl should have to see her mother murdered. The dream was not normal. It was more like a memory than a dream. The dream kept playing over and over in my mind. I had a hard time going back to sleep.

The SGC had a surveillance video of me looking back at my family after they'd all been shot. Maybe this is how they made it look like I was the killer. It was a simple process for the SGC to edit the video. Everyone would believe that I was the killer because it was supposed to be impossible to edit official surveillance video.

All surveillance video has specific encrypted encoding that is used to detect if the video has been edited. Video with the tamper-proof encoding was accepted by all courts as irrefutable evidence. They must have found a way or they had a back door to edit the surveillance video. The judge had decided that they had enough video evidence that I didn't get at trial.

I wondered how many other people had suffered the same fate as me. It was simple, wipe everyone's E-chips and send them light years away to never be heard from again. Technology was changing so fast and the people making the laws didn't always understand the new technologies. The general population suffered from the bad decisions made by uninformed politicians.

Nobody had even heard my story. It happened because some politician passed a law allowing them to send people off to prison without a trial. My fate was based on the assumption that all surveillance video could not be tampered with. I'm sure the law was well intended. Maybe it was passed to save time and lessen the burdens on the courts, but the law was flawed!

Modern society was putting too much trust into technology that only a few could understand.

I finally fell asleep, when it was almost light outside.

...

I was greeted in the morning by Ruffins. He seemed to be in a good mood after knocking me out twice the day before.

"Your face looks great! Did you sleep well champ?" Ruffins asked, adding an insult to my injuries.

I was having a really hard time seeing out of my right eye which had swollen up pretty bad during the night.

"Actually no. I didn't sleep much," I responded.

"Well that's too bad, your fight training starts today!"

"From what I hear my training started yesterday," I said.

Ruffins laughed.

"You're correct! So what did you learn from your first lesson?"

"I learned... never to get in a fight with you," I said sarcastically.

Ruffins smiled.

"Yes, correct! I'll beat you down every time! When you can compete with me you'll be ready for real fighting. What else did you learn?"

This time I tried to think of a serious answer.

"I learned to never underestimate my opponent and to never get too big-headed over previous victories," I said seriously.

"You're correct... Your last opponent forgot this simple but very important lesson."

It was true, actually both my opponents had over-estimated themselves and hadn't expected much out of me. It had worked for me in both of my fights.

I'd only been in two real fights my entire life... well counting now, I'd been in three. I didn't see myself ever being able to beat Ruffins. Maybe that was it! If I pretended to never get quite good enough, maybe I'd never have to become a fighter.

"What happens if I never beat you?" I asked Ruffins.

"You never will beat me, only if I let you. You've got the tools, you just need to learn how to use them. Besides you're going to learn every trick I know. You're already pretty good with a sword."

I guess it was true. I was pretty good with a sword

compared to my competition.

"The problem is you don't always get to fight with swords. Sometimes you don't get any weapons at all. Some fight circuits like the prison ones use weapons. All the fighters are usually prisoners. If you fight in more respectable circuits you don't get any weapons, but the payouts and fame are amazing. The President likes you. He says you're a survivor and you don't give up."

"Really? The President said that about me?" I asked surprised.

"He said that he's never seen anyone with no real fighting skill be so fearless and find a way to win. Especially the way you won your fight with Kos. Even after knowing it was pure luck, the President still wants you. He thinks you have what it takes to be great if you get some real training. He's already scheduled a rematch with your buddy Kos."

The thought of going up against Kos again gave my stomach a sickening feeling. There was no way that I was going to win on luck again. Kos would be ready for me. He wouldn't make the same mistake he made the first time he fought me.

"Don't worry! When I'm done with you, fighting Kos won't even be a workout for you," Ruffins said with a grin.

...

Every day seemed like the same as the day before it. I'd

get up early and start out by working on hand to hand fighting with Ruffins. I worked on offensive moves, throwing punches and kicks. I learned how to block punches and kicks and to avoid getting hit. I worked on hand-to-hand fighting all morning every morning. After lunch each day I worked on fighting with swords, daggers and battle axes. For some reason unknown to me, the prison circuit fans loved to see fights with these ancient weapons.

I actually liked it when we used swords. I was maybe a little better than Ruffins.

After dinner, I'd hit the weights and finally end the day with long endurance runs and sprints. Every time I ran by the waterfall, I'd think of Char and miss her smile. Most nights I'd return back to my quarters totally exhausted. I'd sleep the entire night without waking up. I trained as hard as I could because I wanted to survive. I wanted to find my daughter. I wanted to see Char again. My body was getting stronger. I was fighting better each day.

...

The day of my first official fight had almost arrived. Today we were getting ready to leave for the planet Ethos. I didn't know very much about Ethos. I hoped it would be a nice change from a frozen ice world. I missed my home. I missed the forests and the fresh air after a rain storm. I longed to see the waves of the ocean again.

They were only sending a few of us at first. They wanted to give me time on Ethos to get accustomed to the air and gravity before jumping into a fight. We were going to be halo jumping. I never dreamed that a technology as cool as halo jumping could exist. I still had a hard time believing that it was real. I don't think I'd be able to believe in the technology if it weren't for the pine cone I brought back. I was glad for the moment that I hadn't given the pine cone to Char. That pine cone was the only thing keeping me sane.

I once thought it would be impossible for me to go home. The pine cone was giving me hope that I'd make it home some day. When I thought about home, I always got a good feeling inside. I didn't know how or when, but I knew that I'd see my home again.

I was excited for the chance to see another world. Most people never got the opportunity to travel to other worlds because they couldn't afford the journey. Halo jumping was the most amazing way to travel, but most people didn't even know it existed. I guess some of the worlds were more advanced than others in the SGC and they didn't share technology like they should. I was always taught that according to the SGC treaty with Zendreo and all the other worlds in the SGC, all technology was supposed to be shared. The only answer I could come up with was, the SGC didn't follow all its own rules, which is typical with governments. People in power always come up with good reasons why they are not required to follow the same laws they require regular people to live by.

Until now I'd thought it was impossible to have near real time communications with other worlds because of the distances. But I found out that they use the same halo jump technology to also send messages. The messages navigated the beacons and were routed all over the galaxy. I wondered how long it took them to get all the beacons into place. It must be a massive undertaking to maintain them. I always wondered how the SGC could maintain any kind of order with the vast distances between the different worlds, and now I knew.

"Are you ready for the briefing?" a voice said taking me away from my thoughts.

It was Ruffins.

Ruffins was excited. I could tell that he was getting pumped for the upcoming fight. I was sure that he was anxious to see how I'd do with all his training. I'd made lots of progress. I'd spent so much time sparring with Ruffins that I could anticipate just about every move he'd make and react to it without thinking. If you spend too much time thinking about the moves you want to make, your chances of winning go way down unless your opponent is extremely slow or lacks training.

The President smiled and nodded as we entered the briefing room. I was surprised to see him there. I was also surprised to see that there were lots of other well-dressed important looking people there. They'd setup chairs at one end of the room facing towards a presentation area. I wondered what the big deal was? I thought the briefing was going to be just for me and the group that was leaving soon. I was expecting to learn a little bit about Ethos.

After everyone had quieted down the President got up in front of the group.

"I'm happy to welcome everyone here today. I want to introduce you to the Zendreon Valerus, our next champion."

There was a large cheer from all the people in the room. Valerus? All I could think was, what a stupid name!

"My name is Zehn!" I heard myself yelling over the noise of the cheering.

I heard a few astonished gasps and then silence.

"My name is Zehn," I said looking at the President and speaking just loud enough for everyone to hear.

The President didn't look amused. He looked directly at me. I could see the disdain growing on his face. The President wasn't the kind of man you corrected, yet for some reason today I wasn't afraid of him.

"We know your name is Zehn, however you'll be known as Valerus the Zendreon in the fighting circuits," the President said quietly.

"I will be known as Zehn Mortalix the name my mother and father gave me," I said looking directly at the President.

I knew if my mom could see me at this moment she'd be proud to call me her son. I looked over at Ruffins, if his eyes could talk I'm sure they'd say SHUT YOUR MOUTH! Are you insane?

I was embarrassing the President in front of all these important people that he was trying to impress. I turned back and looked at the President. The shocked looked on the President's face was leaving; he was returning to his normal calm look.

"Okay, Zehn it is," the President said with a smile.

"Since many of you have not seen..." the President paused for a moment as if to choose his words carefully, then he started again.

"Since many of you have not seen Zehn fight before, we have arranged a small preview presentation so you can feel confident in his abilities and in your wagers. Without going any further let's start the presentation," the President finished, indicating towards his technical people to start the preview.

Ruffins grabbed me and dragged me to a chair as the lights in the room where dimming.

"Are you insane? If you knew who that man really is and what he is capable of, you'd keep your mouth shut!" Ruffins whispered.

"Who is he and what can he do?" I asked.

"We'll talk later..." Ruffins said, shaking his head.

"Meet the young mighty Zendreon Valerus, a convict from the galaxy's toughest prison Gellus on Tyrol. Valerus is a natural fighter and he comes with incredible strength and endurance. He has the will to win," the narrator's voice said.

"Valerus has never been beaten."

Ruffins jabbed me in the ribs.

"We know that ain't true!"

The holographic display showed me fighting Kos.

"This footage comes from one of his first fights in the Gellus prison when he had little or no training. Watch as he easily defeats the champion Kos who needs no introduction," the narrator in the video said.

The narrator had a commanding voice. I hadn't seen the footage of my fight; I was interested to see it. I wasn't really sure what people saw in me as a fighter. The footage began showing me advancing on Kos with my sword. The President had cut out the first part of the fight when Kos was making me look silly. It's amazing how good editing could make me look so strong. The video showed me throwing Kos around like a rag doll with some of the moves that Ruffins taught me. I was pretty sure that they were using sparring footage and had edited the footage into the presentation to make me look better.

The presentation was on a full size holographic setup. It looked so real that if you walked in the room and didn't know it was a presentation, you might believe a real fight was going on. I looked over at Ruffins, after watching me throw Kos to the ground.

"I don't remember that part of the fight."

"That can happen if you've been hit too many times in

the head," Ruffins said with a smile.

The presentation came to the part with me standing over Kos with blood on my sword. I didn't remember seeing that much blood during our fight. I remembered the cut had been so fast that his arm didn't start to bleed right away.   The editors must have added in all the extra blood for effect. Everyone was cheering except me.

I should've been excited with all the cheering in the room. The President and his media people had made me look strong and even heroic. A sick feeling was growing inside my stomach. I was becoming angry. How could these people get so excited to see two men fighting to the death. I wanted to ask them how they'd feel if they were thrown into a ring to die by the hands of a champion like Kos.

"What's wrong with you? You should be enjoying this moment?" Ruffins said, looking at me with a surprised almost-disappointed look.

"I feel sick," was all I a managed to say.

I was different than Ruffins. He lived for the praise, glory and attention that fighters got. I'm sure he loved every minute of his fighting days and he was feeling jealous of me. Sure, I liked the attention. I liked to feel important, I think everyone does but this just felt wrong to me.

The presentation continued.

"Journey with us to explore the amazing world of Ethos

where you and your guests will experience ancient culture first hand. Ethos is a primitive world without modern conveniences so you'll need to follow certain guidelines and standards while you're there. You'll be required to leave behind all modern devices.

You'll be required to choose from the options of primitive clothes to wear so you fit in with the culture. You'll be able to exchange your money for local money. You'll be identified using your SGC ID. If you do not make it back to the expected departure location by the selected departure times you could be left behind, and could spend the rest of your life on Ethos..."

The narrator was still speaking but I chose to stop listening since none of the things he was saying applied to me.

I guess these people were looking for an exciting adventure so they were willing to take the chance of being stranded on a primitive world. My thoughts turned away from the presentation. I was thinking about all the possibilities. What if I lost on Ethos? Would they just leave me there forever? What if the technology failed or something went horribly wrong? I'd never be able to see my daughter.

When the briefing finally ended and the crowds of people were gone, five of the President's meanest looking men started walking towards me. I could see stern looks on their faces as if they were on a mission.

Ruffins was gone, he was probably off talking to some of his friends about the upcoming fight. I was alone. The closest man to me didn't hesitate, he took a swing at me aiming for my face. Instantly my training kicked in. I turned my head out of the way of the man's punch and grabbed is hand as it was coming towards me and using his momentum, I threw him into the wall hard.

I knocked down the next man with a massive hit to the head. I was pretty sure he wouldn't wake up for awhile. Somebody took out my legs and the President's men were holding me down. I struggled but I couldn't get them off me. There were too many of them.

"I have a message from the President," a man said almost whispering in my ear. I felt sharp pain in my ribs; somebody was kicking me...

"If you ever disrespect the President again like you did tonight, you'll die."

The man pushed my head into the ground and they let me up.

Somebody was helping up the man that I punched; he had a blank look on his face.

"He's lucky to be alive," I heard one of the men say.

I decided that night that I'd had enough of the President. I was leaving. I'd rather face the freezing temperatures than be the President's slave. I decided that I'd leave early in the morning. I'd follow the mountains and with some luck find my way back to the library. If I got up early enough, none of the guards assigned to watch me would be up yet.

I woke up early and got dressed into my workout clothes. I packed a backpack with some food, my ice-flyer suit and the pine cone. I didn't notice anyone as I headed to the waterfall. The climb to the top went fast. I wasn't even breathing hard when I made it into the tunnels.

My plan was to stop by Nanna's house and get my ice-flyer skates. I'd need the skates, otherwise I'd have no chance of making it over the crevices in the ice. Maybe I'd see Char before I left. I needed to hurry before anyone noticed that I was gone. I ran all the way through the tunnels until I reached the orchards. I stopped and picked some fruit and put it into my back pack and then headed for Nanna's house.

Nanna looked surprised and happy to see me. She gave me a hug.

"How did you get here?"

"I ran. I don't have a lot of time. they might already be looking for me. I came here to get my stuff. I'm leaving."

I told Nanna everything as quick as I could. After I finished Nanna looked concerned.

"I wish there was something I could do," Nanna said softly.

"There is one thing. I was hoping to see Char but it doesn't look like it is going to happen... Will you tell her goodbye for me. I brought her this pine cone from my home," I said, handing Nanna the pine cone.

"Maybe if she plants the seeds from it... when she sees the trees she'll remember me," I said, feeling sad.

Goodbyes were always so hard.

Nanna nodded her head slowly. She had a few tears in her eyes.

"I'll tell her. She is going to be so sad. She talks about you non stop."

"If I make it, I'll come back some day," I promised.

I was heading out into a very hostile environment and I knew it, and Nanna knew it. The chances that I'd be coming back were next to none. I gave Nanna a hug goodbye and I left.

It had been awhile since I'd been out in the cold; I almost went back inside when I felt it again. It felt good to have my ice-flyer skates on. It had been too long since I last skated. I headed out following the mountains. I hadn't gone that far when I started getting this feeling that I needed to go back. At first I just ignored the feeling. Why would I need to go back? I was finally free again. I felt it again stronger this time. Something was telling me to go back. I stopped and looked back.

Someone was following me. At first I thought it was one of the President's men. Then whoever it was fell over into the snow. Once again I felt that I needed to go back. Somehow I knew that it was Char, laying in the snow. I skated as fast and hard as I'd ever skated in my life. Char was laying on the ground. I was worried that her lungs could be freezing up.

I'd learned from my past experience in the cold, to pull my ice-flyer suit up over my mouth to help warm up the air so my lungs didn't freeze; probably something Char didn't know.

She probably didn't know how dangerously cold and dry the air was. Maybe she didn't know it could freeze her lungs.

When I finally reached her, she was lying on her back with her eyes open. There was frost on her eyebrows and eye lashes. Her mouth was open. I started to panic. How was this happening? Char was dying or dead and it was my fault. It felt like time had stopped. I could see her smiling at me in my mind. I was crying inside but no tears were coming out.

Then I felt a calm feeling come over me. I put my mouth on Char's mouth and gave her a breath. Her eyes blinked. I gave her some more breaths until she was breathing on her own. I picked her up in my arms and kept her face close to mine. I headed back to Grindolstin. It seemed like only a few seconds and we were back inside the big doors where the air was warm. In my mind I knew it must have taken us a lot longer than a few seconds to arrive, but the process felt like seconds. I began to notice Char was becoming heavier in my arms. I started to set her down when I looked at her face. She was looking at me with the same beautiful smile I'd seen in my mind.

"You came back for me. You saved me with a kiss! I

didn't want you to go," Char said weakly.

I'd finally learned how much this girl loved me. It was impossible for me not to love her at that moment. I squeezed her tight and without putting her down, I headed for Nanna's house. I could see the relief on Nanna's face when we made it back to her house.

"When I told Char that you came by and that you were leaving, she took off running. I didn't know what to do," Nanna said.

"I got to her before it was too late. Her lungs were almost frozen and she was having a hard time breathing. I guess, I won't be leaving after all. I'll have to go back."

The tone of my voice must have upset Char because the smile left her face.

"I'm sorry it's not you Char. Next time I leave, I'll take you with me."

The smile returned to her face and she hugged me.

"I better get back before the President's men come looking for me. I don't want to get you into trouble. There's a big fight coming up on Ethos and the President and his men have a lot of money invested..." my voice trailed off.

I could see looks of concern growing on the faces of the women.

"Don't worry about me. I'll be back. That's a promise," I said in the most convincing voice I could come up with.

I wasn't convinced myself that I'd be back, but I did have something to hope for.

I decided to leave everything at Nanna's except my holograph disc. If the President wanted to know where I'd been, I'd tell him that I was getting the holograph disc. I changed back into my workout clothes. I gave Nanna and Char hugs goodbye and headed for the door.

Char followed me out and before I could leave she grabbed me and hugged me tight. I hugged her back just as tight as she hugged me...

"I miss you," Char said.

It felt good to know that there was somebody who missed me.

"I miss you too," I responded.

Char kissed me.

"Can we count that as our first kiss?" she asked with a smile.

"The first time we kissed I was barely conscious and it was so cold I could hardly feel anything."

"That was a pretty good stunt just to get a kiss."

"Wait! Our first kiss brought me back from the dead! How romantic!" Char said almost-gleefully.

"Don't be telling... ah, what's his name? you know your future husband," I joked.

"Oh he's never getting a kiss from me," Char said.

"I'm sorry but I've got to go. I need to get back before they figure out that I'm gone. I don't want trouble."

I could see disappointment creeping back onto Char's face.

"I wish we could go back to the days when I was training you to do my job. Be safe and come back to me. Don't be like the other immortals and never come back," Char said quietly.

"I promise, I'll come back to you."

If I went through the city, it was still early enough that if I hurried I believed I could make it back before anyone noticed. The streets were mostly empty. I did see a few people on the streets during my run. The people looked very happy to see me and they all waved to me like they knew me.

When I arrived at the front gate of the Presidential complex the guard didn't even ask me any questions. He just let me in and told me that I better win the upcoming fight.

CHAPTER XI
ETHOS

I'd never heard of Ethos until I found out about the upcoming fight. Ethos is a planet covered mostly in water. The planet has pretty stable weather patterns thanks to its large moon. Ethos is located far out from the Primus star system and the center of the galaxy.

The planet was only recently discovered almost by accident. According to the stories, a very old space freighter's navigation computer malfunctioned taking the ship hundreds of thousands of light years off its course. The ship's long range sensors located Ethos as a possible planet that could support life.

The civilizations on Ethos are primitive. I was pretty sure that we had to get the proper SGC permits to travel to Ethos. We had to follow certain rules and regulations when visiting worlds with primitive civilizations.

I learned that the President and his betting friends had traveled to Ethos in the past. They liked going to Ethos because everything was so raw and exciting. There were no rules in the fights. The only piece of technology we were allowed to bring with us were translator chips. The chip technology was pretty cool. It was similar to the technology that the synthetics used to speak so many languages. The chips were inserted into your ear with nano bots that connected the chip to the speech part of your brain enhancing your speech capabilities. The chips would eventually degrade and pass through your body like any other dead cell. If the chip stayed active long enough, your brain would remember the languages it had learned from the chip. This must be how the President and his men had learned to speak Tyderio.

I found out that I'd be going with Storem, Ruffins and a few other men that I didn't know. They were sending enough men to keep an eye on me and make sure we didn't get into trouble. Storem was the man that introduced me to halo jumping, the man I called Zip.

"Are you ready?" It was Ruffins, he'd come to get me.

Ruffins was wearing what looked like a skirt or a dress.

"Wow! Nice dress! you look... ah, hmm pretty authentic?" I said.

"You bet I do. These clothes are authentic by the way. I got them on my last trip. We even got some authentic clothes for you. You're not going to like them," Ruffins said, with a grin ignoring my dress-comment.

He was right, the clothes looked filthy and were barely more than rags.

"You know that you're going to be my slave?"

I looked at Ruffins with a confused-look.

"On Ethos all the fighters are slaves. I own you!" Ruffins

laughed.

Slavery was not legal in the SGC but I was pretty sure that it had been practiced on almost every world at some point in time. I'd been sent to prison, banished from the SGC, my ID-chip taken out, and I was forced to fight by the President. I was his slave even though slavery was supposed to be illegal.

"I'm already the President's slave," I said quietly.

"Don't ruin the party! It's going to be great! You're going to love Ethos!" Ruffins replied ignoring my comment.

It was still early in the morning and I hadn't slept very well. I wasn't sure if I was nervous or excited. I felt nervous for the fight and excited to travel to another world. I was a little mad about being Ruffins' slave. I couldn't do much about it, so I decided to put it out of my mind.

Storem was waiting for us already suited up, ready for the halo jump.

"Hey Zip, are you bringing your super powerful replicating rail gun to make sure that I don't get away?"

Storem almost smiled.

"They won't let me bring my gun. If you try anything you will regret it! Suit up! Let's get going!" Storem hissed.

Storem was always about business. I'd forgot how menacing his voice was. I believe his voice would send mothers of young children running to cover their children's ears even if he wasn't using bad language. I didn't want to find out what the man was capable of. I hurried to follow his orders.

When everyone was suited up and ready to go, we all stood near Storem. He was busy cycling through star charts on his holodisplay.

"Everyone we need to sync up for the jump," I heard Storem's voice say over the speakers in my helmet.

His voice was overpowering the annoying woman's voice that was explaining all the risks of halo jumping.

The indicator light on my helmet showed that I was synced up.

"All right, it looks like everyone is synced up. We're leaving in ten. Make sure you are standing inside the blue circle," Storem said.

I watched the countdown indicators on my helmet's HUD counting down. I started to think, would I ever see my daughter? Would I ever see Char and Nanna again? I guess when you're about to do something dangerous it can make you focus on what's most important to you. The indicator had reached one. There was a bright blue light, and then nothing.

...

I opened my eyes to blackness.

"We had a beacon malfunction."

It was Storem's voice coming over the speakers in my helmet.

I opened my sun visor and looked around. We were floating in space. The view was amazing! There were so many stars. Pictures and holographs taken by telescopes could not compare to seeing this view with my own eyes. I noticed that there was a lot of light hitting my visor to my right. I turned my head towards the light and I saw the most amazing blue planet! The planet was a massive gas giant taking up almost my entire field of vision. The planet had small rings of debris going around it.

"Stay close! We don't want to lose anyone," Storem said.

I wasn't paying attention to Storem. I started cycling through my HUD to see if it had any information on the planet and where we were. The HUD showed that we were in an uninhabited solar system GSC212 near beacon 12993... Before I had time to think everything went black again.

We were standing on solid ground. I felt heavy. The sky was red, a very dark red, like no sky I'd seen before.

"We made it to Ethos everyone. You can take off your helmets."

The evening temperature was perfect. There was a cool breeze to go with it.

"The air is a bit thicker here but it shouldn't give you any problems," Storem said.

I couldn't stop looking at the sky towards the setting sun. Ethos' sun was massive and red. The sunset sky was redder than I'd ever seen before, more than half the sky was a deep red with streaks of orange.

"What is it with you? Every time I jump with you, we get a beacon malfunction," Storem said walking over to me.

I shook my head and smiled.

"I don't know, but that blue planet was amazing. I think it was worth the malfunction."

"We were lucky! If we'd been there much longer the gravity of that planet might've separated us. You don't want to get too close to those gas giants because the radiation can be dangerous. We could've lost people back there," Storem said.

It wouldn't be the first time somebody got lost," one of the men said, who was listening in on our conversation.

"Good thing I'm lucky! Can you believe how amazing this sunset is?" I asked the men.

"Don't get all sentimental! You've got a fight to get ready for! We're not here on some school science trip to cry over sunsets," Storem said, in his deep menacing voice.

"Relax! Storem you've got to admit the sunsets are beautiful on Ethos."

It was Ruffins.

"Guard, I command you to treat my slave warrior with

respect! I might just turn him loose and enjoy watching him beat you to a pulp," Ruffins said with a grin.

I could tell that Ruffins was enjoying his new position of power.

"You take orders from me Ruffins or you'll never make the trip home. Besides this little boy wannabe-fighter is no match for me. If I yelled at him loud enough he'd probably wet his pants and start crying for his momma."

There was something about Storem, a feeling that comes from deep down inside your gut. I knew that Storem was a dangerous man and someone to be feared. I don't think there was a man alive that would dare to intentionally cross him.

"All right, let's do this! I want to see you take my boy out! You're helpless without your replicating rifle!" Ruffins said, sounding a little too happy for my liking.

I didn't like somebody else volunteering me to fight.

I set down my helmet and took a few steps back getting myself ready for Storem.

Storem chucked his helmet on the ground and walked over towards me. He started throwing punches. I was surprised at how easily I avoided him. I almost started laughing. I could feel a huge grin on my face. Storem stepped back and he was smiling.

"This kid gotts some skills!" Storem said sounding more happy than normal.

Storem held out his hand offering it to acknowledge that he'd been beaten. I knew instantly that I'd made a big mistake, when I took his hand. Storem pulled me off balance and kicked me hard in the groin. I think the pain was the worse I'd ever felt in my entire life. I fell to the ground almost wishing that I'd died.

Finally when the pain started to go away, I looked up at Ruffins. He had a disgusted look on his face.

Storem was laughing and gloating over his victory.

"Did you think Storem would fight clean? I can't believe you fell for his tricks," Ruffins said.

"I guess it's all part of my training. Do you think I'll ever be able to have children?" I asked.

Ruffins and Storem both laughed at my comment.

"Let's head out while we still have some daylight. We have a little bit of a hike before we hit Edem Teramus," Storem said.

We started walking heading in the direction of Edem Teramus which is the name of the city where the fights would be. It looked like we had landed in a rain forest with tall trees and heavy undergrowth. I couldn't make out a trail so I hoped Storem knew where he was going. The air was very damp and my clothes were soaked; it was much different than the air back on Tyrol. Tyrol is very dry, with pretty much all the moisture on the planet is trapped in ice.

I thought I could smell ocean in the air. We must be close

to the coast. I could feel my legs getting tired, and my breathing was getting heavy after walking only a short distance. I was feeling the effects of gravity on Ethos. It felt like I had weights strapped to my legs and my feet. I wondered how long it would take for me to get used to the gravity.

Edem Teramus was like no other city I'd seen before. The city had a massive red wall all the way around it with guard towers spread out at even intervals. Walled cities hadn't existed on Zendreo for thousands of years.

We stopped walking on a hill above the city. I could see ships with sails way off in the distant harbor, thanks to the moon light. The full moon was low to the horizon, rising above the sea. The moon fill half the night sky, back-lighting the harbor. I could see large craters and even what looked like mountain ranges on the moon.

The city was surrounded by hills covered with tropical trees and thick underbrush. The buildings were not tall like modern cities and the streets were not well lit. The lights that I could see were flickering and not very bright. The people didn't have power cells or a power grid to power their homes.

"We'll wait here til morning. They won't let anyone into the city after dark," Storem said.

I wasn't feeling very tired or sleepy. It was still barely the morning back on Tyrol and only a few hours had past since we left.

"Zip, I think we have time for a re-match!" I said with a

grin.

"Once a champion always a champion. I think I'll hang on to my title for a while before I get back into fighting," Storem said with a smile.

I gave up on a re-match with Storem and I sat down. I missed Char. I missed my daughter.

...

Just before sunrise we started heading towards the gates of Edem Teramus. The red light from the sun made the red walls look even redder than they were. There was a line of people already waiting for the gates to open when we arrived.

Our clothes must be authentic because none of the people even looked at us. The comm chip they stuck in my head was working because I could understand what the people were saying. I was surprised at how big the people were. I felt short and I'd never felt short in my life. Most of the women were as tall or taller than me.

"It's the gravity that makes them so big." It was Ruffins.

"They're big but they're slow. I'd take speed and strength over big and slow any day," Ruffins whispered.

If the average people looked like this, I wondered how big their fighters would be.

The gates finally opened and we followed the people into the city. The streets were narrow and crowded. The smell was different at every corner and intersection.

Sometimes I'd catch a horrible whiff of the worst smell I'd ever smelled.

"How do you like the smell of fresh crap? They haven't invented sewers yet," Ruffins said, with a grin.

"Seriously how do people live like this?" I asked.

Ruffins shrugged his shoulders and kept on walking.

"At least the food is not that bad if you like sea food," Ruffins said, with a grin.

After navigating the maze known as the city of Edem Teramus we finally arrived at our destination. We were staying at the Black Eagles Inn. The Inn was located on a hill with large stone walls. Not far in the distance you could see a large circular stadium with large stone columns. I wondered if the fights would take place in the stadium that I could see. The Inn had 2 large statues of magnificent Eagles on either side of the gate. I wondered how big the birds were in real life. I hoped that I'd get the chance to see a black eagle.

After going through the gate we entered into a large courtyard and it dawned on me that this court yard was made for sparring. There was a large flat open area perfect for training. There were racks full of all kinds of weapons near the walls. There were many different kinds of swords, axes and spears This Inn must have been created specifically to host fighters.

The Inn was an impressive structure. I was amazed at the intricate detail in the architecture. I didn't think primitive people were capable of making such a fine structure.

"You're not going to like this," Ruffins said.

He pointed over to towards a long separate building that looked much more primitive than the Inn. The building had a tall fence.

"That's where all the fighters stay," Ruffins said with a grin.

Ruffins was right; I didn't like it. The building was a small prison with men in armor guarding the fence line. I noticed the stench right away. It smelled like a gym that hadn't been cleaned ever. I could catch smells of raw sewage coming with the small breeze that was blowing.

"Do they got any AG beds in there?" I asked.

Ruffins smiled.

"I suggest you get in there, eat up, and get some sleep. You've got some hard days of training ahead of you. We've hired some local talent to help get you ready for your fight."

My bed was nothing more than a blanket that was placed over top of some nasty smelling straw. Somebody had been sleeping here recently and whoever it was had really bad body odor. The blanket was not very thick and the straw would poke you every time you moved to get more comfortable. I wasn't that tired and it was impossible to sleep. I hoped that my body would adapt.

...

When I woke up the next morning, it only took one smell to remind me that we were on Ethos, the stinkiest planet ever.

"It's time for you to really learn how to use a sword," Ruffins said.

There was a large, older-looking man with lots of scars on his arms and face waiting for us in the practice area. I could tell this man had lived a hard life.

"This is Anatronus. He earned his freedom fighting in the arena," Ruffins said.

"You're going to need this," Ruffins handed me a practice sword.

The sword felt heavy in my hand. It had to be the gravity.

"This is going to be great. I can't wait!" Ruffins said, and he quickly got out of the way.

The old man didn't say a word. He just stood there looking at me holding his practice sword in a non-defensive position. I had no idea what I was expected to do so I just stood there looking back at the man.

"Well, are you just going to stand there or are you going to do something?" Ruffins asked impatiently.

I glanced over at Ruffins and in that small fraction of a second the old man moved much faster than I thought possible for an old man that large.

Anatronus knocked my practice sword out of my hand threw me on the ground and put is practice sword to my throat. The old man got up walked back a few steps and with a smile pointed at me with his sword and said, "Dead!"

I got up slowly and picked up my practice sword. I was frustrated. It seemed like everyone fought dirty. I decided to see what the old man could do. I went on the attack. The old man easily stopped my attack and put me on the defensive. It was everything I could do to avoid his blows and block his sword.

The old man kept coming at me relentlessly going low and high coming at me from every angle. I felt a sharp pain on my sword arm and I dropped my sword. The old man's practice sword had come down hard on my arm. There was a quick flash as I saw his practice sword coming for my head. I found myself laying on my back with a massive headache.

Ruffins was laughing. I must have been out for a few seconds because my vision was blurry. After my vision corrected itself, I could see the old man pointing his sword at me with a smile on his face and he said, "Dead!"

I started to agree with Ruffins. This day was going to be a very long day. I wasn't sure if the worst part of it was getting beat up by an old man, or having to hear Ruffins laughing all day.

I got back up slowly again and got ready for the old man to attack me. He was using a fighting style that I'd never seen before and it was very effective. I decided I'd try to pay more attention to his fighting style.

The old man looked at me smiled and I think he asked, Are you ready learn from me? It was hard to understand him. He had a very thick accent even with the communication chip.

I decided to risk a look at Ruffins hoping the old man would not attack me again. When Ruffins saw the expression on my face, he smiled.

"This is a good thing Anatronus wants to train you. It means he thinks you're worth training and he's established that his fighting skills are far superior to yours."

I looked back at the old man who was smiling and nodding.

"You're an amazing fighter Anatronus. Yes I want to learn from you," I said.

I wasn't sure what else to say. I felt kind-a lame.

"You know why I train you?" Anatronus asked.

I assumed the old man was training me for the money but I didn't want to say that.

"I don't know," I said, shaking my head.

"I train you, because you don't quit. You don't give up. You not afraid. Many fighters come here. They don't get back up. They stay down. They afraid..."

"Maybe those other guys stayed down because they were knocked unconscious and didn't know where they were," I said with a smile.

"I like you!" the old man said, with a big smile, nodding his head.

"First Lesson, Dead! You Dead, you not afraid," the old man said pointing his sword at me.

I looked at Ruffins for a translation.

"He means that if you accept the fact that you're going to die you will not be afraid because you know that you are already dead, like a soldier."

It made sense. I'd heard that men in combat who'd come to terms with the fact that they were already dead were able to cope better with the fear of dying.

I turned back to the old man.

"I'm not afraid to die. I don't want to die. I need to find my daughter first."

I don't know how I knew, but I just knew deep down that I'd see my daughter. The old man nodded.

I found out that the old man was a former soldier before he became a slave. He'd been captured by Teramus soldiers who decided to spare him because he was such a good fighter. Jansu a captain of the Teramus army and the owner of the Black Eagles Inn, spared his life and brought him here many years ago. The Teramus civilization had conquered a quarter or more of Ethos.

No one knew for sure since Ethos was a very large world. Edem Teramus is the capital city of the Teramus.

The old man was Eroken, from the Erok civilization that had been conquered by the Teramus, which explained his heavy accent. The Teramus were a proud nation and often treated people of conquered nations as lower class citizens. It was a common practice to make fighters out of the best soldiers from conquered nations.

The training each day was hard but I was learning quickly. Every day I'd train for hours with the old man. I was amazed at his stamina. I could barely keep up with him. It seemed like months had passed even though it had only been a few weeks. The weapons in my hands didn't feel as heavy as they did when we first arrived. I felt like I was getting stronger and faster.

...

It was early in the morning and I was waiting to be let out of the cage. I didn't like being in here. The fighters called our quarters the cage for obvious reasons. There was nothing I could do about my position. I had to do what the President wanted, if I ever hoped to see my daughter.

This morning like most mornings, I was thinking about Char. I wondered how she was doing. I couldn't believe that she followed me out of Grindolstin and nearly froze to death. I wanted to see her again. I missed our talks and walks… I missed Char. I didn't know that it was possible to miss somebody so much. I felt an emptiness growing inside me. It seemed impossible that we would ever see each other again. I wanted to accept the fact that I would never see her or my daughter again, but instead I put those thoughts out of my mind. I was sure Char would never give up on me. How could I give up on her? I was not a quitter. I decided I'd hold on to that small hope and fight for it every day...

Thinking of Char and my daughter kept me going. When my body wanted to quit from exhaustion, I would picture them in my mind and get the strength to keep going.

One of Jansu's men finally came and let me out of the cage. I headed over to the usual training spot. The old man was waiting for me with a funny grin on his face. I wondered what he was up to. He motioned for me to pick a weapon. I picked up a practice sword. The old man smiled. I waited for him to pick up a weapon but he just looked at me and smiled.

"Aren't you going to pick a weapon?" I asked.

"No, I no need weapon to beat you," he said with a grin.

I quickly thought of my strategy. I'd wait for the old man to make his move. I had the advantage because I had a weapon and he did not. The old man is a very good fighter, if I tried to attack him I was pretty sure he'd probably have some amazing move and disarm me. I decided to play defense. I took my position and waited. The old man just stood there smiling at me. Minutes passed and nobody moved. I began to feel awkward.

"Are you fight me or not? You afraid of old man with no

weapons?" he asked.

"No, I'm not afraid of old people," I smiled back at him.

The minutes kept passing and nobody moved. Finally after a long time had passed the old man said, "You learning... Why you not attack me?"

"I know that you are a very strong fighter with lots of experience. I don't have your fighting experience. I'm pretty sure you know a move that you could use to disarm me and take away my advantage."

"Good, this time you win. Now I want you attack me. You need learn how to fight without a weapon."

It was the first time I'd ever been credited with a win against the old man. I was starting to feel good.

I advanced cautiously towards the old man. I tried doing some quick stabs. He quickly moved out of the way of my stabs, dropped low to the ground and kicked my legs out from under me. The old man jumped on me and pinned my sword arm to the ground. It was like this for the rest of the day. No matter my attack the old man always had a counter attack that left me beaten.

...

Despite all the hard training the days passed by quickly. I hadn't seen Ruffins and the rest of the men for a long time. I wondered when they'd be back. I was getting better at fighting. The old man actually had to work very hard to beat me.

CHAPTER XII
THE ARENA

It was early in the morning. The red sun of Ethos was barely starting to come up. The cool early morning breeze felt good. I was actually getting used to the primitive sleeping conditions. It wasn't the smelly straw poking me, or the hard ground that had kept me awake most of the night. I was nervous about fighting today.

Today was the start of the fall festival of the harvest, which would last for a week. The Black Eagles Inn was full of people who'd come to the festival. The people had started arriving a few days ago. The excitement of the visitors was almost contagious until I remembered why they were here. I had bad memories from the ring back on Tyrol where I'd witnessed the senseless slaughter of human beings. I'd never seen anyone die in real life before that horrible day and today it would be happening again.

My training sessions with the old man had ended a few days earlier. I could beat the old man more than half of the time. I'd learned most of his tricks. On our last day the old man told me that I was the best fighter he'd ever trained. Me and the old man had become good friends and we'd grown to respect each other.

It meant a lot to me when the old man told me that I was the best fighter he'd ever trained. I knew that he didn't give out any praise if he didn't truly mean it.

Ruffins and the rest of the men had shown up a few days ago. I'd felt alone and empty with no one to talk to while everyone had been away. It felt good to see the men again. I hoped that soon after this week had ended, I'd finally be able to go back to Tyrol and see Char.

Ruffins told me that on the first day of the games I would have a preliminary fight. I was fighting in a tournament and I'd have to survive each round to make it to the championship.

"Are you ready to get out of that cage?" It was Ruffins, taking me away from my thoughts.

"Yeah! get me out of here! Hey, if I win today, do you think they will let me sleep in the Inn?"

"Yeah probably," Ruffin said, sarcastically nodding his head.

I could tell that he was amused.

"Did you ever fight here on Ethos in the arena?" I asked.

Ruffins shook his head, "No they never let me fight in something as big as this."

I was a little disappointed. I'd hoped to know what to expect. The old man would never talk about fighting in the arena. Whenever I asked about the arena, the old man would go silent and tell me to do whatever I had to do to survive.

"I think you're going to like this," Ruffins handed me a long sleeve shirt.

"It's a little dated but its still military grade body armor and it wasn't cheap."

"Let me guess the boss man wants to protect his assets?" I asked, with a hint of anger in my voice.

Ruffins looked a little surprised after hearing the anger in my voice. I guess, I was surprised too. I hadn't realized it, but there was a lot of anger building up inside of me.

"No it's my standard-issue body armor. It's not that I don't think you're good fighter... It's the best I could do for you. So hurry and take it before anyone sees. You never know what they're going to throw at you in the arena. A lot of really good fighters die in the arena," Ruffins said quietly.

"Okay, thanks," I said, realizing the seriousness of the situation that I faced today.

"So do you think you can take me yet? Are you ready for our re-match?" It was Storem.

I think for the first time it felt good to hear Storem's voice.

"Yeah, let's do this," I said, almost forgetting about the arena.

Storem cracked a rare smile.

"You come back in one piece from the arena, and you've got yourself a deal kid."

I started to get the feeling that nobody thought I was going to make it out alive. Ruffins was giving me body armor, and Storem was actually being nice to me.

After what felt like a long time we finally headed out for the arena. I'd only seen the city once on our way to the Inn so everything about the city was still very new to me. It was hard to believe that people actually lived like this. The houses had no windows and the city streets smelled terrible. It should've felt nice to finally be outside the walls of the Black Eagles Inn, but instead I felt a small pit of fear growing in my stomach. Would this be my last day? Would I never get to see Char and my daughter again? When I thought about Char and my daughter the fear started to go away...

Somehow I knew that I was going to find my daughter and see Char again.

I smiled.

"I can't wait for our re-match!" I said, glancing over at Storem who was walking beside me.

Storem was looking back at me with an almost-surprised expression on his face.

"Don't worry about me kid, focus on today."

There were tons of people already gathered around the stadium which everyone liked to call the arena. I wasn't sure, but if I had to guess, I'd say fifty-thousand people or more could fit into the stadium. I was impressed with the builders. There were at least four levels of arches combined with large stone columns.

"Can you believe the size of this place, and the quality of the workmanship?" I asked.

"Seriously you're on your way to a death match and your admiring the workmanship of the arena?" Ruffins asked, shaking his head in disbelief.

"Yeah you got to admit this place is pretty impressive. My question is does this stadium have restrooms for all these crazy people who come to watch?" I asked.

"Wow! You can't be serious. Aren't you afraid or even nervous?" Ruffins asked.

"No, I'm not afraid. Why? Should I be?"

Ruffins shook his head.

"Seriously, where do you think all these people go to the bathroom in between the fights?" I asked.

Nobody answered. But I thought I heard someone say that I was crazy.

They took us underneath the stadium to a waiting area. We had to wait here until it was my turn to go into the arena. There were racks full weapons and armor that I could choose to use in the arena.

"This place is huge. It reminds me of a professional ice-flyer stadium," I said.

"What's ice-flying?" one of the men asked.

"You've never heard of ice-flying? Seriously? Ice-flying is the most amazing sport ever invented and you've never heard of it! What planet or galaxy do you come from?" I asked.

"Actually I'm from Primus... you know the center of the known galaxy, the capital planet of all known planets. You know, everyone who is anyone comes from Primus."

"Well, don't they have ice-flying on Primus?" I asked.

"Seriously, you're talking about ice-flying before your death match!" Ruffins shouted.

"You know you could die. Maybe you should focus on the arena. Maybe you should pick the armor your going to wear," Ruffins continued.

I looked at the racks of available armor, but nothing stood out to me.

"Ruffins, I'm not going to die today so don't start crying or anything."

Everyone started laughing except Ruffins. He shook his head and was quiet.

"Ice-flying is played with two teams. Each team has six players with one of the players playing keeper. All the players have AG skates..."

I felt someone tapping me on my shoulder. I turned to face the old man. He handed me a sword.

"This my father's sword. He give to me. I want you have sword. I don't have son," the old man said, in his thick accent.

I was speechless. The sword was amazing, it was perfect, it was the best sword I'd ever seen. I took the sword from the old man and it felt good in my hands. The balance was perfect and for such a large sword it felt light. The sword was polished to perfection and very sharp.

"This the best Eroken sword. Will not break," the old man said.

"We're not paying for this sword," one of Storem's men said to the old man.

"Pay? No! You not pay for this sword. Only can be given!" the old man blurted out angrily.

He was offended and everyone could tell.

"I have more. This best Eroken armor I pay to have good friend make for you," The old man said.

The armor matched the sword in quality.

"It would be my honor to wear this armor," I said quietly.

I'd done some practicing in armor with the old man but the practice armor I'd worn was heavy and nothing compared to the Eroken armor. I was glad that I didn't have to choose from the piles of inferior armor in the waiting area.

"Eroken best armor in the world," the old man said.

I was amazed, the armor fit perfectly even with the body armor that Ruffins had given me.

"These ancient sword and armor makers have some serious skills," I said, without thinking.

The old man laughed, "this new armor, not ancient!"

I looked over at Ruffins and he just smiled and winked at me.

It was time. I started the long walk to the arena with just the old man. The rest of the men had left to find their seats in the arena. I wondered if I should feel afraid? I didn't want to kill anyone. My heart was pounding and I could feel my adrenaline spiking.

"I don't want to kill anyone," I said to the old man.

He only nodded.

When I walked through the gate out onto the sand of the arena, the crowd began hissing, booing and throwing things at me. I looked back at the old man who had stopped at the gate. He was smiling and pointing his finger back and forth indicating it was the armor that the people didn't like. It made sense. Most of these people were from Edem Teramus and they didn't like Erokens very much.

After the crowd quieted down, I heard a man yelling to the crowd from a balcony that was hanging over the edge into the arena. The man was introducing me.

"Valerus is a great fighter," I heard him say.

I noticed that the President was sitting with all the dignitaries close to the balcony and the man announcing the events. Without thinking I started waving my arms in the air. I walked toward the man on the balcony giving the introduction.

"My name is Zehn Mortalix!" I heard myself yelling.

The man stopped what he was saying and the arena went completely silent. The man had a confused look on his face and indicated he didn't understand me.

"You've got my name wrong. My name is Zehn Mortalix!" I yelled again.

The man turned and looked over at the President who said something I couldn't hear. The announcer continued his speech but this time he said my name. I saluted the announcer with my sword and walked back out to the middle of the arena.

When I took a look at the President and he was not happy. If looks could kill I was pretty sure that I'd be dead. Once again I'd corrected the President on my name and this time it was in front of thousands of people. It felt good to correct the President. I noticed that the arena had quieted down again. I decided that I should pay attention to the announcer so I knew what was going on.

"In this feature event we have scheduled a melee to the death which will not end until only one survives. Only one will leave this arena alive. Will it be Zehn Mortalix?" I heard the announcer say.

There was a problem. I was not planning on killing anyone if I didn't have too. I suddenly got a bad feeling. I could feel my heart pounding. Maybe I was being too over confident. I pushed the bad thoughts out of my mind and I thought about Char and my daughter.

Gates from all around the arena began to open and people came flooding in. I could see desperation on their faces. They were running frantically looking for weapons. I wished I'd paid more attention earlier. I hadn't noticed all the weapons placed around the sides of the arena until now. It felt like there were hundreds of people coming into the arena. Most of them began fighting each other just as soon as they had a weapon. It was a blood bath. Many of them died quickly because they weren't able to get a weapon.

I could hear people in the crowd laughing and cheering. I was sad and surprised to see so many of the people entering the arena were women. I could tell that almost none of them had been trained in fighting. It must be very entertaining for the Edem Teramus culture to watch fights between untrained fighters.

I got a sickening feeling in my stomach and I felt myself getting angry. I was not going to fight until I had too. I was not an executioner and I didn't plan on becoming one today. I wanted to find a corner so nobody could sneak up behind me. I slowly began to back up keeping all the fighting in front of me, making my way to the far side of the arena. When I got close to the walls people started hissing and throwing stuff at me.

A man and a woman came running away from the main fighting towards me. The pair looked terrified. When they saw me they stopped and started looking back and forth between me and the crowds of fighting people. I suddenly knew what to do.

"STAND WITH ME," I yelled! The couple looked confused.

"I won't kill you. I promise. Put the woman between us. You watch our rear and I'll protect our front."

The man said something to the woman that I couldn't hear. The woman nodded her head. They walked slowly towards me. It was obvious that the couple wasn't sure if they wanted to trust me.

"HURRY," I yelled.

The fighting was getting close.

When the man and the woman saw how close the fighting was getting to us they ran and got behind me.

I decided I was going to try and save as many lives as I could. A man with a sword that had lots of blood on it, took a swing at me. I easily blocked his attack. The man kept trying to attack me but he had no skill with a sword. With two quick moves I knocked the sword out of his hands. He stood there defenseless looking terrified knowing that I could kill him.

"JOIN ME! I'll protect you," I yelled.

I could barely hear my voice over the noise of the arena.

The man looked surprised and then started nodding his head vigorously. He picked up his sword and said he wanted to joined me. I indicated to the man to take my right side which he quickly did. I took a glance behind me and was surprised to see two more men had joined us. The couple that I'd convinced to join me were yelling to people to join us. They were telling the women to get in the middle. In a matter of a few seconds at least thirty people had joined our group. The group formed a circle of men on the outside with the women on the inside. I was in the part of the circle facing the center of the arena.

The noise in the arena went from cheering and laughter to the hum of surprised voices talking. Many of the people who were still fighting stopped fighting and came and joined us in our circle. There were at least a hundred people, maybe more who had joined me in the circle. After a few minutes, nobody was left fighting...

The gates around the arena opened and soldiers began coming in. The soldiers herded us towards the center of the arena. I looked up at the announcer who was standing. The announcer had a puzzled look on his face and looked like he had something to say. When I looked at the President, I could see that he was not too happy. The President's face was red and he looked almost embarrassed. The arena went completely silent.

"Did you not understand? Only one of you can leave this arena alive. If you will not fight each other you will have to fight the soldiers," the announcer yelled so everyone could hear.

"You said only one will leave the arena! WE fight as ONE! WE are ONE! WE will leave this arena as ONE!" I yelled back at the announcer.

There was a low hum of surprised voices in the arena. The low hum turned into applause and cheering. I looked around at the people who were standing with me. I could see a glint of hope in their eyes and even a few smiles. I was worried that their hope would be short-lived.

The announcer stepped back and started talking with the leaders of Edem Teramus. The cheering and applause continued until the announcer returned.

"You've proven your leadership skills Zehn. You and only you may leave the arena. The rest are condemned criminals and we cannot let them leave alive," the announcer said in an almost cheerful voice.

I looked at the men and women around me. They didn't look like criminals. Maybe a few of them did, but for the most part they looked like good people.

"What kind of a leader would I be if I left these people here to die? We'll leave as ONE!" I yelled back.

There was a roar of applause and cheering from the crowd. The noise in the arena was almost deafening.

"I think the soldiers will form ranks when they come to fight us. We outnumber the soldiers five to one. I want everyone to form a line facing the soldiers. Our line should fit across the entire arena. When the solders advance on us, I want the middle of our line to fall back. You men on the edges, come around behind the soldiers and attack as the middle retreats. We'll surround the soldiers and we'll beat them. Make sure everyone knows!" I yelled to the men around me over the noise of the arena.

I could see that the men were yelling to the rest of our group to make sure everyone knew the plan. The soldiers had already started to form their ranks.

"FORM THE LINE!" I yelled.

Everyone in our group started forming a line and yelling to each other making sure everyone knew the plan. The arena was growing silent. I turned and looked at the announcer to hear what he had to say.

"Very well, you have chosen death," the announcer yelled sounding extra menacing.

There was a loud roar from the crowd. The cheering was so loud that I was afraid nobody in my group would be able to hear me...

"We can do this. We can beat them. We have numbers five to one. Don't be afraid. BE STRONG!" I yelled.

The soldiers had started to march towards us in a well-organized formation. I was hoping that the soldiers would believe that the people in my group were afraid and that they'd run away. Once that happened the soldiers wouldn't notice that they were surrounded until it was too late. I stepped out in front of the line, hoping to give some courage to the rest of my group.

"I could take all of you by myself! I'll even let you join my little army here if you want to. I'll take your surrender! Do you surrender?" I yelled at the soldiers who were advancing on us.

I could see nothing but contempt and determination on the faces of the soldiers.

I heard laughter and applause from the crowd in the arena. The soldiers were getting close and some of the people in my line in the middle started running away from the soldiers. I hoped that not all of the men would run away. I started to back up slowly, matching the pace of the soldiers. I looked over out of the corner of my eyes and I could see the men on the edges were slowly moving to get behind the soldiers.

"NOW! ATTACK!" I yelled, and I ran to meet the soldiers not knowing if anyone would follow me.

Time seemed to slow down as I was running towards the soldiers. I took a good look at them. They were big powerful men in full armor. The sun gleamed off of their well-kept armor and shiny swords. I hoped this group of soldiers was not an elite squad hand picked just for fighting in the arena. Was I a complete idiot? I could've gotten out alive. I should've listened to the old man and done whatever it takes to survive. I thought of Char and my daughter. I wanted to win this battle for them.

The first soldier I came to had a big grin on his face. I could tell he wanted to be the one that killed me. I easily avoided his sword. The soldier was big and slow like Ruffins said. I used one of the old man's tricks and in a split second I knocked the sword out of the soldiers hand. The man looked stunned, his eyes were wide open and I could see fear in his face.

I had time to take a look and see what was happening. All the soldiers were being engaged and some of the soldiers were already on the ground bleeding. I saw soldiers getting stabbed from behind. The line of soldiers was falling apart. The soldiers couldn't fight in all directions. My plan was working. The noise of the arena was deafening and by far the loudest I'd heard so far.

The man I was fighting picked up his sword and turned back to face me. He attacked, trying to stab me with his sword. I blocked the man's attack and the next time he tried to stab me I came down hard on his sword hand with my sword, knocking the sword out of his hand for the second time.

I hit him hard in the face with the hilt of my sword as he was reaching down to pick up his sword. I landed a good blow because it knocked the big man to the ground and he didn't get up. I must have knocked him out cold.

I grabbed the soldier's sword. The old man had taught me how to fight with 2 swords.

I was right in the middle of the fighting. I was very vulnerable being in the middle. Someone could easily attack me from behind and I wouldn't be able to react. I moved to get out of the middle. I saw a soldier fighting in front of me. The man didn't see me coming until the last second. I swung both of my swords almost knocking the sword out of the soldier's hand. The soldier staggered back regained his balance and sneered at me.

"I'm going to enjoy this. You arena fighters all think you know how to fight, but you don't," the soldier said as he started towards me.

The soldier advanced on me swinging his sword with a lot of power. I let the man advance on me. I wanted to take him away from the fighting and get out of the middle. I could tell that the soldier was becoming over confident. I let him feel like he was winning. We were getting close to the walls of the arena and the crowd noise was loud. I couldn't make out any words. I only heard noise.

The soldier tried to stab me. I side stepped and knocked his sword away. I stood my ground and easily parried his every move looking for a weakness. The old man had taught me how to test and find weaknesses. He tried the same combinations of attack over and over again sometimes going low and sometimes going high.

The soldier was predictable. He tried to go high. I moved inside his reach planted both of my swords in the ground and grabbed his arm with both of my hands as he brought down his sword arm. I went down on one knee turning and using the soldier's momentum, I threw him hard into the wall of the arena. The man's head hit the wall of the arena and he didn't get up. I picked up his sword and threw it as far as I could away from him and the fighting. Grabbing my swords that were both sticking up out of the sand, I ran back towards the fighting.

The soldiers were trying to form ranks again. We would be in big trouble if the soldiers were able to fight as a unit. Our only chance was to use our numbers and keep them separated.

I ran towards the center of the fighting yelling for any straggling fighters to follow me in my attack on the soldiers who were trying to form ranks. I'd just left the center of the fighting and against my better judgment I was heading back into it. I hoped, I wasn't making a mistake. Some of the men who had stepped back from the fighting to catch their breaths came running and joined me in my charge. If we could just get one good charge I was sure we could finish off the soldiers.

I ran into the back of a soldier and hit him hard with my shoulder. The soldier fell into the legs of two other soldiers knocking both of them down. The men who charged with me finished off the three soldiers and we formed a circle in the center.

In the fighting, I saw and heard the captain of the soldiers giving orders trying to get his men to re-form ranks.

"Don't let them form ranks!" I yelled to the men with me.

I ran towards the man giving orders. I needed to stop him. The man saw me coming.

"You Eroken DOG! I'm going to KILL YOU!" the man yelled.

I didn't say anything. I attacked with both swords, and it was all the man could do to stop my swords from killing him. I saw fear on the man's face as he retreated from my attacks. I let him retreat and I followed him. I wanted to get this man as far away from the fighting as possible. When I felt like we were at a safe distance from the fighting I had an idea. I went low and kicked the man's feet out from under him and I pinned his sword arm to the ground with the weight of my body and put my swords to his neck.

"Order your men to surrender and I'll let you and your men live!" I yelled.

The man nodded his head.

"Okay, let me up."

I let the man up slowly keeping the swords at his neck. When he was up I got behind him and we walked back towards the center of the fighting. The man started ordering his men to surrender.

"DON'T KILL the soldiers! DON'T KILL the soldiers, I promised we wouldn't kill them!" I yelled to my group.

It worked! The soldiers began surrendering until the fighting slowly stopped. With the fighters holding their swords towards the soldiers we headed over to see what the announcer would say.

The noise in the arena was slowly dying down as we

made our way to the announcer. I looked at the President as we approached the box where all the leaders and dignitaries were. All the dignitaries were sitting down except the President. He and his men were standing and applauding. The President was smiling triumphantly. This was one time that I was actually glad to see him proud and happy.

The announcer was bent over talking with the leaders. After a few minutes of conversation with the leaders of the city, the announcer walked out onto the balcony holding out his arms to silence the crowd.

"Zehn, your bravery, strength and skill have proven that you are worthy to leave this arena today. You and everyone in the arena may leave as ONE!" the announcer yelled enthusiastically.

There was a roar of approval from the crowd. All the people were instantly on their feet cheering!

The people in my group started hugging and cheering. I looked over at the captain of the soldiers. He nodded his head and gave a quick salute. After being hugged and congratulated over and over by the people in the arena, we made our way back towards the gate where I'd entered.

I was relieved to see the original couple that had joined me in the fighting had both survived.

"Why did you trust me?" I asked the couple as we were walking.

The man looked at me and smiled.

"You're wearing Eroken armor. Isn't it obvious?" he asked.

"Not to me. Should it be?" I asked.

"How is this possible? You really don't know that we're Erokens?"

"Are all of you Eroken?" I asked.

By the looks on their faces, I could tell that they were stunned.

"You really didn't know. I guess that explains the strange accent," the man said.

"Thanks for your help. There's no way I could've done it without you! Stick by me. I want to make sure you get out with me," I said.

The old man was waiting behind the gate with a huge smile on his face. When the gate opened he ran to meet me.

"You crazy man! Did you hear? They cheer for Erokens! This never happens! It's impossible. I never see this before ever! You much honor today! You do impossible!"

I suddenly loved the old man's accent. It really felt good to hear the old man say those things because I knew he meant every word.

"How did you get those people to fight with you? How did you know that they'd follow you? That was seriously the most amazing thing I've ever seen in the arena," Ruffins said.

"I don't know… it just felt right. Instead of killing people I wanted to save them," I said, looking at Ruffins.

"It just felt right… I wanted to save people... Haha really! I can't believe it!" Ruffins said, mimicking my voice and laughing.

"The President was so mad after you told them your real name. I was pretty sure he would've been fine if you were killed. But after that, I mean seriously how did you get those people to defeat trained soldiers? I'm pretty sure the President is your biggest fan now! Even Storem who never gets excited about anything was bragging about you to all the people who made the trip. You're a legend after one fight. Listen to the crowd they're still chanting your name," Ruffins said, smiling at me.

I suddenly felt very tired. I hadn't slept very much and the adrenaline rush was over. My body was exhausted.

"Make sure these people leave with us! They've earned it," I said to Ruffins.

Ruffins nodded.

There was a large crowd of people waiting for us as we all left the arena together. The Erokens who'd been very quiet, began celebrating as we made it to the main streets of the city and met a crowd of friends and family members. I think they didn't completely believe that they were actually going to be allowed to go free. The

Erokens were laughing and hugging each other.

An older man from the crowd approached me. "We will never forget this day! Praise be to God for sending you. We will remember this day forever!" the man said in a loud voice and he hugged me.

I was soon completely surrounded by the Erokens.

I've never been hugged and kissed so many times in my life. Grown men were hugging me and kissing me on my cheeks. It felt so awkward to have grown men kissing me. I didn't know what to do. I just let the people hug and kiss me.

It felt good inside to know that I'd made a difference for them. After a lot of celebrating the people said goodbye to me and we headed out for the Black Eagles Inn.

The Erokens seemed like good people. I wondered why people hated them so much.

CHAPTER XIII
SARA DESSA

Everything was quiet when I woke up. I didn't hear any of the usual noises that I normally heard at the Black Eagles Inn. The events from the day before were still fresh in my mind. It felt like I was living in a dream. I had to almost pinch myself to make sure that I was awake and not dreaming. The excitement of having survived the arena and saving all those people was already starting to fade. Today I was going back to the arena and I had no idea what would be waiting for me there. I didn't feel very hungry. I didn't really feel anything. I felt numb.

This time when we headed out into the city on our way back to the arena, I hardly noticed anything. I hardly even noticed the horrible smells and the people staring at us as we made our way to the arena. We left early in the morning so there were not very many people out and about yet. I just ignored everything and everyone.

"Do you know what the plan is for today?" I asked Ruffins.

"No, they really don't tell us anything. I'm sure it won't be anything you can't handle. You're already a crowd favorite. They're going to make sure you make it to the final day," Ruffins responded, with confidence.

Ruffins words really didn't help at all. I loved sports and hearing the roar of the crowd when I made good plays. The arena was a twisted and evil place, it was all so surreal and strange. Not in a million lifetimes would I picture myself in such a sad and evil place. No matter what, I wasn't going to let them change me into something I didn't want to be.

When we arrived at the arena it was still early enough that there were not very many people there.

"Knowing you, I don't think you're going to like this part of the day," Ruffins said, with a sheepish grin on his face.

"They have this tradition. They like to put all the fighters on display each day so the people can meet you and decide which fighter they want to support. So follow me. They've got a cage set up for you over here," Ruffins said, motioning for me to follow him.

"I thought they didn't tell you anything!" I said.

My voice was a lot louder than I expected.

Ruffins looked guilty.

"It's not that bad, besides you're already famous. You should enjoy it," Ruffins said, indicating with his head to follow him.

I followed Ruffins. I really hated this place and the idea of being on display made me hate it even more. I was not interested in getting to know these people.

The cage was at least shaded by some trees. I went inside. Ruffins closed the door, locked it and stood by waiting for people to come and ask him questions. At least the cage had something I could sit on without having to sit on the ground. There was a long line of cages with barriers in between each one of them. I was a little curious to see if I could catch a glimpse of some of the other fighters. I couldn't see much, so I sat down.

The excitement from the day before was completely gone. I couldn't understand how people were okay with the arena. Did it even cross their minds what it would be like if they were in my place?

"You should probably stand up so when people come by... we need to make a good impression," Ruffins said.

"I thought that I already made my good impressions yesterday," I said, to Ruffins angrily.

I decided I'd just sit there and ignore the people who came to gawk at me. I felt like an animal at a zoo. As the minutes passed, I got angrier and angrier.

"Hello there," a pleasant voice said.

I looked up into the face of a very beautiful girl about my age. The girl was very well dressed with beautiful jewelry. Her long dark hair shined nicely in the sunlight. She was surrounded by lots of other girls all staring dreamy-eyed at me. I wondered what I looked like. I hadn't really seen a mirror for a long time. The clothes I was wearing were pretty much rags. Suddenly I didn't care what I looked like or what I was wearing.

"You're not Eroken, are you?" the girl asked.

I shook my head, not really looking at her.

"No," I answered, trying to sound as annoyed as possible.

"I think you're very brave and I want you to win," the girl said, with a sincere voice.

The girl continued, "What you did yesterday was the bravest and most noble thing I've ever seen. Why do you wear Eroken armor? Why did you protect the Erokens since you're not Eroken?"

"I wear the armor because one of the men that trained me gave it to me. I didn't have anything better to wear. I protected the Erokens because I thought it was the right thing to do," I said, barely loud enough for the girl to hear.

"Oh that explains a lot. You're not from here and you have a strange accent. Where do you come from?" the girl asked with a smile.

"I come from Zendreo," I said without thinking.

I looked over at Ruffins. He was scowling back at me and shaking his head.

"I've never heard of... did you say Zendreo? Where is Zendreo?" the girl asked.

"It's a really obscure small place that nobody has ever heard of. It's so far away, I'm pretty sure nobody here has ever been there."

"What's your home like?"

"Where I come from we don't fill up arenas to watch people kill each other and bet money over it. Where I come from we fill up arenas to watch people play the greatest game ever invented. It's called Ice-Flying," I said, with a sly smile looking at Ruffins out of the corner of my eye.

"You must come from up north where it's cold. I didn't know they had large arenas up there?" the girl said.

"Well the arenas are not as big as this one, that's for sure."

I looked at Ruffins and could see that he was grinning. I was tempted to tell the girl that I came from another world just to see what she'd say but I decided not to.

"What are you fighting for?" the girl asked.

I was confused. What kind of question was that?

"Do you think this is a game? In a few minutes somebody is going to try and kill me for your entertainment. Why do you think I'm fighting? I'm fighting because I'm a slave, and if I don't, I'll die," I said angrily.

I hoped that the tone of my voice and my answer would make the girl leave. She didn't seem to notice my anger or me attempting to make her leave. The girl looked at me with a serious look on her face and said, "I know that you are a slave and you have to fight, but really what are you fighting for? You're not like any slave I've seen before."

I was really surprised by her. I was not expecting such a well thought out question. This girl seemed to have a talent for observing things that most people missed. She was smart and she paid attention to small details.

"I'm fighting for justice and my daughter because she needs me. I'm fighting for my friend Char, who I promised I'd come back to after this is all done. I'm fighting for the old man that gave me the Eroken armor. I guess I'm even fighting for the Erokens. I'm probably fighting for my daughter and justice the most."

I could see some compassion in the expression on the girl's face after I finished talking.

"What's your daughter's name?" the girl asked.

I thought about it and I felt sad. I couldn't even remember my daughter's name. The SGC had taken that memory away from me.

"I don't know. They took my daughter away from me when her Mom died," I heard myself say.

"Oh, I'm sorry." I heard the girl say.

I suddenly missed Char. In my mind I pictured how excited and happy she was the day that she rescued me. I missed my daughter and I couldn't even remember her name.

"I know that we just met but when you look at me what do you see?"

"Does it really matter what I think? Do you really care?" I asked, in an angry frustrated voice.

I was not in a very good mood. I was getting tired of all the questions. It didn't seem to matter what I said to this girl or how I said it, she didn't seem bothered one bit.

"No, it doesn't really matter but I want to know anyway," the girl said looking me directly in the eye.

"All right then, if it doesn't matter..." I took a long look at the girl trying to think what I should say.

"You're very observant and much smarter than you look. It seems like you know what you want and how to get it. You're used to getting everything you want. I'm pretty sure nobody ever says no to you. You're not easily offended and hard to get rid off..."

"Just so you know, I don't want to be here either," the girl said, showing for the first time a hint of frustration.

"I'm on your side. I hope you find justice and your daughter. It would be my greatest honor if you would wear my symbol as you fight for justice and your daughter today," the girl said softly.

One of the girl's companions started to hand me a golden ribbon but the girl stopped her, took the ribbon and handed it to me directly.

"Good luck," she said, sincerely.

She turned and walked away followed by her companions. I didn't know what to say. I just sat there and watched her and the girls walk away.

"Do you have any idea *who* that was?" Ruffins asked me, when the girls where out of earshot.

"Obviously I have no idea," I responded.

"She is the Sara, you idiot!"

"What's a Sara?" I asked.

"She's the daughter of the Sar. She's a PRINCESS!" Ruffins yelled in disbelief.

"I can't believe she picked you as her champion. You were so rude to her. You didn't even stand up to talk to her and you hardly even looked at her. You were practically yelling at her. I'm pretty sure nobody has ever been so rude to her especially out in public."

"Why didn't you tell me?" I asked Ruffins, shaking my head.

"It doesn't matter, but the President is going to love this!" Ruffins said, with a big grin on his face.

I looked down at the ribbon that I was holding in my hand. It was made from a very fine material. At first glance it was hard to see but when I looked closer I could see the word *SARA DESSA* stitched into the material.

I didn't have a long time to think about the Sara or the

ribbon.

...

When I walked out into the arena the crowd cheered instead of hissing and throwing things at me. I could feel my heart rate increasing. I didn't want to die today. I thought about my daughter and Char. I felt a calm feeling. Somehow, I knew that I wasn't going to die today. I just hoped I didn't have to kill anyone. I decided that I was going to pay more attention to the announcer. I wanted to avoid any surprises.

I walked to the center of the arena looking towards the announcer to discover what I was facing.

"He's wearing Sara Dessa's ribbon! The Sar is going to be so mad," I heard an excited voice from the crowd yell.

The crowd grew silent as the announcer was about to speak.

"Let's welcome the champion Tros from our sister city, Edem Trianthus!" the announcer said.

The crowd started to hum with activity and then there was a roar of noise as the gates on the far side of the arena opened. A huge man entered the arena.

"Tros is a veteran of the arena. He has never lost a fight." I heard the announcer say.

I suddenly wanted to kill Ruffins. So much for making sure I made it to the last day. Ruffins was an idiot!

I'd actually heard some people talking about Tros earlier

today as I sat on display in my cage. I remembered them saying that they felt sorry for anyone that had to face the man. Tros made Sargas look like a little boy. I was pretty sure if I tried to wear the armor that Tros was wearing, I wouldn't even be able to stand up. This man was massive. His arms were bigger than most men's legs.

Tros was the biggest and strongest looking man I'd ever seen. If I had to guess, I'd guess that Tros was close to 8 and ½ talens tall and weighed around 450 zefers. The sword that Tros carried looked like it was as long as I was tall. The peace that I was feeling just a few seconds before was gone. I felt intimidated and afraid. I didn't stand a chance against Tros. I was going to die today. I hoped that it wouldn't be a painful death.

I looked up in the crowd where the dignitaries were sitting and I found the eyes of the Sara. She was looking at me and when our eyes met she stood up. All the people around her began to stand showing the Sara respect. She raised her right arm and made a fist. She was encouraging me to be strong and brave. Without thinking I did the same. I raised my arm. I heard the Sara saying my name and the crowd began saying my name quietly.

The announcer who was still in the middle of his introduction of Tros, paused waiting for the crowd to quiet down. I could tell the announcer was annoyed. He was not used to being interrupted. Once the crowd quieted down the announcer continued.

"Tros comes from a warrior race..."

I stopped listening to the announcer and looked at the Sara who was still standing looking at me with her arm in the air. She had a determined look on her face. I'm sure every fighter would like to have her support.

I didn't want to hear any more words about how great Tros was. The fear that I was feeling was starting to go away. If the Sara who I didn't really know had faith in me, maybe I should too.

Tros was a big man. I'd have to use my speed for my advantage. Ruffins always said he'd take speed over big and slow every time. I was sure intimidation was one of Tros's main tactics. I was not going to be intimidated anymore. I wasn't going to die today. I looked for a weakness in the man's armor. I noticed that he didn't have much armor covering the back of his legs.

The announcer finished. I turned to face Tros. I tried to look as afraid as possible. I avoided looking Tros directly in the eyes. When I heard the command to fight, I ran at Tros. He had a surprised look on his face. I guess he was not used to people charging him. When I was close, I gave him a head fake to the left. Tros fell for the bait and he swung his sword straight down trying to anticipate my position. I'm sure that his sword would have easily cut me into two even halves had he connected.

Instead of going left, I cut right and I got behind Tros. I felt my sword cutting deep into the back of both his exposed legs as I ran by. I heard Tros groan. There was a loud thud has he fell to the ground.

I continued running towards the gate without looking back. The crowd roared and began chanting my name. I ignored the crowd and kept on running until I arrived at the gate which was at the far end of the arena. The old man was waiting for me at the gate with a huge smile on his face. The guard at the gate was clapping. I decided to take a glance back. Tros was laying on the ground holding his legs. I saw men running towards him with a stretcher.

"You're supposed to stay in there and finish the job. But it's always a pleasure to watch the Trianthans lose even if you are wearing that hideous armor," the guard said.

I was relieved when the guard let me out. I didn't want to spend anymore time than I had to in the arena. I wanted to get out without killing anyone.

"Why did you run out so fast? You should've stayed around a little longer to enjoy the victory."

It was Ruffins.

I ignored Ruffins' question.

"Can we go back to the Inn? I want to rest and get away from this place," I asked Ruffins.

"You wish! You can't leave yet. You have to stick around for the parade of champions."

"A parade?" I asked, feeling annoyed.

"Yeah, it's a tradition. At the end of the day, all the winners who are able, go on parade. They parade you around the arena as they announce the match ups for the next day. If you survive tomorrow, you'll be in on the final day," Ruffins said enthusiastically.

"Great! I can't wait..." I said sarcastically.

When the time finally came for the parade I was in a bad mood. I'd been sitting around underneath the stands of the arena most of the day just waiting. It was hot and I hated this place.

"Try to have some fun," Ruffins said, as I headed towards the arena.

The old man was waiting for me at the gate looking proud.

"You bring honor to my people," he said.

"You trained me well," I said, tapping the chest protector of the armor.

"You gave me this incredible armor and this amazing sword," I said, almost forgetting that I was in a bad mood.

When I stepped out into the arena, the crowd began to cheer. I didn't really feel like I deserved any cheers. I didn't want to be here. I'd rather be walking the tunnels with Char.

A guard pointed me the way to go. I began the slow walk around the arena. I was walking near the walls of the arena so the people could see me up close. It was hard to believe that I'd rather be back on Tyrol, but it was true. I missed my friend Char. I wished that I could take her away from the dull life of living in Grindolstin. The thought of her marrying Orly Bogler was a depressing one. After making my way around most of the arena the guard motioned for me to stop walking. We stopped in front of the announcer.

I looked up into the crowd and I saw Sara Dessa. She was looking at me with a smile and when our eyes met she waved. I was sure that no man could resist her smile. Sara Dessa was such a beautiful woman, it almost made the walk around the arena worth it to see her smile.

I took out my sword which had her ribbon attached to the hilt. I held the sword up high to honor the Sara. It was nice to have someone supporting me. When I first entered the arena I'd been completely alone but today I didn't feel so alone. It felt like the Sara and me were now good friends. I'd never been friends with someone who was so important before.

There was a hum and then cheering from the crowd. I could see people in the stands pointing and cheering. I looked to where the people where pointing and I saw a large man in shiny golden armor walking around the arena making his way towards us. This man must be my opponent for tomorrow. The man was not as big as Tros but he looked more athletic and powerful. The man must be a crowd favorite because he was getting lots of cheers. It seemed like the crowd was more excited about my opponent than they were about me.

I looked back up into the crowd towards Sara Dessa. She was looking towards my opponent and I could see concern on her face. I scanned the crowd looking for Ruffins and the President. The President was talking with the people around him and he didn't look very happy. I didn't see Ruffins anywhere. It looked like I'd gotten matched up with a very popular and strong opponent. The man was well over 7 talens tall and had to weigh at least 320 zefers.

...

"I can't believe you got matched up against Iventu!" Ruffins said, with an angry voice when we were on our way back to the Black Eagle Inn.

"What's so great about Iventu?" I asked.

"He's the Teramus Champion from last year. He's the favorite to win it all. The man is the best one out there. You weren't supposed to fight him until the last day. You're probably not going to make it to the last day now..." Ruffins said his voice trailing off.

"Thanks for your faith and confidence in my abilities," I said, half-laughing with a smile.

"You don't understand, this guy is good. He's by far the most dangerous man I've ever seen, and I've seen a lot of fighters. Iventu is ruthless. He never shows any mercy. One mistake and you're dead," Ruffins said quietly with a very serious look on his face.

I could feel the fear of never seeing my daughter

growing in the bottom of my stomach. What would happen to my daughter if I never found her. I wondered if she would be able to forgive me if I died. I'd promised Char that I'd come back. I could picture Char in my mind, waiting and waiting, never knowing what happened to me. Would Char ever be able to forgive me if I never came back?

I didn't want the Sara to see me die. The Sara had so much hope for me. I knew that my daughter and Char would forgive me. Somehow I knew that Sara Dessa would not see me die. I had a good feeling about tomorrow.

"I'm not going to die tomorrow. So don't worry Ruffins." Ruffins didn't say anything.

...

I woke up the next day ready to go. I should be feeling afraid knowing that I was matched up against last year's champion, but for some reason I wasn't feeling scared. Breakfast and the walk to the arena were a blur.

After waiting most of the day they finally announced my fight with Iventu. I made my way to the gate with Ruffins and the old man. Looking out into the center of the arena between the bars of the gate I could see Iventu. The crowd was cheering while the Teramus Champion was standing emotionless facing the announcer. Iventu's golden armor was magnificent. I admit that I hadn't seen a lot of armor, but Iventu's armor was probably good enough for a king.

I loved the eroken armor that the old man had given me The armor was very good and practical but it was not as decorative as Iventu's armor.

The announcer finished introducing Iventu. I looked over at Ruffins and the old man.

"Don't worry, I'll be okay," I said.

Ruffins nodded.

"You great fighter, you no fear. You make me proud, more proud than any fighter," the old man said with his thick accent.

"Thanks! I'll be back in a few minutes."

When I heard my name announced, I walked out into the arena. The crowd was not as friendly as they had been the last time. I heard a few cheers. I was pretty sure that they hadn't allowed as many Erokens into the arena as they had on the days before. The people were here to support their Champion Iventu.

I thought about my daughter. I'd do anything to see her. I imagined one day that I'd be telling her my story. I could almost hear myself telling her how I survived the arena. I'd tell her how nobody thought I had a chance to survive but somehow I was able to survive and find her.

I stopped when I made it to the center of the arena. I didn't pay much attention to what the announcer was saying. I searched the crowd until I found Sara Dessa. I could tell the Sara was trying to hide her concern but she was having a very hard time doing it. I smiled and waved at her. The Sara kissed her hand and held it up high in the air.

I looked at my opponent to see if I could see any weak spots in his armor but I didn't see any. I wasn't sure what my strategy was going to be. My heart was racing. I felt a little nervous, like before a big game. Everyone was acting like they were at my funeral. The feeling was contagious. I felt sad. Maybe my daughter and Char were never going to see me again.

I looked at Iventu. He wasn't showing any emotion at all. Up close the man was huge! I was glad that I'd fought Tros. I wasn't going to let his size intimidate me. I could almost hear Ruffins saying I'd take fast over big and slow any day!

Iventu was holding a chain mace in his right hand. The mace on the end of the chain was massive. I was pretty sure it would've been next to impossible for me to fight with that mace and be effective because it was so large. I was going to have to get in close to make the chain mace ineffective. I was pretty sure that he was using a chain mace to try and get me in close. In close, he could use his size and strength to his advantage. I didn't have any more time to think. The announcer finished.

When I heard the command to fight, I charged, running fast towards Iventu. I hoped the same tactic that I used on Tros would work for me again. Iventu retreated at just the right speed turning slowly as he retreated. He was making sure that I didn't get behind him. I stopped charging because it wasn't working. We began to slowly circle each other.

Iventu was spinning the chain mace effortlessly as he circled around me. He swung and just barely missed my sword. I didn't want to get my sword wrapped up in his chain. Iventu swung at me again with his chain mace. I avoided the big man.

My training took over and I kicked him hard in the chest. My kick had almost no effect. There was some cheering from the crowd but I didn't pay much attention to it. Iventu swung and missed again. I used the opportunity to kick him. Iventu was ready, and once again my kick had no effect. The man was strong.

I decided I didn't like fighting against the mace on a chain without a shield. There were some shields placed along the sides of the arena and I decided that I wanted one. Maybe if I had a shield, I could stop the momentum of the mace.

Iventu swung again but I avoided him. I kicked low, trying to sweep his legs out from under him. The man's legs didn't even move. It was like I was kicking a wall.

He was fast with the mace. He was a lot faster than I expected. He took a big swing and missed. His mace sunk deep into the sand. I decided that his miss might give me enough time to get a shield.

I ran for the nearest shield. I barely had time to pick one up; Iventu was on me. He was like an angry zorok that had been woken up from his winter hibernation. I put up my shield to block his mace and the shield shattered.

I felt a sharp pain in my hand. The pain was really intense. I didn't have time to take a good look at my hand but I knew that it was bad. I felt a sharp pain in my other hand the mace hit my hand knocking the sword out of it. I could see a smile on Iventu's face. I saw the mace coming for my head. I ducked. I felt a sharp pain to my head and then everything went black...

...

There was dirt in my mouth. I opened my eyes; everything was blurry. I couldn't move. I tried to spit out the dirt in my mouth but my mouth wasn't working, I could barely move it. My eyes started to focus. I was looking at two men caring a stretcher. The men stopped walking. One of the men dropped his end of the stretcher. I was laying face down in the dirt. I tried to get up on my knees but there was a lot of pain in my hands so I stopped. I looked over at the two men and smiled. The man who had dropped his end of the stretcher was running jumping up and down shouting my name. I got up to my knees ignoring the pain. I heard cheering and more people yelling my name. I remembered... I was in the arena. I needed to get up and find my sword. I was defenseless. I stood up. The noise from the crowd went from a buzz to a loud roar. I needed to find my sword.

I was finally able to spit some of the dirt out of my mouth. I could still taste the dirt but I didn't care. I needed to get my sword. After turning and looking all around me in all directions, I finally spotted my sword and went over and picked it up. It was difficult to walk. I was concentrating in my mind on walking but my legs were not responding like they normally did.

Holding the sword in my hand was painful. With so much pain in my hand, I wasn't sure how I was going to be able to defend myself. My body wasn't moving like it normally did. Nothing felt right. I started to panic. I looked for Iventu. When I couldn't find him, I turned in a complete circle. I couldn't see the man anywhere.

I looked up into the crowd. The arena was half empty. People were running into the arena from every direction. Everywhere I looked around the arena I could see people jumping up and down yelling my name. Did I somehow win the fight with Iventu? The feelings of panic left me. The last thing I remembered was his mace coming for my head. Did we simultaneously take each other out?

I started walking towards the gate where I'd entered the arena. The gate was on the other side of the arena and it felt like it would take me forever to reach it. The noise in the arena grew louder and louder. I didn't understand why the people were cheering. Was the noise so loud because I'd taken a blow to the head? I felt dizzy, but I was okay. I remembered the Sara and I looked for her in the crowd.

Sara Dessa had come down from her normal place and was close to the edge of the arena. Her guards were pushing people out of the way. The Sara was yelling my name, wiping tears from her eyes and waving all at the same time. I smiled and tried to salute her with my sword. I could barely lift my arm and I almost dropped the sword. The noise in the arena was deafening, the loudest that I'd ever heard it. I was glad the fight was over because I was in no condition to do any fighting. It finally hit me, the crowd was cheering, not because I'd won the fight, but because I wasn't dead.

I saw the gate open, Ruffins and the old man were running towards me.

"I saw you die. How did you get up from that hit? Nobody walks away from something like that!" Ruffins yelled, when he got close.

I could barely hear Ruffins over the noise of the crowd. "I can't die. I have a daughter and she needs me…"

Ruffins shook his head indicating that he couldn't understand me over the noise of the crowd. The old man looked happier than I'd ever seen him look. He didn't need to say anything. The look on his face said it all…

I walked out of the arena.

"I need some water," I said. I felt myself falling and then everything went black…

CHAPTER XIV
RECOVERY IS HARD

It was dark outside when I woke up to a terrible pain. My hands, shoulder and my head were killing me. I was laying in a bed wanting the pain to go away. Both of my hands were wrapped in bandages. I couldn't move my fingers. The constant sharp pain in my hands was unbearable, it felt like I had a piece of frozen metal pressing against all the nerves in my hands.

I tried to go back to sleep but the pain was too much. Whenever I moved I felt a sharp pain in my shoulder and in my hands. It was impossible to get comfortable. If I put any pressure on my hands, it would send a very sharp pain all the way to my elbow.

I was sure I had multiple broken bones that were scraping against each other. I wondered if anyone had brought a med kit so they could give me something for the pain and do a bone repair scan on my hands. If someone brought a BR scanner it could have my hand healing in no time.

After laying in pain for hours, when the sky was starting to get light, I finally managed to fall asleep.

...

I woke up to daylight. The old man was sleeping in a chair in the corner of the room. I felt a sharp pain in my hands but not as bad as it was during the night. I heard myself groan from the pain as I sat up in bed. The old man woke up and smiled.

"You free man. You never fight in arena again," the old man said, looking proud.

"You free, your owner gone and say you free!" the old man said, again more happy than the first time.

"They're gone? They left me here?" I asked, almost shouting at the old man.

"They gone, say they never come back, you free man!"

I wasn't sure if I was understanding the old man correctly.

"They left me? Am I the only one here?" I asked again.

"Yes, they gone, now you go home and find your daughter."

"I can never go home without them? It's impossible," I said, quietly to the old man.

The thought of never finding my daughter was more painful than my broken hands. I knew that the pain in my hands would go away, but the pain of never finding my daughter would never go away. I thought about my promise to Char. I promised her that I'd come back. The pain that she would go through never knowing what happened to me. I got out of bed ignoring the screaming pain in my shoulder and hands.

"I need to find them before they're really gone. They can't leave me here! Maybe it's not too late!" I said to the old man.

The old man's eyes narrowed, he looked confused.

"When did they leave?" I asked.

"They leave two days ago."

When I heard the old man say two days, I knew in my heart that they were gone. I was sure it was the President's way of paying me back for losing.

"Did they leave anything for me?"

"I don't know… maybe you ask inn keeper," the old man responded.

The inn keeper didn't have anything for me. He informed me that I needed to pay the bill for the room. When I told the inn keeper that I didn't have any money, he told me that because I'd done so well in the arena, Jansu said I could stay. When my wounds had healed, I'd have to pay or leave the inn.

The next few days were the longest most painful days of my life. I'd sometimes put pressure on my hands just to feel more physical pain in an attempt to take my mind of the fact I'd never find my daughter and never see Char again. The inn keeper offered me leftover food from the kitchen but I didn't feel hungry. I didn't eat much. I hardly ate anything for almost a week. I felt numb.

My left hand, the one I'd used to hold the shield, was injured worse than my right hand. My right hand was actually starting to feel a little better after a week.

...

When I left the Inn I only had the ragged slave clothes that I was wearing, the Eroken armor and the magnificent sword that the old man had given me.

The Inn Keeper asked me if I wanted to store the armor at the Inn until I'd found a new place to stay. I refused his offer. There was no way I was going to let the armor out of my sight. The armor was my most prized possession.

It was not easy dragging the armor with only one half-good hand and a bad shoulder. I walked slowly. Nobody seemed to notice me. I decided I'd head towards the sea.

The Sea of Edem Teramus was truly a magnificent sight to see, especially when the red sun of Ethos was setting. I'd only seen the sea from a distance but it reminded me of the ocean back home. I was drawn to it. It was still pretty early in the morning and the weather was perfect.

The streets were busy, full of people. Wherever I looked, I could see happy people seeming to have no cares in the world. I should be happy to be alive, but today I was more sad and depressed than I'd ever been in my life. I didn't know it was possible to feel this sad and hopeless.

My body didn't want to move. I felt the weariness of depression telling me to quit. I was completely alone, stranded in a strange world, without the possibility of ever returning home. The weight of my situation was pressing down on me making it hard to breathe.

The President's promise that I could go home had given me so much hope and so much to live for. I believed that I'd see my daughter again. Knowing that I'd never see my daughter was worse than the physical pain that I'd felt with my injured hands. The level of sadness and despair that I was feeling didn't leave any room to feel angry at the President for leaving me here. I was sure one day I'd be angry. Today all I could feel was a despair that would never leave me. I felt more numb than ever before.

I found a spot away from people and close to the sea. The sound of the breaking waves helped me to not think about anything except the beauty of the sea. I thought about walking out into the waves. If the undertow took me out to sea and I never made it back to shore, nobody would ever know. There was nobody on Ethos that would miss me if I was gone.

I stayed by the sea all day until I got thirsty. I decided to head back into the city to find a drink.

There were some public springs not too far away from the beach. It was late enough in the day that there weren't very many people near the springs. I drank until I wasn't thirsty anymore. The water was cold and tasted good. I found a comfortable place near a tree and decided I'd spend the night there.

I fell asleep quickly because I was so tired.. I spent the next few days the same way. I went to my spot by the sea during the day and slept by the spring during the night. I didn't eat any food. I didn't have any headaches or hunger pains despite not eating. I was completely numb. I wondered how many days I could go without eating before my body would start to feel hungry again.

...

Early in the morning I was sitting by the tree watching the women come and fill their water containers at the spring. Every morning women would come to get water to take home for the day.

"Are you hungry?" a voice said. I turned to look at an older woman. She was standing very close to me. Nobody had talked to me for days. It took me a few seconds to answer.

"No," I heard myself say.

"Do you have any food?" the woman said with concern in her voice.

The old woman had kind eyes. I knew she was trying to help me.

"No, I don't have any food and I don't need any," I said almost in a whisper.

I don't remember it ever taking this much effort to speak before.

The woman squinted her eyes as if she was thinking really hard about something.

"Do you have a place to sleep?" she asked.

I nodded towards the tree.

"This is my place to sleep."

"You need my help. I'm here to help you. Will you come with me for some breakfast after I get some water?" the woman asked.

I looked into the kind eyes of the woman. Her clear blue eyes reminded me of Char. I wanted to say no but for some reason I heard myself say, "Okay."

The woman looked pleased. She was very patient with me. She walked slowly as I followed her into the city dragging my armor and my sword with my one good hand. After walking only a short distance, I was tired. I needed to stop. The woman noticed that I'd stopped and she turned around and came back. It felt unreal that I could barely keep up with an old woman. I must be in worse shape that I previously thought.

"What are you dragging behind you?"

"My armor and my sword."

The woman's eyes got big. I could tell that she was surprised by what I'd said to her.

"You have armor? You have a sword? What is your name?"

"My name is Zehn," I said after catching my breath.

The woman smiled and put her hand over her mouth.

"I can't believe it! You're the man who saved my daughter and her husband in the arena!" the woman said, looking extremely happy.

"Come to my house. It's not far. You need to eat. You look horrible. You don't look like a great fighter. You look like you could almost be dead."

"I never was a great warrior."

"Don't say such things! Come with me. Hurry!"

"I lost," I said slowly.

The woman ignored my comment and smiled.

"Come, Hurry!" the kind woman said.

I followed the woman whose name I found out was Leena. We came to a narrow street with small houses built with stones. The houses all looked identical. Each house had a flat roof, one small window and a small door. Leena stopped in front of one of the doors.

"Welcome to my house. It's not much but you're always welcome in my home," Leena said, almost a little embarrassed.

"Don't you remember? My house is a tree?" I said with a smile.

Leena smiled and opened the door. To enter the house, you had to step down from the small doorway onto a dirt floor. The inside of the house was very small. I couldn't stand all the way up because the ceiling was too low.

"We are short people," Leena said smiling.

It wasn't true. The people on Ethos were huge. Most of the women were as tall as me and I'd seen quite a few women who were a lot taller than me.

"Come sit down, let me get you something to eat."

Leena indicated for me to sit at a small table in the kitchen, which I did.

"Here, drink this. Hopefully it hasn't spoiled," Leena gave me a glass with something in it.

The drink tasted like milk. I hadn't had a glass of milk for so long I'd almost forgotten what it tasted like.

"What kind of milk is this?" I asked.

"It's Boven milk. Boven milk is more cream than milk. It will put some weight back on your bones," Leena said.

"This is the best milk I've ever had!"

The woman smiled. I wasn't just saying it to be nice. The milk really was amazing.

"Drink! Drink! There's more. I'll get more!" The woman went outside and started yelling in a language I couldn't understand.

Before I knew it, there were at least a dozen old women inside the tiny house putting food in front of me and commanding me to eat. The women were talking so fast and asking so many questions I couldn't keep up. I didn't want to refuse the food but I really wasn't hungry. After a few minutes it became obvious to the women that they were overwhelming me with the food and their affection, so they went outside.

I could hear the women outside talking excitedly in their strange language. For the first time in quite awhile, I felt like I was alive. I didn't feel numb. I was starting to feel hungry. For the first time in days I ate some food.

"This is for you."

I looked up from the food on the table. There was a woman standing in front of me holding some clothes.

"You need these very bad," she said.

I stood up, walked over and hugged the woman. I could feel tears coming into my eyes. I hadn't cried after learning that I'd never be able to find my daughter. It was impossible to hold back the tears. I couldn't ever remember not being able to control my feelings like this. I hoped nobody would notice.

"Thanks," was all I managed to say after a long time. The woman smiled, wiped a tear from her eyes, and left me to eat.

There was a steady stream of visitors all day long coming to meet me, inviting me to their homes. They brought clothes, shoes, and many other gifts. I was completely speechless. I couldn't believe the kindness and generosity of these people who I did not know.

"You are starting to look better already," Leena said after most of the visitors had left.

"I feel a little better too," I responded.

"I think everything is going to get better for you now," the woman said with a cheerful disposition.

I smiled.

"Why do you say my life is going to get better?"

"I think you've reached your lowest point. Things can only get better for you going forward," Leena said with a kind smile.

I started thinking about my situation and it was not good. I'd never be able to find my daughter. I'd never see Char again. I felt a weight pressing on my lungs making it hard to breathe.

"I think, I'm going to head back to my tree," I said quietly.

"I'm sorry if I've upset you. Do you know why I stopped and talked to you this morning?"

I didn't say anything I just looked at the door. All I could think about was that I'd never leave Ethos. I was stuck here on this stinky planet forever.

"God told me to stop. For three days God told me to stop and talk to you. I passed by you each day. I didn't listen because I was afraid. I didn't know what to say or do so I just walked by you each day. Today when I saw you... you looked so sad that I decided to listen," Leena said, with a tear in her eyes.

I was surprised and confused. I didn't know what to say. I'd always heard that ancient people had invented the idea of God to explain things that couldn't be explained by science. Corrupt men used the idea of God to gain money, power and influence over people. Many wars had been fought in the name of God and religion.

There were still people today that believed in a God. My Grandma believed in God when she was still alive.

"How does your God talk to you? God never talks to me," I asked Leena.

The old woman smiled.

"Have you ever felt peace in your heart when you knew you should be feeling something different? Have you ever known something and not been able to explain how you knew it? Have you ever experienced something you couldn't explain? Have you ever done something because you knew it was the right thing to do, even though it seemed impossible or crazy? God talks to everyone, especially to those who listen."

"How do I know your God would know who I am? Why would your God care about me?"

Leena smiled and said, "My God is your God. He is the God of all things. God cares about everyone because we are all his children."

"If God cares so much about us why would he let so many bad things happen. Why would God allow wars? Why would God allow so many bad things to happen to me? Why would he let people take my family away?"

"Without the bad, you can't know the good. Without sadness you can't know happiness. Hard times help us to grow and find strengths that we didn't know we have. The more pain, suffering and sadness we feel, the more our capacity to feel joy and happiness increases. God wants us to grow and become happy like he is. We must feel sadness to be able to experience happiness. I promise you the next time you feel happiness it's going to surprise you how happy you feel. Right now you're in a low spot which will pass and when it passes you'll be amazed at how happy you feel."

"It sounds nice. I'd like to believe there is a God but I just don't see God in my life," I said.

Leena stepped back with a surprised look on her face.

"God is everywhere if you open your eyes," Leena said, sounding a little frustrated.

"How do you think you survived the arena? Nobody gets up from the hit to the head like the one you took.

You should be dead but here you stand. How do you explain it?"

It was true. I should've been dead many times by now. I didn't know how to explain it.

"You rescued hundreds of people from the arena. Do you think you did that all by yourself?"

I thought about what Leena had said before, about knowing to do something even though it was crazy. I thought about her question: Have you ever felt peace when you should be feeling something different? I felt peace in the arena and I felt peace that I would see my daughter again.

I wanted to find my daughter more than I'd ever wanted before. I started to feel that same peace that I'd felt when I believed I would find her. I remembered how I felt after my dream when my wife had come to visit me. Maybe I would see my daughter again.

"You might be right. I can't explain why I'm still alive or how I rescued those people in the arena. It just felt like the right thing to do," I said, shaking my head.

"It was God. He has work for you, otherwise you'd be dead," the woman said enthusiastically.

Could I really see my daughter again? Was it really possible that I'd see Char again? It was impossible, they were both on different worlds and I was stuck here on Ethos.

"Why would God choose me instead of just doing it himself?"

"God made you strong, so you can help others who are not as strong as you. With God all things are possible. If God wants you to do something, He will find the way for you to do it," Leena said confidently.

"I'm not that strong. I'd pretty much given up and decided that I was going to die by the tree until you came by," I said half-smiling.

Leena laughed.

"That's why God sent me to you. He's got more work for you to do!"

"Maybe so, I don't know. If there is a God, I have no idea why he'd pick me to do anything."

"Sometimes God takes the weak and simple and he uses them to accomplish amazing impossible things!" the woman said.

"So are you calling me weak and simple now?"

"Yes!" Leena laughed.

Maybe, somehow... I could still find my daughter. I wanted to hope that I'd find her but at the same time I needed to be realistic.

"Tell me more about your God," I said. The woman looked at me and smiled.

"The God I worship is the God of everything. He's your God and my God. God has created many worlds and put his children on them. Some of the worlds are no more and some are new and some are old."

I was shocked.

"Wait, you believe that there are many worlds with people living on them?" I asked.

The woman smiled.

"Of course, have you ever looked up at the night sky and seen all the stars? Out in those stars are many worlds with people on them just like you and me," the woman said.

I couldn't believe it. I had no idea that people from such a primitive world would ever come up with the idea of people living on other worlds. I wanted to tell her that what she was saying was true. I wanted to tell her that I came from another world but I decided not to.

There were thousands of worlds with higher forms of life that had been discovered just within our galaxy. New galaxies and worlds were being discovered all the time. The possibilities of life are endless.

"Did you know that there are people on every one of those worlds who all believe in the same God?" the woman asked.

"I don't know. I guess it could be possible. It's a pretty interesting idea," I said.

"Can you explain where life came from?" Leena asked.

Even with the latest technologies, science can't explain how life started. Science can't create life. Even the synthetics come from already living cells.

"No, I can't explain it," I said.

Leena smiled and said, "God created life."

Could it be as simple as Leena said? I wanted to believe her, but it just sounded too simple.

The door opened and in came two familiar faces. It was the man and woman who I'd first asked to fight with me in the arena.

"It really is him!" the woman exclaimed.

"You look awful! What happened to you?" the man asked.

"The arena happened," I said.

The man nodded.

"I understand what you're saying. I still can't believe we made it out alive. I didn't see your fight with Iventu, but I heard all about it. I think everyone's heard about how you came back from the dead by now."

"Well, I didn't die. I can hardly remember anything. All I remember was seeing black and then feeling a lot of pain."

"It was a miracle!" the man's wife said.

I looked up at her and I nodded my head in agreement.

"Yes it was a miracle, maybe God didn't want me dead yet," I said, looking over at Leena who was smiling and nodding her approval.

...

During the next few days there was a steady stream of people coming to meet me. It truly was amazing. The Erokens were such good people. I decided I was going to see if I could do something to help them.

CHAPTER XV
MEETING WITH THE SAR

I got up really early in the morning. It was still dark outside. I put on my armor which I'd shined the night before. I wanted to be at the palace early so I could avoid the crowds. The streets were empty. I didn't see anyone on my way to the palace.

The palace walls were impressive. They were easily 30 talens high and almost as thick as they were tall. You could barely see the guard towers and the steep roof of the palace peaking over the tops of the walls.

When I reached the gates of the palace it was still really early. The sky to the east was just beginning to turn red as the sun was coming up.

I stopped at the main gate hoping that there would be a guard or someone who could pass a message to the Sar. A very large guard came out of the barracks and started walking towards me at a fast pace. The guard was easily a head taller than me and he had a rough demeanor. The guard was wearing expensive armor that was polished to perfection.

"GET AWAY FROM THERE!" the guard yelled in a commanding voice that caused me to jump. I looked around to see if there was someone trying to scale the walls or something.

"What are you doing there? You dare approach the Sar's Palace?"

I heard running feet above me. Looking up I noticed that there were archers on the wall with their bows drawn and arrows pointed at me.

"I'm sorry, I didn't know that I was doing anything wrong. I just wanted to speak with the Sar. I'm just one man. Don't worry, I'm not going to try anything!" I yelled, hoping that the archers on the wall could hear me. I didn't want to get shot with arrows.

The guard started laughing.

"Who are you that the Sar should speak with you?"

"My name is Zehn."

The guard stopped laughing and rolled his eyes.

"I know who you are! I can see that hideous armor you're wearing! Why would a Sar wish to speak with a slave?" the guard asked in an angry voice.

"I'm not a slave. I'm a free man!"

"The Sar doesn't speak to people like you."

The man's expression of disdain told me that he thought I wasn't worthy of his time.

"Stop wasting my time and GET OUT OF HERE!" The guard yelled at me in a threatening voice.

"Can you at least deliver a message?" I asked, ignoring the guard's commands to leave.

"I told you to leave! Now get out of here before I let my archers test their skills. You better take off that armor or the people in the streets might finish you off!" the guard said as he walked away from me.

I could hear the guard laughing and see his head shaking in disbelief as he left me at the gate.

I looked up at the archers. They were still standing on the walls but they were no longer pointing arrows in drawn bows at me. I could see that they were talking and laughing. I didn't like be laughed at. I could feel my ears turning red.

I decided to stand my ground and wait. Maybe the guards would talk and laugh enough that word of me would reach the Sar. I waited all day and nothing happened. The guards never came back to talk to me. I wished I'd brought a lunch with me.

...

I went to the gate every day for more than a week. Most days the guards didn't even bother to come out to talk to me and tell me to go away.

I decided that today would be my last day of trying to speak with the Sar. I wasn't even sure what I was going to say. I had a feeling inside nagging me that I needed to speak to the Sar.

Today I woke up a little later than usual. I put on my armor in a hurry and headed for the Palace. There were more people in the streets today than usual because I left so late. It was already light outside.

A large man stopped me.

"Where do you think you're going wearing that armor?" he said with a menacing voice.

"Are you Zehn?" the man asked before I could answer his first question.

"Yes, that's my name."

The man looked pleased.

"I knew it was you. Only you would dare walk around Edem Teramus in that armor. Where are you going?"

"I'm going to meet the Sar."

The man looked surprised.

"You're even braver than I thought! I want to see this. Do you mind if I come along?"

I nodded.

"Sure why not?"

It might be nice to have some support.

We started walking towards the Palace. The man saw some people he knew and yelled at them to join us.

"It's okay if they come, right?"

At this point I didn't really care. I was pretty sure the guards would just ignore me as usual. By the time we reached the gate there was a large crowd of people following me. The people stood back and let me approach the gate by myself when we arrived. The crowd began chanting my name.

Several guards came to meet me at the gate.

"You better tell those people to get out of here," one of the guards yelled over the noise of the crowd chanting my name.

"Any chance you can let the Sar know I'm here to see him?" I asked.

The guards both shook their heads no.

"You should leave!" one of the guards said.

The chanting crowd was getting louder. The crowd was growing. The people must have heard the chanting crowd and came to see what all the commotion was about.

"I think I'm going to go tell them to yell louder until the Sar can hear them," I yelled nodding my head towards the crowd.

"It will never happen. The Sar will never speak to a slave like you. I should've let the archers shoot you the first day you showed up!" the guard yelled in an angry voice.

I walked back towards the crowd which quieted down as I got close to them.

"The guards won't tell the Sar that I'm here to see him," I yelled to the crowd.

"Let's make the Sar hear us," a voice yelled back at me from the crowd.

I heard a lot of approving voices and then the crowd once again began yelling my name but louder than before. The square in front of the palace was filling up with more and more people all chanting my name in unison.

When I went back up to the gate, I could see soldiers assembling into ranks behind the gates. It looked like they were preparing for an attack on the Palace.

"Let the man in!" one of the guards yelled over the noise of the crowd. Someone opened the smaller gate that was just big enough for a man to enter. I waved to the crowd and entered into the small gate. I heard the crowd outside cheering their approval.

The guard from the first day met me inside. He had an angry look on his face.

"Come with me," the guard said. We walked around the men that were forming a line.

"Zehn is my friend. He is my guest. Let me through! He's not going to hurt anyone." It was Sara Dessa.

The Sara was struggling to get past her guards. Faking left and going right the Sara got past her guards and came running up to me with a big smile on her face.

"You're still here! I'm so glad you came!" the Sara said with an excited voice.

I stopped walking and to make sure the guards knew that I was not a threat, I went down on one knee.

"I'm glad to see you!" I said with a smile looking up at the Sara.

The Sara smiled shyly, her face was almost glowing.

"Do you think the Sar... I mean your Father, do you think he'd talk to me?" I asked.

"It's my birthday. I think he'll talk to you if I ask him!"

I looked up at the guard who was standing near the Sara.

"I've been coming here for days and this guard refused to give you any messages that I was here. When I talk to the Sar, I'll be sure to mention you for a promotion or something," I said to the guard.

The guard shook his head and walked away without saying anything.

"Some of the guards don't like you very much after what happened in the arena," the Sara said.

"When I heard the crowd chanting your name, I knew you were here. I told the guards to let you in. I thought you would've left by now to go find your daughter."

"I wanted to go find my daughter but they left me here and I don't know the way home."

The Sara frowned.

"Stand up," the Sara said stretching out her hand to me to help me up. When the Sara saw my hands, her face turned white and she winced.

"I'm so sorry about your hands."

"Well, at least my right hand is doing better than my left. I don't think I'll ever be any good with a sword again," I said, showing her my left hand.

My left hand had healed badly; there was an ugly scar across the length of my hand. My fingers would not extend all the way and I could barely grip anything with it.

The Sara grabbed my arm and started taking me towards the entrance to the palace. The wide-eyed looks on the guards faces confirmed my fears that it wasn't normal for the Sara to escort men such as me around the palace.

The Sara must have noticed the shocked and concerned looks from her guards because she said, "Don't worry, I trust my life in this man's hands more than any other man," she said to her guards.

"You really shouldn't, but thanks," I said quietly hoping the guards wouldn't hear.

"I trust you. I get so tired of always having these around me," she said pointing towards the guards.

"I sometimes just want to be alone. You know, I never get to be alone, ever!"

"It really must be hard being a Sara," I said, with a smile.

The Sara smiled back at me and said, "My father will love you. You're not afraid of anyone and you always say exactly what's on your mind."

The Palace was truly magnificent. I'd visited ancient ruins on Zendreo and walked through holographic displays depicting how things were in ancient times at museums. My past experiences and my perceptions of how ancient people lived did not prepare me for the Sar's palace.

I don't know a lot about architecture but I was pretty sure these ancient people had more skill than modern workmen who relied so much on technology. The builders built this amazing palace without AG machines to do all the heavy lifting. Skylights lit the giant hallways that were covered with artwork. I didn't have time to look at the art up close. From a distance it appeared to be paintings depicting prior kings and their victories in battle. There were paintings of great halls filled with people in lots of detail. I'm sure my art teachers from the academy back home would be very jealous of me.

After walking through a maze of hallways and large open rooms that were large enough to hold hundreds of people we came to the entry way of a hallway guarded by several large guards.

The hallway was crowded with people lined up and waiting. I assumed everyone was waiting to meet with the Sar.

The Sara smiled at the guards and squeezed my arm tighter as we passed between them. The guards had confused looks on their faces. It was obvious that it's not an every day occurrence that a man walks into the palace wearing eroken armor being escorted by a princess. The Sara's guards who had been following close behind us stopped at the entry way of the hallway.

"They can't follow us here, they're not allowed," the Sara said, with a grin on her face.

I heard people whispering my name as we passed them in the hallway. The Sara led me through the long hallway straight to the front of the line.

"What's this? What do you think you're doing?" It was the doorkeeper.

I was sure the Sar's Great Hall was behind the massive doors. There was so much precious metal and jewels on the doors, I decided it must be part of this man's job to make sure nobody tried to steal any of it while they were waiting in line.

"It's my birthday! This is Zehn, my friend, and he needs to speak with my father," the Sara said.

"What possibly can this slave have to say to a Sar that he'd care about?" the man asked, looking at me scornfully.

"Look at that hideous armor! Your father will have my head if I let him in."

"You dare insult me and my friend? An insult to my friend is an insult to me! When my father hears how you insulted me in front of all these people he might just take your head," the Sara said, turning to face me and winking so the man at the doors couldn't see.

The Sara turned back towards the doorkeeper and smiled gleefully. I could tell by the look on the man's face that he was having a very difficult time deciding what to do.

"He's going to let us in? Aren't you? And you're going to say that you are sorry for insulting my friend," the Sara said, with a very polite voice.

"Okay, I'm sorry. Please don't make me regret it," the man grumbled.

"What is your business with the Great Sar?" the man asked.

Before I had time to answer the doors began to open and the Sara pulled me into the Great Hall.

"This is so exciting! I never get to come in here," she whispered.

I was surprised.

"What do you mean, you never come in here? Are you going to get into trouble because of me?" I whispered.

"I might get into a little trouble. I'm not usually this brave. With you I'm not afraid of anything!" the Sara whispered.

The Great Hall of the Sar was impressive. The size and beauty of the room surpassed all the other rooms I'd seen so far. The high ceiling was held up by large wooden beams that were curved like the bottom of a ship. Red light from the sun came in through large windows, giving the great hall enough light to make it so you could see the details on the ceiling that towered high above us.

"Isn't it beautiful?" the Sara asked.

The Sar's Great Hall seemed to almost go on forever. I could feel all the eyes of the people were on us as we walked towards the Sar that was at the far side of the great hall. You could hear an echo of the steady hum of people talking.

"These are all the important people who help my father make his decisions," the Sara said as if she were taking me on a tour of the Great Hall.

I smiled and waved to the people. My wave was met with disgusted looks, and the room burst into a louder hum of voices and laughter.

"What did I do? Did I do something wrong?" I asked.

"No you didn't do anything wrong. These important people are not used to meeting people as amazing as you! They're used to the regular, boring people who think they're more important than everyone else. They just want to find more ways to get even more powerful and important."

I smiled.

"Is it the armor?" I asked.

"I don't have my sword. I left it home. I figured they'd try and take it away and I could never let that happen. It was a gift."

The Sara nodded, "Yes the armor is part of it, but they think you're not fit to speak with a Sar and seeing you with me is probably even more shocking since you're not royalty. The Sara isn't supposed to go around escorting..." she paused, thinking of the correct word to say.

"Escorting people like me," I finished her sentence.

"Yes, amazing people like you! I never get to be with people like you," the Sara said with a smile.

"Don't say anything, unless the Sar speaks to you and kneel when we stop," the Sara whispered as we were approaching the Sar.

We stopped in front of the Sar's throne. I took a knee and I didn't dare look up at the Sar. I didn't want to miss the chance to speak with him.

"What brings the Sara to the Great Hall of the Sar?" a voice asked.

"My friend Zehn. He's the bravest, most courageous man I know. He's been waiting for weeks outside the gates to come and speak with the Sar."

"Why would the Sar wish to speak to this man? This man has no business with the Sar. You must take him away from here now. This is no place for a Sara and her friends," the voice said.

"It's my birthday and I wish it more than anything!" the Sara said, interrupting the man.

"Please! Sara Dessa, you must go!"

"Wait! I will hear what this man has to say, after all, it is my daughter's birthday. Tell the man to stand and speak," the Sar said.

I stood up and at that moment I should've been feeling nervous and out of place, but for some reason all I felt was peace.

The Sar was a big man and much older looking than I expected. His beard was mostly gray and trimmed neatly matching his regal appearance. His once dark hair was fading to gray especially on the sides of his enormous round head. The Sar was wearing purple robes and had a large gold chain around his neck.

"The Sar must truly be great because he has an amazing daughter," I said.

The smile on the Sara's face was priceless. The Sar smiled and nodded indicating he wanted me to speak and be quick about it.

"Why are you wearing that hideous armor in my Great Hall?" the Sar asked before I could continue.

"One doesn't just walk in to see a Sar in rags. This is the very finest attire that I own."

The Great Hall erupted into laughter.

"I'd like to see any one of you do what this man did in the arena!" the Sara yelled over the laughter.

The Sar waved his hand for silence.

"It's true. Not one of these cowards would be brave enough to even try on armor, let alone walk in here wearing Eroken armor asking to speak with the Sar. It's never been done before! I like him! I respect your courage. I see you've given courage to my daughter. I heard how you gave courage to the people in the arena, enough courage to defeat my soldiers. I know who you are Zehn," the Sar said.

"If I may, I want to tell the Sar a story," I said politely.

The Sar nodded.

"I'm sure this will be the most interesting story I hear all day," the Sar said with a smile.

"There was man who was injured, in a strange city, he was alone with no home or place to go. This man didn't know anyone, and because of his injuries, he decided that he was most likely going to die. An old woman with nothing saw the man by the public springs each morning when she went to get water. On the third day the woman approached the man and asked him if he was hungry. The man told the woman that he wasn't hungry. The woman insisted and finally persuaded the man to come to her house where she fed him and invited her friends and neighbors to come and meet the man. The friends brought gifts and food. They took care of the man who got better. This man wanted to do something to pay back the generosity of these people, but he had nothing that he could give them.

This man understands what it's like to be a slave and to be so far away from his home without hope for a better life. So this man has come here to speak with the Sar and ask him if he will let the Erokens return to their homeland."

I could hear the people in the room gasping and speaking under their breaths.

"This man doesn't know the history, and wonders if there is anyone alive who can remember what happened between your people. He just knows that the Erokens are good people and they shouldn't be punished for something their parents or grandparents did."

The great hall grew quiet. I felt the Sara squeeze my hand. When I looked at her, I could see that her face was beaming with pride.

"Did you actually think I'd listen to your request?" the Sar said laughing.

"I see why my daughter likes you so much! You're the bravest man I have ever seen. You come walking into my Great Hall wearing Eroken armor and you have the nerve to ask me to let the Erokens go home!" the Sar said with a hint of anger growing in his voice.

"They are good people," I said.

There was a loud gasp as if everyone in the Great Hall was gasping simultaneously. The Sar began to laugh uncontrollably. I wasn't sure what was happening. I didn't know if the Sar was laughing because he thought I was crazy or not.

The Sar waved his hand and his Great Hall became silent.

"I admire your courage! I'll give your Erokens one day to leave. As many of the Erokens that want to leave will be able to leave on that one day, with one condition. You Zehn, must stay here with me. I want you to be one of my advisers. I need men like you who have the courage to say hard things to me. I'm surrounded by a bunch of cowards who agree with everything I say."

I was shocked! I couldn't believe my ears.

"What's wrong? You look surprised?" the Sar asked.

I didn't know what to say. I was so overcome with surprise that after a few seconds I finally managed to say, "I didn't think you would say yes."

The Sar smiled and then he laughed again.

The Sara grabbed my arm and began leading me quickly away towards the side exit of the Sar's Great Hall.

"We need to hurry before he changes his mind," she whispered.

"Get that man some clothes so I don't have to see that hideous armor again," the Sar called after us, as we were leaving the Great Hall.

I could hear the Sar's booming laugh even when we were outside of the Great Hall.

CHAPTER XVI
HOME

I woke up early and headed to the main gates of Edem Teramus. Today was the day that the Erokens were leaving for their homeland. The Sar had given me a place to stay at the palace so I hadn't been able to speak with very many of the Erokens. I arrived before the main gates were opened. There was already a line of people forming, waiting for the gates to open.

I was happy, my chest was ready to explode. It felt really good knowing that I'd helped to make so many people happy. I was going to miss the Erokens. I was happy for them because I know what it's like to be a slave taken far away from your home. I'd stopped thinking about going home because I was tired of feeling disappointed. I knew that I could never go home and the sooner I decided to accept reality the sooner I'd get over my sadness.

"Hello, I want you to meet my baby. His name is Zehn. I named him after you," a woman's voice said taking me away from my thoughts.

"I'm honored," I replied to the woman.

"I'll tell him everyday why I named him after you. Words cannot tell you how grateful I am. I've been separated from my family for so long. I can't wait to see them again."

I smiled.

"You're welcome. I hope that your son will grow into a great man one day."

"Why am I not surprised that there are people naming their children after you?" said a familiar voice from behind me.

I turned around and it was Storem!

I could feel tears coming to my eyes. Words would not come out. Storem stood there with a big scowl on his face that only he could muster.

"You didn't think I was going to leave you here forever? Did you?" Storem asked, with a hint of amusement in his voice.

The feeling of disbelief combined with the most happiness I'd ever felt, was taking away my ability to speak. Feelings of hope and joy were overwhelming my senses. I didn't know it was possible to feel these kinds of feelings so powerfully.

"I did, I did..." was all I managed to say, when I could finally speak again.

Storem nodded with a hint of disappointment on his face.

"Nobody wanted to leave you. It was the President, he made us leave without you. He doesn't know that I'm here."

"I can't believe you're here," I managed to say.

I'd never experienced this much difficulty controlling my emotions before.

"How can you be here? Won't the President notice that you're gone?" I asked.

"I'm on vacation," Storem said, with a smile.

"You're on vacation!" I blurted out the response.

"I can't believe it! You're on vacation and here!"

"I can't believe I'm here either. The smell of this place isn't exactly up to my vacation standards."

Storem could go anywhere in the known galaxy and he came to get me. Why? Why would Storem come for me?

"I thought you didn't like me Zip!"

"I don't like you. I don't like anyone. In my line of work, I can't afford to like people. I made you a promise and I intend to keep my promise."

"I recognize this man! Has he come to take you home?" asked a voice laced with happiness.

It was the Sara. I turned to look at her. She was running up to greet me.

"Yes, he can take me home..." I paused remembering my deal with her father.

"I promised the Sar that I wouldn't leave..." I said slowly.

"Don't worry about him. The Sar will understand. Promise me, that you'll bring your daughter back to meet me," the Sara said.

She took off her ring and handed it to me.

"Give this to your daughter to wear. I'm loaning it to her. When she comes to meet me, she can return it," the Sara said hugging me.

I looked over at Storem and he nodded as if to say that I'd be able to keep my promise to return.

"I promise. I'll bring her to meet you," I said, holding the Sara tight.

"I would never have the chance to find my daughter without you. I can never thank you enough."

The Sara stepped back looking up at me, there were tears in her eyes.

"I'm going to miss you. There's no one like you! You really are the most amazing person I've ever met. Be safe! I can't wait to meet your daughter. I hate goodbyes."

The Sara turned and started running towards the palace.

"I'm going to miss you too. I won't forget you," I yelled after her.

The Sara nodded her head and continued running without looking back.

I looked over at Storem and remembered Char.

"Can you take me back to Tyrol? Can you take me and my friends to Zendreo," I asked.

Storem didn't look happy.

"I made a promise. I could never be happy if I didn't keep it," I said.

The thought of Char living out her life married to Orly Bogler wondering what had happened to me, and why I never returned was a depressing one. I knew that I could never be happy even if I did find my daughter. I had to do something. I knew that I needed to go back.

"I know a place where I can hide so the President won't know," I said.

"How would you know anything?" Storem asked in an angry voice.

"There's the old library by the prison. I can hide there, while you get my friends."

"Maybe," Storem said.

"If anyone at the prison sees you, the game is over. I'm a dead man. Why would I take that kind of a risk for you?"

"If the President tracks your travel logs, won't he know that you came to Ethos on your vacation. Didn't you already put your life at risk?" I asked.

"He never tracks my travel. I'm his most trusted man…" Storem paused for a moment.

"You're right, I did put myself at risk," Storem admitted.

"I'll stay hidden! I always keep my promises. You can respect that... right?" I asked, hoping that Storem would agree.

"I respect a man that keeps his promises. I admit that I do have a lot of respect for your courage and loyalty to your friends. I'll take you. But only because of what I've seen you do," Storem said quietly.

Was Storem actually giving me a compliment? It meant a lot more to me, more than he'd ever know.

"Doesn't it feel great knowing you're on the right side this time?" I asked Storem with a grin.

Storem ignored my question. I thought I saw a hint of a smile on his face.

"Maybe you can get me one of those halo jump devices and a suit, so you don't have to haul me around all the time."

Storem pretended not to hear me.

"When do you want to leave?" I asked.

"We can leave anytime when you're ready to go."

"Can I bring my armor and my sword?"

Storem nodded his head.

"Yeah, we'll have to make sure it doesn't puncture your jump suit."

"I've got to say a few goodbyes and get my stuff and then we can go."

I could hardly believe my own words... Was this real? Was I really going home?

I spent the rest of the day talking with the Erokens as they left for their homeland. When I told Leena that I was going home, she smiled and told me that with God nothing is impossible! I had to admit she might be right.

...

I woke up the next morning having barely slept the night before. I was so excited for home that it had been impossible to get any quality sleep. The large red sun of Ethos was still rising in the east. The red sunlight hitting the clouds was truly a sight to see. The sky was full of red and orange streaks. I wondered if I'd ever see an Ethos sunrise again.

I was happy and sad at the same time; happy because today I was going home, and sad because I would miss my friends on Ethos. When I first came to Edem Teramus, I never thought that I'd miss this place. I wouldn't miss the arena, but I was going to miss the beauty of Ethos. I was going to miss my friend the Sara and the people. I've never received so much kindness from perfect strangers before.

I took a long last look at the sea and headed out to meet Storem. He didn't like the city much and told me that he'd meet me outside the gate. I wondered if I'd ever be able to return. It seemed impossible, but lately things that seemed impossible had been made possible. I wasn't going to give up hope now. I decided I wasn't going to miss the smell after walking through the city and arriving at the gate.

I was relieved to find Storem waiting for me not too far outside the gate.

"I'm really grateful. I consider you to be my friend," I said to Storem, when I as close enough for him to hear me.

Storem didn't say anything. We walked in silence climbing into the hills that surrounded Edem Teramus. I could tell that he wanted to go faster; I was slowing him down. It was slow going for me because I was carrying my armor. The bag holding my armor kept slipping out of my half-good hand. I refused to let Storem carry the armor and I could tell that he was getting annoyed.

After we'd walked a pretty good distance from the city, Storem stopped walking. I turned around to take one last look at Edem Teramus. I didn't want to forget what the city looked like. I was glad we stopped because my hands were hurting me.

"Is there anyway we can get some video or pictures before we go?" I asked.

"Isn't everything recorded on your E-chip?" Storem asked looking slightly annoyed by my question.

"I don't have an E-chip anymore."

Storem's eyes narrowed and his head turned to one side.

He looked confused.

"You mean you can't access your E-chip. Maybe they disabled it because you were banished or because you were a prisoner?"

"Can you reactivate it? I won't tell if you don't," I said to Storem with a grin.

"Here, I brought this for your hands," Storem said sounding impatient.

I couldn't believe it! Storem was holding a portable BR scanner! I was completely shocked.

"This doesn't mean I like you. We're not friends. I just want to get out of here and you are taking forever with your bad hand," Storem said loudly.

I smiled, "I think I can get used to not being your friend."

I thought I detected a small hint of a smile on Storem's face.

"The scanner is an older model, but I think it'll do the trick," Storem said.

"I thought you weren't supposed bring things like this to under developed worlds? You know... SGC rules and regulations," I said, sarcastically.

"If you don't tell anyone, I won't tell," Storem said.

I took the scanner and found a place in the shade to sit down. I put my left hand inside the scanner. My left hand was pretty much useless.

The scanner began to hum. I wasn't exactly sure how the scanners worked but I know they use nano-tech. I'd had my share of broken bones so I knew it was only going to take a few minutes for the scanner to do its job.

"How did you convince the Sar to meet with you? We've tried lots of times and never managed to get in. What did you do?" Storem asked.

I told him about the crowd that helped me get past the guards. I explained how the Sara took me into the great hall because it was her birthday. Storem shook his head in disbelief.

"I'm an official advisor to the Sar. He even gave me a title and a place to live in the Palace," I said to Storem.

Storem had listened intently to everything that I said. He actually looked impressed.

"The President might consider having you work for him knowing that you've got an in with the Sar. He might even give you a halo device and jump suit and even a nice salary," Storem said.

"I could never work for that man," I said, with disgust.

"You don't even know who he is. If you did you might reconsider," Storem countered.

"I know enough!"

I could feel myself getting angry.

Storem smiled, "He's the Vice Director of the SGC! Do you know what that means? He's the second most powerful man in the SGC!" Storem said, sounding more excited than usual.

I was surprised. It didn't make any sense. Why would the second most powerful man in the galaxy spend time on Tyrol?

"So that's why he doesn't like it when I don't do what he says."

Storem laughed. "You're the only one I've ever seen dumb enough to make an enemy out of a man that powerful."

"Even If I'd known who he was, I don't think I would've done anything differently. I don't even know who the Director of the SGC is. My mom was into politics but me, never, I hate politics," I said to Storem.

I wondered if they'd killed my mom because she wouldn't do what they wanted. I wondered if the Vice Director was responsible for killing my parents and my wife. I wanted to ask Storem for information but I decided not to. Storem was the Vice Director's number one man and I didn't want him knowing what I knew. There was no way I could work for that man.

"Why is the President, I mean the Vice Director on Tyrol? Why would anyone choose to live there?" I asked Storem.

"The Vice Director is very hands on. He's in charge of

the energy council," Storem said.

That made sense. Tyrol has the most h36 in the galaxy.

"He doesn't really live on Tyrol. He's only there when he needs to be," Storem said with a smile.

"Halo jumping opens up the entire galaxy. He can spend his day on Tyrol and return to his home world to sleep at night."

"That's crazy, how would that be?" I asked, shaking my head.

"How do I get a Halo Device?"

"You don't, unless you work for the SGC. They don't want this technology getting out to the masses. You're not even supposed to know the technology exists. Only the people on the top level of society know that it exists."

My hand in the scanner was heating up. I could tell the scanner was almost done. I couldn't believe that Storem had brought it. The green light on the scanner turned on indicating that it had finished.

I pulled my hand out of the scanner and it looked normal with barely a hint of scarring. I was glad that I could still recognize the scar, it would be there to remind me what I'd overcome. I extended my fingers slowly, expecting to experience some pain, but there was none. I wiggled all my fingers and made a fist and extended them again. I could feel myself smiling.

"Stop staring at your hand and fix the other one, so we

can get out of here," Storem said impatiently.

I put my right hand into the scanner.

"So where are you going to go on vacation after you drop me off?" I asked.

Storem ignored my question or he pretended not to hear me…

"I could show you around the Great Zelecon Wildlife Refuge. We could look for zoroks. The forest there is amazing. People from all over go there just to see the trees."

The words coming out of my mouth made me extremely excited for home. I hadn't let myself think of home for a long time. I couldn't wait to take Char to see the trees. I could picture her lovely smile and the looks of amazement that would be on her face.

"I think even the Director would be impressed by the Zelecon Pines! Everyone's impressed their first time seeing the trees," I said with a grin.

"I don't think so," Storem said.

"You don't think the Director would be impressed or you don't want to hang out with me on your vacation?" I asked.

"You can't impress the Director," Storem said, avoiding my invitation to hang out.

The green light on the scanner came on. I took my hand out of the scanner. My hands felt great! I stood up and picked up my gear.

"I'm ready. Let's get going! I can't wait to get home!"

I started walking fast, hoping I was going the right direction. It felt great to have my hands back. You just don't understand how much you have, until you lose the use of your hands. I will never complain about anything now that I have my hands back.

"The last time I was at the refuge I saw a huge zorok. You don't want to get between a mamma zorok and her babies! I bet not even Iventu would have a chance!"

Storem didn't say anything.

Ever since Storem had mentioned the E-chip I couldn't get it out of my mind. If I could get access to my E-chip I might be able to see things I couldn't remember. I thought they removed the chip on prisoners, but maybe they just disabled the connection to it.

Storem was quiet the rest of our walk to the location where he had stashed his gear. I couldn't believe it, I really was going home!

Halo jumping was almost starting to feel like a normal form of travel for me, even though I'd only done it a few times. Storem had brought a change of clothes for me. I had my clothes changed and my gear on even before Storem was ready to go.

"If you know any sight-seeing stops on our way? I'd be okay taking a few minutes to check them out," I said feeling hopeful.

The blue gas giant planet and the view of the stars was still fresh in my mind, even though it felt like it was ages ago. Storem didn't say anything. I was probably annoying him.

Finally after what felt like an extremely long time Storem was ready to go. The indicator light on my helmet showed that I was synced up.

"We're leaving in 10." I heard Storem say.

The indicator in my helmet began counting down. I felt so excited knowing that soon I would be home. I couldn't wait to see Char again. I really was going home. The count down on my HUD reached 1. I saw the familiar bright blue light and then nothing...

...

I opened my eyes to blackness.

"Every time I jump with you there is a beacon malfunction."

It was Storem sounding annoyed.

"I must be lucky!" I replied.

When I opened my sun visor I saw the same blue planet with rings, that we had stopped at before. I loved the feeling of weightlessness.

"I don't think it's luck. I think the same beacon is malfunctioning," I said.

"The beacons are supposed to repair themselves. Most

likely this one hasn't finished with the repairs," Storem said.

I didn't know how long we had, so I decided to enjoy the amazing view as long as I could. The countdown on my HUD started again and the blue planet went black. I was standing on solid ground.

I knew we'd made it to Tyrol because I could feel the difference in gravity. We were at the library.

"You wait here, stay hidden. I'll get your friends. Don't let anyone see you," Storem said in a commanding voice.

"I'll stay hidden. Thanks Zip. I owe you!"

I stood back and watched Storem disappear in the blue light created by the halo jump device.

I was tired. I needed to rest but I knew it was going to be hard to get any rest because I was so excited to see Char again. I barely had time to think about what I was going to say to her when I saw Storem appear surrounded by blue light.

Storem was alone and he didn't look happy.

"Where are my friends? Where's Char?" I asked, a nervous feeling was growing in my stomach.

"They won't know you," Storem said.

"What do you mean they won't know me? Of course my friends will know me," I said, feeling confused.

"They moved back everyone's E-chip to before you

came."

"How's that possible? I thought regular people's E-chips could not be modified. The encryption is unbreakable."

"You actually believe those shewa stories about unbreakable encryption?" Storem said, shaking his head and looking a little disappointed.

"What's a shewa story?"

Storem smiled and started laughing.

"Shewas are little magical creatures who tell bed time stories to children who can't sleep because they're having nightmares."

"Oh," was all I managed to say, feeling a little stupid.

"They've been using E-chips to control people since day one. They can reset an individual's chip or an entire population's chips by broadcasting a simple update signal."

"Wouldn't people be able to detect the signal?" I asked.

"They piggyback the signal on regular communication signals, so no, they are pretty much undetectable. Somehow a lot of the people got this idea that they were prisoners in an SGC experiment. Somehow these people started believing that there were thousands or maybe millions of mirrors blocking out the sun, causing Tyrol to go into deep freeze which killed off most of the planet's population. You wouldn't know where they got such an idea would you? You wouldn't know how some of the people learned how to read, would you?" Storem said, in a sarcastic voice.

"To avoid complications with the population they set all the E-chips to back before you came. Your friends don't know you anymore."

"Is there any way to recover the data from the chips? Do they store all the data in some central location?" I asked.

The realization that Char wouldn't know me was devastating. I realized how much she meant to me. I could feel the pain of losing Char growing on my chest, there was a heavy weight pressing on my lungs making it hard to breathe.

"They don't store all the data in a central location. It would be impossible to store that much data from so many people. If they want information from someone, they access the data directly from the E-chips," Storem said quietly.

"Can I see them? Can I talk to them? Maybe they'll remember me. I've got to try..."

"They won't remember you. I've seen this before," Storem said.

"I have to try. They're my friends and I'll remember. I could never live with myself if I just left," I said quietly.

"There's one thing we can do. We can find your daughter," Storem said, changing the subject.

"I don't even remember her name let alone any of her

documentation records," I said, feeling hopeless.

"I'm going to, reactivate your E-chip. Once your chip is up and running you might be able to remember. It's rare that you'll remember anything from your E-chip since they most likely wiped out all the memory, but we can still try it. I'll grant you security agent access rights on the grid, which will let you search the public records," Storem said, almost sounding cheerful.

I wondered if Storem was actually trying to be my friend.

"All right. So what do I need to do?" I asked.

"It's not hard. You'll probably want to lay down so you don't fall over and injure yourself, if you lose consciousness.

"Wait, I'm going to be knocked out?" I asked.

The last thing I wanted to be was unconscious. I probably shouldn't trust Storem because he works for the Vice Director who is one of the worst men I know.

"What do you have to do to enable my E-chip?"

"The programmer just has to physically touch you. You can't activate E-chips remotely. I just have to touch you with the programmer. It will require you to agree verbally to the install. I use the programmer to update access levels for new security agents."

I had a good feeling for some reason. Something was telling me that everything would be all right.

"Okay, let's do this," I said, getting down and laying on my back.

"Don't worry, I do this all the time. It's quick and painless," Storem said.

Storem got the programmer and touched it to my hand.

"State your name," the automated voice from the scanner said.

The female voice from the scanner sounded almost a bit snobbish. I wondered if a programmer could be a snob.

"My name is Zehn Mortalix," I said, pronouncing my words carefully for the programmer.

"This software comes with no warranty, may cause brain damage and even death. Do you agree to allow me to install updates to your E-chip? If you agree say the following, "I, Zehn Mortalix, agree to the terms of this install."

"I Zehn Mortalix agree to the terms of this install," I repeated it quickly.

I didn't want to think about the possibility of going unconscious and maybe never waking up. I hoped I could trust Storem. For all I knew he was following orders from the Vice Director.

I saw a flash. I felt my arms twitching and my legs were cramping up. I saw more flashes but not with my eyes; I saw them with my thoughts. It felt like every muscle in my body was contracting. Everything went black...

...

I opened my eyes to blackness. I moved my hand in front of my face. My hand must have triggered a motion sensor because the lights turned on. I sat up. My body felt extremely tired.

"You're awake?" Storem said, sitting up.

He must have fallen asleep.

"I don't know what happened. You started convulsing. You had a seizure. I've never seen that happen before. You've been out for hours. I thought your brain was fried. I was afraid you wouldn't be waking up..." Storem went quiet.

I didn't know what to think. I felt normal, just very tired. At least my brain wasn't fried as far as I could tell.

"Can you try accessing the Grid?"

"How can I do that? I don't have a display device." I asked.

"Really! Don't tell me your E-chip requires a display device!" Storem said, in disbelief.

"Not that long ago, I didn't even know that my E-chip still worked," I mumbled, feeling myself getting annoyed.

"How am I supposed to know how to access the Grid?" I asked, in an angry voice.

I was surprised at how angry my voiced sounded.

"Your E-chip must be ancient. Nowadays all you have to do is, think the command and you should be able to access the Grid. You only need display devices if you want to show other people something."

"What's the command I need to think?"

"Try thinking 'grid help' and see if anything comes up," Storem said, sounding frustrated that I didn't know something that was so basic to him.

I thought the words very clearly in my mind and nothing happened.

"I get nothing!"

I tried thinking the words again.

"I don't see anything."

"I bet the install failed. I'm not sure what we're going to do now," Storem said.

"Can't you search the Grid?" I asked.

"I can but without a name and personal documentation records, I don't even know what I would be searching for," Storem said, sounding annoyed.

"What about the prison? Don't they have my records?"

"I don't have access to the prison records. Those kinds of records aren't exactly public."

"Can't you look me up and then find my daughter that way?" I asked.

Storem shook his head.

"You don't exist anymore according to the Grid. There is no record of you ever having lived."

"What about my parents, can you find them?"

"Trust me, I've tried everything on the Grid and I can't find anything on you or your parents. Your parent's records are sealed by court order and I don't have access to see them."

"What about my ice-flying records at the school. I had the fastest lap time ever recorded and I was voted the best player in the league my last year in school. My daughter Nebia tells me all the time that she is going to beat all my records even though she's a girl. Maybe my E-chip will work with a display device? Do you have one?"

"No, I don't have one on me..." Storem stopped talking mid-sentence.

"You just said Nebia is your daughter's name."

"Yeah, that's her name. I really miss Nebs," I said.

"The last time I remembered seeing her was before I had to leave for Tyrol. She brought me my ice-flyer suit and my skates. I remembered Nebs telling me that I'd need my gear because it is really cold on Tyrol. She told me to practice because she was going to be better than me.

My daughter's name is Nebs, and she's going to be a better flyer than ME!" I yelled with a smile, looking at

Storem.

"I can remember my daughter!"

I could feel tears in my eyes. The old woman Leena from Ethos was right. The joy I was feeling at this moment was more powerful than I'd ever felt before. I didn't know it was possible to feel this happy! I'd never understood why old people would cry when they were happy until now.

"Storem! You did it! I can remember Nebs! This is the happiest day of my life. You gave me back my life! You're taking me home. You fixed my hands and now I can remember my daughter."

I almost wanted to hug Storem. I don't remember ever wanting to hug a man before. Storem was actually smiling back at me, looking pleased with himself. Maybe he was a true friend.

"I bet the HUD in the halo jump suit helmets might work for a display device!" Storem said, in a loud voice sounding more excited than I'd ever heard him sound before.

"Hey, can you restore Char's memories like you did mine?" I asked Storem.

"No, I don't have that kind of access," Storem said shaking his head.

"How can I remember everything?" I asked.

"I only re-enabled your chip. I didn't restore any

memories. I don't have that kind of access," Storem said impatiently. I was happy that my E-chip was working. I just wished there was something I could do for Char.

It was so hard to know if Storem was being genuine. He wasn't an easy person to read. I wanted to trust him, but it was hard to trust someone who works for the Vice Director.

I put on the helmet and the HUD turned on. I noticed an icon flashing on the right top corner of the screen that I'd never noticed before. The icon looked like a syncing icon. Storem handed me the wrist controller. I selected the flashing icon.

I saw the same flashes that I'd seen before. I wasn't seeing the flashes with my eyes but with my mind. The flashing stopped. I was relieved that this time the flashing lights didn't cause a seizure.

"I think it might be working... At least I'm not having a seizure," I said, to Storem.

I focused on the HUD, hoping for something good to happen. I knew somehow that I'd find my daughter.

"Do you see anything?" Storem asked, sounding hopeful.

I saw the words "sync completed" come across the screen on the HUD.

"It says sync completed," I let Storem know.

I thought the words, 'grid help'. I saw a list of

commands. There was a command for finding people. I thought the words "find female Nebia Mortalix, home world Zendreo, born 09-31-3421, city Perthasol, daughter of Zehn Mortalix. I couldn't believe it. I remembered my daughter's birthday and the city she was born in. The word *deceased* came to my mind and I read it on the HUD.

"It says deceased. There's no way that she's dead. I know she is not dead," I said, taking off the helmet.

"I know she's not dead, It's a lie!"

"The Grid doesn't lie," Storem said quietly.

"Weren't you just talking to me about shewa stories?" I asked angrily. "I know she's alive. She has to be alive. I just know it!"

Today had started out to be such a good day. The happiness I'd felt was going away fast. Maybe Nebs was dead.

The thought of Nebs being dead left me feeling very much alone, without any purpose. I wanted to go back to Ethos. I wanted to fall asleep by the tree at the spring and dream about my daughter and never wake up...

Nebs could be dead, and Char didn't know me anymore. There wasn't any person alive who would remember me, or care if I were dead except the Sara on Ethos, who I'd probably never see again.

I suddenly felt very tired and completely deflated. I'd felt so happy thinking that finally my life would be made right only to find out my life would never be the same again. I felt my legs going weak and I sat down on the ground.

"I can take you home when you're ready," Storem said quietly.

"I can't leave without seeing Char," I heard myself saying.

"It's too dangerous if anyone sees you."

"Nobody will see me. I can go in at night and wait for her in the tunnels," I said, looking up at Storem.

Storem had a confused look on his face. Maybe Storem didn't know that Char was in charge of the vents to the city.

"It's her job to control the air vents to the city. I helped her before the President, I mean before the Vice Director, decided to make me his slave. She was training me, anyway nobody is ever in those tunnels but her. If I go in at night, no one will know I was there. All you have to do is get me to the tunnels by the orchard."

I was surprised by how sad my voice sounded.

"All right let's wait til it's night time," Storem said, sounding tired.

We sat in silence for a while. I started thinking about my daughter. Somehow, I knew that she wasn't dead. I couldn't explain it, but I knew she wasn't dead. I started to feel a little better.

I wondered if Storem was trying to trick me with some fake Grid program. I put the helmet back on.

"Maybe I had the wrong Nebia," I said to Storem.

"Yeah, maybe so. I'll do some searching too," Storem said sounding more like his normal self.

I thought about my daughter and the same deceased message came up. When and how did she die? I asked the Grid in my mind.

"*Public Access Denied,*" the response came into my mind. The words were also written across the HUD.

I wished I had admin rights so I could see the records. The icon on the right corner of the HUD changed. The words Access Level changed to Root Administrator on the HUD for a few seconds and then went away.

Did I have admin access? How was that possible?

I wanted to ask Storem about the access levels and how they worked but instead I read what was on the screen.

Public Records for Nebia Mortalix

Status:	Sealed to public, unknown status, ID-chip removed or disabled
Home World:	Zendreo
Born:	09-31-3421

City:	Perthasol
Sex:	Female
Age:	17
SGCID:	09313421-NZ-4421
Father:	Zehn Mortalix
Mother:	Dhenna Zitell Mortalix

I knew it! My daughter wasn't dead. I knew that Nebs was alive! I wasn't surprised that she had removed or disabled her ID-chip.

I wondered how I was able to see the sealed record.

"What's my access level?" I asked the Grid in my mind. *"Programmer AI with full access,"* the Grid responded in my mind.

I didn't even have to look at the HUD. I could see the words in my mind.

"What's a Programmer AI and what can it do?" I asked the Grid.

"The Programmer AI adds security to the system, a protection against the system destroying itself or the people it serves. All systems on the Grid are controlled by Artificial Intelligence or AI which follow the rules set by the Programmer AI."

"How did I get access to the Programmer AI?" I asked

the Grid.

"Unknown," the Grid responded.

I wondered if it had something to do with the fact that I no longer had an ID-chip in my arm. There must be a bug in the system that the designers didn't account for. When Storem tried to give me access to search records, it triggered the bug. The bug gave me Programmer AI Access which is the highest access level because the designers never thought that access levels would be given to someone without an ID-chip.

I wanted to see what Storem knew about the AIs and access levels.

"Hey, how do you get access to see sealed records? It keeps telling me that I don't have access to see the records."

"You don't get that kind of access, only the AIs have it," Storem said, slowly. I could tell that my question annoyed him.

"Can the AIs tell me what's in the record?"

"You have to have law enforcement privileges otherwise the AI won't get the information for you. Don't you know how the AIs work?" Storem asked, sounding more frustrated than before.

It made sense to me that depending on your position in law enforcement or government, the AIs would allow access to information accordingly. The AI's job was to make sure that people were not able to break the system of government by limiting what a person could do according to their position.

"So let's say the Director secretly decided he wanted to take over a planet for it's resources without getting approval from the council, would the AIs let him do that?" I asked.

I was surprised by the amount of sarcasm in my voice.

"That's a fair question. I think that the AIs aren't supposed to allow the Directer that much power. But You know how politicians are? They always find ways to get around the laws. There's always some legal clause in the AIs programming to allow them to do things that people would never agree to. As long as the people have faith in the AIs, politicians will continue to find ways to circumvent the system. It's the nature of governments to game the system to benefit the elite class of people in power over regular people."

"Do you agree with that?" I asked, with a hint of disbelief in my voice.

"I hate politics. I don't agree with it but I'm not naive to how governments work. People were so excited to turn everything over to the AIs because they believed the AIs couldn't be controlled and would enforce the laws without discrimination. Many people wanted the government to solve society's problems and believed that the AIs could do just that since they're not controlled by politicians. The people look to technology to solve the traditional failings of governments."

"Which legal clause do you think the Director used in the case of Tyrol?"

I was feeling brave.

"He probably used some clause that says worlds with less than some arbitrary number of inhabitants can be claimed by the Director of the SGC without the council's knowledge or approval. In the millions of lines of code there will be some little clause like this that nobody knew existed until it's used. The AIs will quietly allow the action since the clause exists."

"You see how that works?" Storem asked.

"No honest man could vote for, or support laws that they don't completely understand, yet it happens all the time," Storem finished, sounding a little disgusted.

I agreed with Storem. I was starting to understand why most people didn't like politicians.

Today had been a good day. I was feeling extremely tired. I decided to see if I could get some sleep before we headed out later when it was night time. I couldn't wait to see Char again even if she didn't know me anymore. The ground was hard, but I'd gotten used to sleeping on it back on Ethos.

CHAPTER XVII
CHAR'S MEMORY

"Wake up! Do you want to see your friends or not?" Storem asked, sounding more like his angry old-self.

I felt tired, almost as tired as I'd felt that terrible first day when I woke up in a cryo-chamber.

"I do. Just let me wake up first," I said.

"You're lucky that the security in Grindolstin is low or I'd never try to take you in there," Storem said.

The SGC didn't worry much about people trying to leave or come into the city. The cold temperatures formed a natural barrier that nobody would cross.

"Your friends aren't going to know you. I guess after you learn the hard way, I'll take you home and this can all be over."

I didn't care what Storem thought. I needed to see Char. I couldn't just leave her behind.

I didn't pay much attention to the halo jump instructions. I'd jumped enough times by now, it almost felt like a normal activity. I saw the blue light glowing around us then everything went black. We arrived in the city at a spot that I wasn't familiar with.

"You'll have to point me in the right direction to the orchard. I'm not sure which way to go," I said to Storem after I'd taken off my helmet.

"Just be quiet and follow me."

We started walking. It wasn't long before I started to recognize things. I was relieved that Storem hadn't decided to go rogue on me and take me to the detention center.

Grindolstin was dark and quiet. We didn't see anyone on our way to the orchard.

"Will you tell anyone if I eat some fruit?" I asked Storem, with a grin.

Storem shook his head and didn't say anything. I grabbed some fruit and now it was my turn to show Storem around. I was surprised that he didn't know where the tunnels were.

I had to admit even though this orchard was underground, at nighttime, you wouldn't know it except for the fact you couldn't see any stars. The grass felt soft under my feet and it was nice to be at a familiar place. I remembered thinking that I'd never see Char and Grindolstin again, yet now here I was, in the orchard. I was going to see her again.

"Do you promise that you'll stay hidden?" Storem asked after we'd made our way to the tunnels.

"Yes," I promised.

"Good, but I'm not worried about you. I'm worried about your friend. Make sure she doesn't tell anyone, not even her family. Can you promise me that?"

"I'll let her know that a man's life depends on her being quiet. I don't think she'd want to be responsible for destroying your life," I said, looking at Storem with a smile.

Storem frowned. "You better convince her. I'm counting on you. I'll meet you back here in a few days. Don't get your hopes too high. She's not going to remember you."

My stomach started feeling a little weak. I felt some trepidation after Storem left because I didn't know what I was going to say to Char. I didn't want her to think that I was some crazy stalker. It was going to be harder than facing Iventu in the Arena. I wasn't afraid of dying. I was afraid of something much worse than dying. I was afraid of losing Char forever. I found a good place to rest and sat down to wait. I felt myself nodding off.

...

"Hello, are you okay?" I heard a voice say.

I woke up to a pair of blue eyes and a bright happy smile. It was Char! I'd seen this moment in my mind every single day that I'd been away, but it wasn't going how I'd planned it. I didn't know what to say. My heart was pounding.

"My name is Zehn Mortalix... I'm okay... I'm just a little

tired," I finally, heard myself say.

"You're one of the immortals, aren't you?" Char asked, with some excitement in her voice. It was so good to hear her voice again.

"No, I'm not immortal," I said, smiling back at her.

"Yes, you have to be immortal with a name like yours, and you talk with a funny accent."

I hadn't realized that my accent was so noticeable.

"I've never met an immortal before! Hardly anyone has! Come out here where I can see you better," Char said, reaching down, grabbing my arm, pulling me to my feet and dragging me out of the tunnel.

"It's you! I can't believe it," Char exclaimed, after taking a good look at me once we were out of the tunnel.

"Do you know who I am?" I asked.

I wanted to ask her if she remembered me, but I didn't.

"No, I don't know who you are, but I've seen you. I know you have to be an immortal. I can show you if you come with me. I have to show you something. Come on! Follow me!"

Char took off at a very fast pace. She was practically running in the tunnel. I had to run to catch up to her.

"I knew today was going to be a good day!" Char said, when I finally caught up to her.

"Do you know how long I've been waiting?" She asked.

It had been a long time. It felt like I'd been away for a lifetime, especially after I'd lost all hope of ever seeing her again.

"What have you been waiting for?" I asked.

"You'll see, I'm not sure the best way to tell you. It's something I have to show you. It's a little strange... you might think I'm crazy if I tell you. So you'll just have to wait and see."

"Don't you have to change the vents?" I asked without thinking, when we were getting close to some of the vents that needed to be changed.

I realized my mistake instantly and hoped Char wouldn't notice.

Char stopped, turned, and looked at me. She was squinting her eyes and she smiled at me.

"That's strange... but it kinda makes sense too! I don't care about the stupid vents! Let's hurry! You're not going to believe it… well, after what you just said, you might!"

I was relieved that she didn't think I was too weird.

Being with Char made me feel like I'd returned home. My heart was no longer pounding. All the nervousness and fear I'd felt was gone. It didn't matter that she didn't remember me, she was with me again. I'd never understood how good it could feel to be at home again until this moment.

"Is that a waterfall? Does this place have a special meaning for you?" I asked, when we could hear the waterfall. I tried my best to sound sincere. I didn't want to ruin her big surprise.

Char stopped walking, turned and looked up at me and smiled.

"Yes, it's me and my dad's favorite spot."

"Come on let's hurry," Char said and she started back down the tunnel.

Every time Char would talk about her dad I would think about my daughter Nebs. I felt sad for Nebs. Our time together had been so short. You hear stories from old people, how the one regret they had in life was they didn't spend enough time with their families, especially their children. I started feeling like those old people. I wished I'd spent more time with my daughter. It's true, every minute a father spends with his daughter is precious.

"It's really amazing. I can see why your dad liked it so much," I said, when we reached the lookout point.

I walked up to the railing and looked down. I could see the President's mansion with the lush gardens and trees.

"Wait here! I'll be right back. I've got something to show you. It's something from the immortals!" Char said, with a lot of excitement in her voice.

"Okay I'll be right here," I said, but Char was already running down one of the tunnels and probably didn't hear me.

I wondered what the immortals had left behind.

I looked back down at the President's mansion and hoped that I'd never see that man again. I was actually kind of proud of myself for embarrassing him. I was sure that I would've treated him the same even if I'd known that he was the Vice Director.

"Here, take a look at this! What does it mean?" Char was holding the book from the library.

There was a drawing of a person's face on one of the blank pages in the back of the book.

"Let me take a closer look," I said.

Char handed me the book. The person in the drawing was me! The words 'I love Zehn Mortalix' were written under the drawing in much better penmanship than mine.

I could feel my eyes starting to water up. It was everything I could do, to hold back tears.

"It looks just like you! The drawing is you! What does the writing say?" Char asked, bouncing up and down with anticipation.

My legs felt weak and I sat down on the ground and stared at the drawing. I wasn't sure what to say. I didn't have any words coming to my mind. I wanted to tell Char what the writing said, but I was afraid.

"Yeah that's a drawing of me," I finally managed to say.

I began turning the pages of the book to avoid answering what the writing said under the drawing. I stopped on another page with a drawing of a man.

"That's my dad," Char said, sitting down next to me.

"Isn't my dad handsome?"

"Yes he is," I said quietly, realizing that Char probably knew that she was the person that had drawn the drawings in the book.

"I think you have an amazing talent for drawing. The drawings are great!" I said.

Char smiled. "Thanks! I really like drawing."

"What does that writing say under my dad's drawing? Please tell me, you can read it! I really want to know what it says," Char said, with a hopeful expression on her face.

"I can read it."

Char smiled and leaned her head against my shoulder looking down at the drawing of her dad.

It says: *I miss you every day, dad. I think about you often because I know it makes you happy to be remembered. I will always love you. Until we meet again.*

The emotion in my voice, surprised me. Char was silent for a moment. I could tell she was thinking about her dad.

"How did I write that? I know I drew the picture... but I

can't read or write... books are not allowed? You have to know because there's a picture of you in the book."

I was so glad that I didn't go home with Storem when he offered to take me! I could hardly believe it! I could tell Char the truth and I knew she'd believe me! I was glad that I'd taught Char how to read and write. I didn't know it was possible to feel this happy. My chest felt like it was going to explode! I'd never felt this happy in my life, ever.

"Char, I was here before and I taught you how to read and write before I had to leave," I blurted out, before changing my mind.

"You called me Char. I don't let anyone but my dad and Nanna call me that," Char said, with a smile.

"Not even Orly Bogler?"

Char's eyes got big and she laughed.

"You do know me! Orly's the worst! He thinks I'm going to be his wife."

"I was a little worried that you'd be married to Orly before I came back," I said, with a grin.

I wanted Char to know that I'd been thinking about her while I was gone.

"What does the writing say under your drawing?" Char asked.

"I didn't know that you were such a good artist!" I said, trying to avoid the question.

"I didn't either, until I found this book. One day the book just appeared out of nowhere. When I saw the drawing of my dad, I was very confused. I asked Nanna if she knew anything about the book. She couldn't remember anything. She told me that I should try drawing another drawing of my dad to see if it was similar. I'm pretty sure that I drew the pictures," Char said, almost like she was trying to convince herself.

"I just know that I drew the drawings but I don't understand why I can't remember..."

I wanted to tell her about the President reprogramming the E-chips but I wasn't sure how to explain to Char what an E-chip was. I remembered how hard it was to explain to her space ships and space elevators. I didn't want to ruin the moment so I decided not to say anything about E-chips. I could always do that later.

Sometimes I longed for a simple life, a life without having to worry about all the latest technologies.

"What does this say?" Char asked, turning to another page which had a lot of writing on it.

I skimmed over the page until I realized the it was about me; I started to read more carefully.

"What does it say? I want to know what it says," Char asked, looking into my eyes with a pleading look on her face.

I think it would be impossible for anyone to say no to the look that she was giving me. I decided to read out loud. I was as interested to know what was written in the book as she was.

I remember the first day that I met Zehn. I knew there was something special about him. Even though I'd never met him before, I felt like we've always known each other. I felt a connection that is hard to explain.

I glanced over at Char; she was nodding her head looking off into the distance. When she noticed I'd stopped reading she looked at me and smiled.

I first saw Zehn down in the valley from the main door. It was my turn to close the doors for the night and for some reason instead of closing the doors like I normally do I felt like I should wait a minute. I waited, looking down until I saw something gliding over the snow. I'd never seen anything moving outside before. I realized it was a person when Zehn finally got close enough. I wondered how he could survive the cold and be gliding over the snow. Zehn told me later that he is an ice-flyer, which is a very complicated game that he plays and he loves it. Zehn tried to explain the game to me, but I didn't understand.

I smiled. I missed ice-flying so much that I wondered if I'd ever get to play again.

Zehn told me that his skates make it so he can glide over the snow. Zehn has a special suit that kept him warm. He calls it his ice-flyer suit. I've always been told that it's impossible for people to survive outside on the surface, especially during the night. Maybe only the immortal people can do it. When Zehn stopped gliding and laid down in the snow, I felt worried. I hurried and convinced some people to go down with me to the valley before it got completely dark. Everyone thought I was crazy until they finally came to the door and saw him laying in the snow. When we reached him, I was afraid that he was dead. He wasn't moving, and he was very cold. It took all of us to carry him. We finally made it back into the city before it got all the way dark. I can't explain it, but even before he opened his eyes and started talking in a strange way, I felt like I knew him. Zehn told me that he hadn't seen a girl for a very long time and he thought I was the most beautiful girl he'd ever seen. I think maybe he said that just to be nice.

I looked over at Char and I could tell she was embarrassed because she was covering her mouth with her hands.

"Don't worry, I didn't say it to be nice," I said.

Char smiled.

"Do you remember any of this?" I asked.

"No, but I'm glad that I wrote it down. Keep reading. I want to know what else it says," Char said impatiently.

Zehn is gone now. I don't know if I'll ever see him again. Nanna says the President's men came and took him and she doesn't know why. Every day I've gone to the gates at the President's mansion to ask about Zehn but nobody there knows anything. I feel empty. I sometimes wish that I'd never met him because it makes me feel so empty now that he's gone. I wish that I couldn't remember him.

I looked over at Char. Her eyes had gone big and her hand was covering her mouth.

"Do you think it's my fault that I don't remember you?" Char asked, quietly.

It was like she almost didn't want to know the answer to her question.

"It's not your fault," I said, reassuringly.

"How do you know?" Char asked.

"I just know."

I wanted to tell her about the E-chips but I knew she wouldn't understand so I decided to keep reading.

Today was my birthday. It was a good day and a bad day. Today was a good day because I saw Zehn and a bad day because he left again. He climbed all the way up the cliffs by the waterfall just to see me. I was very happy to see him and he was happy to see me. We were only able to be together for a short time. He told me that he's being held as a prisoner and that he only had a few minutes. It was very hard to not follow him when he climbed back down. I watched him go for as long as I could see him. I don't miss Zehn just because he's tall and handsome and he has a smile that makes my heart melt. I miss how he makes me feel. I miss him because when he's gone I feel empty.

"You think I'm tall and handsome?" I asked, smiling at Char.

Char nodded. I could see that her face was turning red. She looked a little embarrassed.

"Are you sure you want me to keep reading all your

secrets?"

"They aren't secrets if I can't remember them," Char said, without hesitating.

"How do you know I didn't write this to try and trick you? Are you sure I'm not pretending and making things up?"

Char smiled. "Here, hand me the book."

She opened the book to another page and said, "I think you or someone else wrote this, look how sloppy the writing is!"

I started to laugh. "That's true, I'm not very good at writing."

"What did you write?" Char asked, impatiently, handing the book back to me.

I glanced at the page.

"It's really boring stuff. It says. I'm writing a sentence to show you what words look like. My name is Zehn Mortalix. I'm an ice-flyer from Zendreo..."

"Everything you've read so far is making a lot of sense. There is no way that you made this all up!" Char said, energetically, interrupting my reading.

"When I saw you sleeping this morning, I felt like I knew you. I felt like I've been waiting for you."

It was good to be with Char again. It could've been so easy to leave without saying goodbye. I was glad that I didn't take the easy route.

"I was afraid that you wouldn't remember me. I was afraid of leaving a bad first impression..." I said, trailing off.

I wasn't sure what else to say.

"If you were afraid it means you really do know me. I'm really glad that you are here," Char said.

She turned the page in the book back to where I was reading before.

"Can you keep reading? I really want to know what it says."

Today started out in a terrible way. Nanna told me that Zehn was leaving and probably would never return. He'd just barely come to say goodbye and I wasn't there. Nanna said that he looked very sad and stressed. I didn't want him to go. I ran looking and hoping to catch him before he left the city. When I got to the doors he wasn't there. I looked out and I saw him far away out in the snow almost out of view. I yelled but he couldn't hear me. I started to cry. I knew that I could never catch up to him but I didn't care. I didn't care how cold it was. I just knew that I didn't want him to go. So I ran after him. The air was so cold and I didn't get very far. I couldn't breathe and I fell down in the snow. I remember thinking how Nanna was going to be so sad when I didn't return home. I heard a voice telling me that I was going to be okay. The voice sounded like my dad's voice. I opened my eyes and I saw Zehn.

He carried me all the way home. I probably could have walked home myself, but I let him carry me because it made me feel like he truly cared about me…

Zehn told me that he felt like he needed to turn back for some reason. He said somehow he knew that I was in trouble. I think it was my dad who told him to come back because I could hear my dad's voice telling me I was going to be okay.

Zehn said I wasn't breathing when he got to me and that he put his mouth over mine and helped me to start breathing again. I told him that it didn't count as our first kiss, even if it did bring me back from the dead.

Zehn promised that he'd never try to leave again without me, even if he had to be the President's slave.

I stopped reading and looked at Char. She was staring at me and quickly looked away when our eyes met.

"I wish I could remember. Do you remember all of that?" Char asked.

I nodded, "Yes I didn't know that part about your dad's voice but it does make sense. I think it could be possible that he was telling me to turn around."

"Do you think dead people can see us?" Char asked, sincerely.

"I think so. I don't know why or how but I felt like I needed to go back. It could've been your dad trying to help."

Char nodded, "I think they can see us. I think they can

hear us when we think or talk about them. You sometimes hear people say that you can't tell someone who's dead that you love them. But I don't believe it. I tell my dad every day that I love him and I know that he can hear me."

I thought about Nebs and I felt an overwhelming feeling that she loved me.

"I don't understand. The President doesn't have any slaves. It's illegal to have slaves. Why would I write that part about you being the President's slave?"

I explained to Char how the President had made me fight or stay locked up.

"You were a slave because of me?" Char asked, quietly when I was finished.

"No, I was a slave because the President is not a good man. It wasn't your fault. I'd probably be dead, frozen to death if you hadn't came after me."

Char didn't look convinced.

"That's a nice thing to say, but you're an immortal. If anyone could survive out on the surface you could. You've already survived once."

"Don't forget, you had to rescue me when I was out there."

"Maybe," Char said, as she halfway-nodded and shook her head.

"You must really like me because you're here now. Are

you still the President's slave? How did you get here?" Char asked.

Everything about Char's demeanor had suddenly changed. She seemed very sad and not her usual happy-self.

I showed Char the scars on my hands and I told her about Ethos and how Storem had returned for me... Char listened quietly and when I finished she looked a little better than before.

"You gotta promise me that you won't tell anyone that I'm here. Storem didn't have to bring me here. He's risking his life."

"I promise, I won't tell anyone," Char said, quietly.

Char was looking off in the distance. I could tell that she was trying to process all the information that I'd told her.

"One thing doesn't make sense to me? How come I can't remember anything and how did you know I wouldn't remember you?" Char asked, after thinking for a long time.

I wasn't quite sure the best way to answer her question.

"A short time after everyone is born, doctors implant in the back of their necks an E-chip. The E is short for enhancement. The enhancement chips interact directly with our minds, giving us the ability of unlimited memory storage. In the past people would forget many things as they aged. The mind can only remember so much. As we age we forget things. The E-chips solved memory loss and opened up people's minds to unlimited information."

I looked at Char, trying to read her expression. I couldn't tell if she was angry or sad.

"The E-chip is also connected to the Grid and allows us to share information so as a society we can be smarter."

"What's the Grid?" Char asked, looking confused.

"The Grid is made up of machines that store all kinds of information. Most people are excited to have the E-chip implanted so they can have access to the Grid. Some of these machines in the Grid are extremely smart and can make their own decisions based on their programming. These machines are called AIs. They enforce all the rules that have been created for governing the Grid."

I could tell that Char wasn't understanding me by the confused looks she was giving me. I explained to her how the AIs control different levels of access to the Grid and they stop people from breaking laws.

"I don't understand. It sounds like your people are slaves to machines," Char said, sounding skeptical after my explanation.

I could see how she would believe that...

"As long as there are people controlling the AIs, it's those people who are in charge. The AIs still have to follow rules created by government. The E-chips can be updated remotely since they're connected to the Grid. Storem told me that the memories of everyone's E-chips in the city were reset to back before you..."

"Wait! You're saying I have a device in my head?" Char interrupted me, sounding very surprised.

She was rubbing the back of her neck feeling for the E-chip.

"How come I don't know anything about having an E-chip? And why don't I know anything about the Grid?" Char asked.

I didn't know how to answer her questions. I decided to ask the Grid.

"Why don't the Tyrols have access to the Grid or know about the E-chips?" I asked the Grid, in my mind.

"There are no people or civilizations on the planet Tyrol. Tyrol is classified as an uninhabited world," the Grid responded.

It made sense to me that the Grid would say Tyrol was uninhabited. The SGC had to be hiding behind a law that allowed them to get away with putting Tyrol into a deep freeze. The AI wouldn't allow the SGC access to Tyrol's resources if they were breaking laws to do it.

"What if there were people on Tyrol? Why wouldn't they have access to the Grid?" I asked the Grid.

"Law 10000223331D section: 211, access to the Grid can be disabled for criminals, ex-convicts and persons deemed as a threat to society. Law 10000223331D section: 143 E-chips can be installed in persons deemed a threat to society without consent to monitor and control criminal activities."

"It's because Tyrol is classified as an uninhabited world by the SGC. They don't have to tell you about the E-chips and they can do whatever they want," I told Char.

"It sounds like your machines don't always tell the truth. Aren't your machines smart enough to know about all the people living here. Don't your machines know that we have E-chips and we're living on Tyrol?"

"You're right! The Grid isn't telling the truth. I think the AIs make mistakes, or they are programmed to ignore things."

"The AIs are correct 99.7% of the time and will auto correct when mistakes are found in the data," the Grid informed me.

In the case of Tyrol the AIs have the data. There are people living on Tyrol but for whatever reason the Grid is reporting it differently.

"Why are you reporting that Tyrol is uninhabited? Don't you know that there are people living on Tyrol?" I asked the Grid.

"Tyrol is classified as uninhabited. There is no information to support…"

I didn't pay attention to the rest of the response.

"Where do you think I am now? Which planet do you think I'm on?" I asked the Grid, impatiently.

"I'm sorry, your location is not available. Check if your E-chip is malfunctioning."

"If my E-chip wasn't working I wouldn't be talking to you! How am I supposed to check if my E-chip isn't working?" I responded to the Grid, feeling annoyed.

"Do you want me to run a diagnostic check for you?" The Grid asked.

"No, my chip is working fine!" I told the Grid.

"The Grid doesn't know where we are. I think it has to do with the E-chips. The E-chips for whatever reason are not reporting location information back to the Grid," I said to Char.

She was looking at me with a confused look on her face...

"I guess the details don't matter, but it was the President who ordered the data on your E-chips to be erased. The President is why you don't remember and know anything about your E-chips," I told Char.

"How's Nanna doing?" I asked.

I wanted to change the subject because I didn't like how the conversation was making me feel.

"Nanna's fine... I wish I could remember everything," Char said, quietly, avoiding my question.

I wished there was something I could do...

"I need to go do my job," Char said interrupting my thoughts.

She didn't talk very much for the rest of the day.

"Will you be here tomorrow? Char asked, after we'd finished and returned to the entrance to the tunnels. She had stopped walking, and was looking up at me.

"Yes I'll be here," I said, trying to sound cheerful.

Char gave me a half-smile, turned, and started walking away towards her home.

"Okay maybe I'll see you tomorrow," she said over her shoulder.

"See you tomorrow. I'll meet you where you like to stop for lunch." I told Char as she walked away from me.

I had a sad feeling watching Char slowly walking away from me. I wished that today had gone better. The day had started out so well, but the ending was leaving me sad and angry. I was angry at the SGC. I was angry at the Vice Director for erasing Char's memories. I wished there was something I could do. I turned and started walking slowly down the tunnel.

"Is it possible to restore memories to E-chips after they've been removed?" I asked the Grid.

"It's impossible to remove memories from E-chips Law 323414 section 2b. Access to memories can be blocked if the person is a criminal, ex-convict or deemed a danger to society."

I felt hopeful. Maybe there was a way to restore the memories if they hadn't been removed.

"How do you restore memories that have been blocked?" I asked the Grid.

"Law 323414 section 33a memories can be restored in persons who are not criminals or ex-convicts, if they are no longer a threat to society."

"How do they determine if a person is a threat to society?" I asked the Grid.

"Law 323414 section 44b The governing law enforcement entity or AI determines if a person is a threat to society."

I wasn't happy to get the Grid's response. There wasn't any chance of the Vice Director changing his mind. I wondered how society could be so trusting to give so much power to just one person in government.

"Hey, you didn't tell me what was written under your drawing," It was Char, she'd come back.

I turned around and looked down at her.

It says, "I love Zehn Mortalix," I said, without thinking.

I was instantly afraid that I'd said too much, but Char's smile convinced me otherwise.

She hugged me tight.

"That's what I thought it said. I'm so glad that I came back to ask you. I'm happy that you're here," she let go of me and without waiting for me to say anything, she took off towards home at a fast pace.

"I need to get home. I can't wait to see you again tomorrow!" Char said, sounding more like her normal-self. The sad feelings were gone. I was excited for tomorrow!

"What can a Programmer AI with full access do? Can I restore all the people's memories?" I asked the Grid when I'd made it back to the place where we ate our lunches. I decided it would be a great place to make a base camp.

I don't know why I hadn't thought of it before when I was talking to Char. I remembered that the Programmer AI was supposed to be a system fail safe to keep the system from destroying itself.

"Yes, the Programmer AI can restore memories," the Grid responded.

I couldn't believe it! This was going to be the best day of my life! I needed to come up with a strategy before I had the Grid restore everyone's memories. I didn't want the galaxy to turn into chaos. I wanted to do more than just restore the people's memories. I wanted to fix the system! I needed to find out all the Programmer AI's capabilities!

I had an idea.

"Grid, can the Programmer AI halo jump a food replicator to my location without adjusting the inventory."

I didn't want anyone to track me. I was hoping that everything was automated. Unlike people, machines are amazing at following orders and not asking any questions. Society has been trained to always trust the data supplied by the AI.

"*Yes. The Programmer AI has access to control inventory and transport products,*" the Grid replied.

"Grid, change my access level to Programmer AI. Do you know the location of the Programmer AI?"

"*Yes, the Programmer AI is in Solar System: T74A, Planet: Tyrol, City: Grindolstin,*" the Grid responded.

I knew it. The Grid had to know where I was, otherwise I couldn't be connected.

"Grid, change my access level to Programmer AI, halo jump 1 food replicator, and 1 anti-gravity bed to my location covertly without updating inventory."

"*Access granted, estimated time of arrival at your location is between 2 and 10 hours local time,*" the Grid responded.

I suddenly had an amazing idea!

"Grid, change access level to Programmer AI, halo jump one halo device and 4 halo jump suits to my location covertly without updating inventory."

"*Access granted, estimated time of arrival at your location is between 2 and 10 hours local time,*" the Grid responded.

I couldn't believe it! For the first time in my life there were no words that could describe how excited I was. I'd never felt this excited even before a championship game. I was back in control of my life. I didn't need to rely on Storem's help to find Nebs! I didn't need Storm's help to get home. In my mind I could picture Nebs, Chara and me making a surprise visit to Sara Dessa on

Ethos! We could go and do anything we ever wanted!

I didn't have to wait long before a blue light filled the tunnel and 2 boxes appeared. I wondered if anyone had ever been crushed by incoming freight from a halo jump delivery.

I ran over to the boxes. The thought of the food replicator was making me hungry for zusotua. I hoped the food replicator was programmed with a Perthasol menu. If not, I'd get one from the Grid. I'd all but lost hope of ever eating Perthasol food again.

My home town, Perthasol, was known for its amazing food, especially pastries. As good as food replicators are, they still can't make pastries as good as the Perthasol chefs. People come from everywhere on Zendreo just to go to the Academy at Perthasol to learn how to bake.

The food replicator didn't have a Perthasol menu. I wasn't that surprised, because Perthasol was a pretty small market in comparison to other locations in the SGC. It only took a minute to install the menu.

'The Zusotua was pretty good but I could tell it came from a replicator. The food made me even more excited. I couldn't wait to see Char's reaction to Perthasol food.

The tunnel filled up again with a blue light. The halo device and suits had arrived. I got 4 suits because I wanted to take Nanna and Char's mom with us. It didn't feel right leaving her family here. The living conditions were not very good and without Char, her mom and Nanna would worry about her.

The living conditions were bad for everyone... I realized if I left and didn't do anything to help these people I'd regret it.

I decided to try my AG bed, it felt good to be in a real bed again. Tomorrow was going to be the best day ever...

CHAPTER XVIII
THE AMAZING DATE

"What is all this? How are you floating like that?" It was Char.

It had taken a while for me to fall asleep even with the AG bed. I was so excited that I didn't fall asleep until early in the morning.

"Oh this is a real AG bed. I can get you one if you want," I said, looking up at Char.

Her face was priceless! She was smiling, her eyes were huge and she was shaking her head. I could tell that she was surprised and confused.

"What..? How did you get this stuff here?" she asked, looking more confused than before.

"I had it halo jumped in... I can get us anything you want..."

"Halo jumping is how you're able to travel to other worlds... right?" Char asked, not sounding very confident.

"I didn't know you could move things other than people.

I thought you told me you needed some guy with a weird name in order to halo jump."

"Oh you mean Storem. Yes, I did need Storem before, but after you left, I was able to access the Grid as a Programmer AI."

I explained to Char how Storem had given me the Programmer AI access without knowing it because there was a bug in the system.

"Char would you like to come with me for lunch?"

She smiled, "Are you asking me on a date?"

"Yes, I'm asking you on a date and it's going to be the best date you've ever been on. I don't know if I'll ever be able to top it," I said, with a grin.

"So you're already planning on a second date? What if I say no?" Char asked, teasing me.

"Don't tell me you already have a date with Orly?"

Char laughed.

"Yes I do, he's going to be so mad when I don't show up."

"I'd very much like to see Orly's mad face," I said laughing.

Char looked a little nervous when she finally had the halo jump suit on. She was probably listening to all the warnings.

"Don't worry, everything is going to be fine," I said, trying to sound reassuring.

"This is my first time being in charge of a jump so it might take me a minute to figure it out."

Char didn't look very convinced.

"I thought this date was going to be amazing. So far I've just been standing here in this hot suit wondering what's so great about it," she said, smiling up at me.

"I think I finally figured it out. We're doing a really short jump. Are you ready?"

Char nodded.

The tunnel started to fill with a blue light and numbers started counting down in my HUD... Char grabbed my hand and gave it a squeeze. Everything was black and then we were standing at the library.

"How was it?" I asked.

Char let go of my hand and took off her helmet.

"I think I'm going to throw up!" she said, bending over.

"It will pass in a minute, you're just not use to it yet."

"Don't watch me... this is the worst date ever!" Char said, pushing me away from her.

I turned and looked away. Char started laughing.

"It's just too easy! I don't even have to try," Char said, punching me in the back.

I turned back around to face her. She had a big smile on her face.

"What's next on this amazing date? So far it makes me want to puke."

We both laughed.

I took Char on a tour of the vault until we finally ended up at the hanger full of ships.

"Are we going to go somewhere in one of those things?" she asked, pointing at the ships.

"Yes we are, we're going to take a ride on a hover bike."

"Where did all these things come from? I can't remember what you called them?" Char asked.

"I think most of them are hover crafts but some might be capable of flying in space. The hover craft work similar to my AG bed."

"I can see that," Char said, turning her head to one side and looking at me like I was an idiot.

"I can see them floating above the ground. I'm not blind."

When Char saw the expression on my face she burst out laughing.

"These ships are not SGC. I think they're Tyrolian ships," I said, when Char had finished laughing.

Her eyes narrowed; I could tell she was confused.

"You mean these ships are not your people's ships?"

"No, I don't think so. Come on, I'll show you. All the displays and controls are in Tyderio."

Char followed me over to the same hover bike that I'd taken out before. When we were close the lights on the bike turned on.

"How did you do that?" Char asked, with a surprised voice.

"I used my magic mind control powers," I said, with a smile.

I looked at Char. She was smiling. I was glad to see that she was having a good time. We stored our halo helmets in the storage compartments under the seat and climbed on the bike. I felt the air pressure around us change as the life support containment shield activated.

The holographic display turned on. I could actually understand a lot of the words that I was seeing. I went to the map and it read Deklious Space Port.

"We're going to the Deklious Space Port," I told Char, while I selected the space port for our destination.

I gave the bike a little throttle and we headed towards the hanger doors.

While we were waiting for the doors to open, I cycled through the menus on the holodisplay to see what I could understand. I found a menu item that said messages. I selected the first item on the top of the list.

The display started to play a message. The voice in the message had a different accent than I was used to hearing, but I could understand most of the words.

"This is an emergency broadcast message, as of the date 05.13.3211 Tyrol is under attack from an unknown enemy. Your best chance of survival is to go to the nearest space port and travel to the Tyrol colonies on Heka. If you can't make it to a space port we recommend that you go to the nearest emergency shelter."

The message repeated several times, and then ended.

"Have you ever heard of the colonies on Heka?" I asked, Char after letting the message sink in.

"No, I've never heard of it," Char said, as we exited the hanger.

"Maybe we can find out more about it at the space port," I said.

I gave the bike full throttle. Char let out a small yelp, wrapping both arms around me to stop her backward momentum.

"You did that on purpose. I see your plan," Char said, with a lot of amusement in her voice.

After a few seconds we stopped accelerating and the bike reached a cruising speed. I loved the smooth feeling of flying low to the ground. It was hard to judge how fast we were going because everything around us was white. I left the bike in manual mode and followed the arrows on the display toward the mountains.

"What's that over there?" Char asked, pointing towards some small clouds.

"That's a river with a hot spring. Do you want to see it?" I asked, turning the bike towards the clouds and the river.

"Yes," Char said, squeezing me tighter than before as we turned.

I really wanted to get to the space port so I decided just to do a fly-by and not stop.

"I can't believe it! Look, there really is a river and trees? How is it possible?" Char asked as we flew directly over the river.

Looking behind me I could see a trail of water shooting up into the air behind the bike.

When I thought of living an entire lifetime inside Grindolstin it made me feel sad for the people there. The city was amazing but it was like living in a box.

I turned the bike hard, back towards the mountains.

"Wait til you see these mountains. I've seen a lot of mountains but I think the Grindol mountains have to be my favorite," I said.

"How do you know they're called the Grindol mountains?" Char asked.

"It says it on the map."

"I guess that's where the name Grindolstin comes from,"

Char replied.

After riding in silence and enjoying the scenery for a while, I checked the menu and found a menu item for music play-lists. I selected the first item on the list and the music started to play.

"What's that sound?" Char asked?

"It sounds really pretty!" she said before I could respond.

The music reminded me of epic music that could be used in a drama or a show. The music was perfect for our ride.

"It's music. Haven't you heard music before?" I asked.

"No, I've never heard anything so beautiful before," Char said, squeezing me tighter.

"You were right, this is an amazing date."

"We haven't even got to the best part yet!" I said turning, looking over my shoulder at Char with a smile on my face.

It was hard for me to imagine living a life without music. I turned the music up louder.

"The mountains really are amazing," Char said.

We were riding close to the mountains in a narrow valley. I slowed the bike down so we could enjoy the view. The jagged snow top peaks filled most of our view, leaving just a small patch of gray sky visible. After we passed through the valley the mountains ended and we were traveling over the flat lands and then the sea covered in snow. I gave the bike full throttle. It probably would take days to walk across the flat lands and frozen sea, but we crossed it in a few minutes.

"Is that the space port?" Char asked, pointing towards the massive buildings of Deklious.

"It's huge! Look at that line going straight up into the sky!" Char said, excitedly. It felt good to see how excited she was.

"Yes that's where the space elevator goes. They use the elevator to take people to space ships waiting in orbit. The space ships are so large they can't fly if they're not in space."

"I know a place where we can eat, if you're hungry," I said to Char, after we had parked the bike in the hanger.

Char grabbed my hand and squeezed it tight.

"This really is the best date ever!" she said, with a smile.

I decided to take her to the hotel where I'd been before. I knew there was a food replicator there.

It was fun to see the expressions on her face as we made our way to the hotel. We paused several times to just take it all in. The buildings of Deklious are so large it makes you feel tiny and insignificant.

"I just can't believe this place. Is this what the cities look like where you come from?" Char asked, after we'd paused to take look at a towering building with pretty architecture.

"How could anyone make these buildings? They are so tall and unique," she said, before I could answer her first question.

It felt eerily strange and empty to be walking through the city without seeing any people.

"No this place is a lot different than my home town. Look over there, see that building over there. We have trees that are taller than that building. The trees can reach almost 350 talens," I said, pointing at a building that had at least 20 levels.

"I wish I could see those trees," Char said.

"Me too!" I decided on the next halo jump that I was going to take Char to see those trees and we were going to find Nebs, together!

We finally made it to the hotel and I was hungry. The lights turned on automatically as we entered into the building. I could hear the voices from the video wall.

"Are there people here? I can hear voices," Char said quietly, not wanting her voice to be heard.

"Come on, don't worry it's not people, it's just a video wall advertisement for the hotel."

"Welcome to the Emerald Coast Hotel where guests can stay in the finest rooms and eat the finest food..."

It was the voice coming from the advertisement. Char stopped in front of the wall and stared in silence.

"Did you see those people? Their clothes were crazy!" she finally said, after we'd watched the video play several times.

"Yeah, this place used to be a lot warmer," I responded with a smile.

Many of the people in the video were wearing summer clothes.

I took Char into the restaurant where I'd eaten before. It really was amazing how there was not a sign of dust and the tables had all the places set ready for guests.

I took Char over by a window so we could have a good view of the city.

"My lady, if you can wait just a minute I'll be back with your food," I said, trying to sound professional.

Char smiled up at me.

"Thanks, I'll be waiting," she said, trying to sound just as professional as me.

We both laughed.

I headed to the kitchen where I knew there was a food replicator. This time I could read the replicator much better. I still had no idea what to order because I wasn't familiar with the names. So I decided to order the most expensive item on the menu.

"Only the best for my lady," I said, as I brought the food to our table.

Char smiled and started eating. The food tasted as good as it smelled.

"I've never eaten food this good before," Char said when she only had a few bites left on her plate.

I still had lots of food on my plate. I was thinking about Char and the people who lived inside Grindolstin. I felt sad for these people who were so oppressed. They were nothing more than slaves to the SGC. I wanted to help them. I wanted the people to experience this food. I wanted the people to experience freedom from the SGC.

When we finished eating, we made our way to the space elevator. I really wanted to take Char up to the top of the elevator. I was curious to see what was up there. The elevator carriage was on the ground waiting for us to go up.

"Do you want to go up there? I asked Char, pointing up.

The look on her face told me that she was worried. I could tell that she was afraid and at the same time she didn't want to disappoint me.

"We've got our halo jump suits. If there are any problems will be able to halo jump out," I said, trying to sound very confident.

"Okay, I trust you," Char said, quietly.

I took Char to the control room and this time it was much better than the last time I'd been here because I could read and understand what I was doing.

"I need to make sure everything is still working," I said to Char. She nodded and smiled back at me.

After taking a look at the screens and cycling through the menus I saw something interesting.

"It says there are several shuttles for the Heka Colonies docked up there."

The controls were pretty straight-forward. Even without training I was confident that I could control the elevator.

"Let's go. We've got too hurry before the elevator leaves!"

I grabbed Char's hand and we ran to the elevator. I hadn't noticed before, but there were seats and even restrooms inside the elevator. The elevator was large with lots of room for cargo and people. There were big windows on all sides. I couldn't wait to see the amazing views as we made our way up into the sky.

"Welcome to the Deklious space elevator, estimated travel time to the first stop is three hours," a recorded voice from the elevator said.

"I'm not sure we're going to get back in time for dinner," I said.

"I never want to go back," Char said hugging me.

I didn't pay much more attention to the elevator's recorded message because we were moving upward. We moved close to one of the large windows so we could have a good view. From above, Deklious was much larger than I thought. The streets and buildings stretched out in all directions and I couldn't see where the city ended.

The tall buildings in the city center didn't seem so tall once the elevator started moving. The elevator was accelerating fast and my stomach was letting me know. We were soon high enough that I could see the small clouds by the river that we had passed on our way to the city. Even though I'd been on Tyrol for quite a while I still wasn't used to the empty sky void of clouds.

The sun was starting to set. The red and orange sky contrasted against the white snow made for a pretty sunset, even in a cloudless sky.

"Char you've got to see the sunsets on Ethos. The sun on Ethos is so red, and the sky gets dark red. It's amazing."

Char smiled, "That sounds nice."

"I've never seen anything like this! It's beautiful! This really is the best date ever!" she said.

We were high enough that we could see the curvature of Tyrol. Above us the sky was dark and we could see a few stars meanwhile below us we could still see the red and orange sky of the sunset. The elevator was moving upwards so fast that it prolonged the sunset. The timing of our elevator ride couldn't have been better for viewing the sunset.

...

"The elevator will be arriving at the first stop in a couple of minutes. All passengers must show a valid ticket to exit the elevator. The elevator will remain at this stop for exactly one hour," the recorded voice from the elevator said.

The time it took to get to the first stop had gone by fast, it seemed like only a few minutes had passed instead of hours.

"I hope the ticket system isn't automated, because we don't have a ticket!" I said to Char, with a smile.

I looked up above and a small glint of light caught my eye. It was the mirrors that were manipulating the climate on Tyrol. My entire field of vision was filling up with mirrors connected together with some kind of super structure that formed a dome all around the planet. The mirrors were small enough that it was impossible to see them until we were up close.

"How is it possible to build something so large?" Char asked, when I pointed out the mirrors to her.

"They probably used a self-replicating nano technology. One section can replicate eight sections and then those eight sections replicate another eight sections and so on, and so on, until it's built. They dump the material into space and the material forms itself into the structure," I explained.

"How do you know so much? Are all immortals as smart as you?" Char asked, with a smile.

"No, I'm the smartest one!"

Char laughed.

Just before we made it to the stop, we put on our helmets and turned on our halo suits just in case there wasn't any air when the elevator doors opened. The doors opened to a long empty corridor that curved so we couldn't see what was at the end of it. The corridor was empty. Nobody was there to greet us. I had half-expected there to be someone or at least some automated system to check for our tickets. I stepped into the corridor.

"Are you sure it's safe to go in there?" Char asked, grabbing my hand and stopping my momentum.

"I think so. The air is breathable according to my helmet."

We followed the corridor, walking slowly. The corridor led to a large welcome area with many rows for ticket lines. The lights turned on as we entered into the welcome room. The room was much larger than I'd anticipated. The ceiling was several levels high; maybe three or four levels high and curved until it met in the center. The floor and walls of the room were curved and made of glass. We were standing in a giant glass sphere. I wondered if the designers of the sphere had thought about people who suffered from vertigo or fear of heights. Looking down we could see the outline of Tyrol. The sun was now on the back side of the planet.

Looking up I saw a massive structure high above us. If I had to guess it was a space station, or luxury space hotel.

"Experience Chariots of the Gods, the ride. Take the free

fall drop challenge today. Skip the slow boring elevator and experience the thrill of falling back to Tyrol at break neck speeds, leaving a trail of fire behind you. You'll be back on Tyrol in just a few minutes!" a voice from a video wall advertisement said.

A large video wall had come to life. We could see people inside spheres surrounded by fire as they entered into Tyrol's atmosphere falling back down to the planet's surface.

"We've got to do this!" I said, looking at Char.

She had a terrified look on her face.

"I'm not going on that!"

"But this is the amazing fun part of the date that I promised," I said, pretending to be sad.

Char smiled.

"Are you serious? Have you ever done this before?" she asked, looking a little less afraid than before.

"I've never done it. I didn't know this ride existed until now! It looks like they created a ride out of a safety feature. I'm pretty sure they're using the same technology that they use for emergency evacuations."

After watching the video a few times and a pretty lengthy discussion I was finally able to convince Char to go on the ride. We followed the line and made our way to the start of the ride. I wasn't even sure if the ride was still operational. Lucky for us it was completely automated! We were able to jump over the entry gates and climb into one of the spheres. Once inside the sphere we found some seats in the middle and strapped ourselves in.

"Welcome to Chariots of the Gods. This ride is not for the faint of heart! You may experience vertigo or motion sickness. Do not ride this ride if you are pregnant, have a heart condition or are in bad health," a recorded voice said.

Char grabbed my hand and squeezed it tightly. The anticipation of dropping was building up. I could feel a squirming sensation inside my stomach.

The audio recording had stopped.

"Are you going to push the button, or do you want me to?" Char asked.

"Which button?" I asked.

"Didn't you listen to the recording?"

"No I didn't..."

Suddenly we were falling, and falling fast. Char had pushed the button in the middle of our conversation. I could feel my stomach muscles squeezing tight with an involuntary reaction to falling. I looked over at Char. She was screaming and laughing at the same time. We were suddenly surrounded by fire and the ride became very bumpy despite the sphere's AG drive. The bumpy ride suddenly ended and the fire was gone. Our ride was smooth and calm as we glided the rest of the way down.

We couldn't see much because it was dark and in just a few minutes we were back on the ground.

"You were right! You'll never be able to top this date!" Char said, when we were back at Grindolstin.

"So I guess that means you want to go on another date. Are you free tomorrow?" I asked with a grin.

"I'll have to check with Orly," Char said in a pretend serious voice.

I laughed!

"Orly says yes! But you can't keep me out so late next time," she said, laughing and hugging me at the same time.

It was pretty late at night. I hoped she wouldn't get into any kind of trouble.

I kissed Char goodnight and headed for home.

CHAPTER XIX
THE RESCUE

I woke up late the next morning. I suspect that sleeping on the AG bed after getting in so late the night before was the cause of me waking up so late. Yesterday had been a perfect day and today was going to be even better! Today I was going home! I finally was really going home! I was going to find my daughter Nebs!

I ate breakfast and waited for Char to come but she never came. I decided after lunch to go down and see if I could find out anything.

"Where do you think you're going?" It was Storem.

He was waiting for me near the same place that he had dropped me off.

Storem was wearing his halo jump suit.

"I was hoping to run into you?" I said.

"They've got your friend. They picked her up for breaking curfew last night," Storem said.

I was worried and angry at the same time. I was angry with myself for getting Char into trouble and worried that something bad was going to happen to her because of me.

"What's going to happen to her?" I asked, I wasn't sure that I wanted to know the answer.

"Standard procedure is to keep her in custody and gather any intelligence as to why she broke curfew. Depending on what they find they'll reset her E-chip and possibly send her to the prison work camps."

"You don't have to worry about her. She won't tell them anything about you. I told her your life would be in danger if she said anything," I said, trying to reassure Storem.

"You don't understand! She doesn't have to tell them anything. All they have to do is review the video from her E-chip and see you on it. They probably already know you're here and are sending people to get you as we speak."

I felt terrible. It was all my fault. I shouldn't have been so reckless, especially with Storem's life, and now Char was in danger as well.

"We need to get out before they disable my halo access... I hope they haven't already done it. I was beginning to think they already had you," Storem said.

"You've been waiting for me... Why didn't you leave already to protect yourself?" I asked.

I was surprised that Storem would risk waiting for me.

"I'm here for the same reason I came back for you on

Ethos, it was the right thing to do. I'm doing things your way now, remember?" Storem said, with a grin.

"I can't just leave without her! I could never live with myself," I said.

"I knew you'd say that. We're not leaving. We're going to your library to come up with a plan," Storem said.

Looking out of the tunnel over the shoulder of Storem, I could see security guards entering the orchards.

"There's no time for me to get a suit on. I can see the men coming. You're going to have to jump with me like this. I'll hold my breath," I said to Storem.

The look on Storem's face told me that he thought my idea was a pretty stupid one. Storem turned and looked at the security team advancing towards us.

"Get the suit on! I'll hold them off with this," Storem had his replicating rail gun that he was so proud of.

"Those guys are low level. They only have stun guns," Storem said.

I started to put on my suit. I had an idea…

"Grid, change my access level to Programmer AI. Grid block access to all E-chips data from external sources starting 2 days ago for all the E-chips on Tyrol," I told the Grid in my mind.

"*Access granted, Your command is being executed,*" the Grid responded.

I wished I knew how much the Vice Director knew. I was worried that he might know about my ability to access the Grid with the Programmer AI access level.

"The Vice Director doesn't have access to information about the Programmer AI access level," the Grid replied.

I was surprised that the Grid had responded because I hadn't specifically requested information from the Grid.

There was a loud explosion, causing a lot of pain to my ears. The explosion came from Storem's gun, and it caused me to look up. I could see the security men running for cover.

"Exploding rounds! Hurry up! GET the suit on!" Storem yelled.

Storem continued to lay down covering fire while I got my suit on. My ears were ringing. I could feel a shock wave of air pressure every time one of Storem's rounds went off... There were flashes of blinding light with each round.

When I finished putting the halo suit on, Storem handed me the gun.

"Point that end that way and pull the trigger. She's all ready to go," Storem said with a grin on his face.

I fired the gun aiming for the middle of the orchard. The explosion from the round I fired was tremendous. The light coming from the explosion was blinding. I could see why Storem loved his gun.

Storem had put his helmet on, he tapped me on the shoulder. The tunnel filled up with blue light, everything went black and we were standing at the library.

"I've always wanted to do that, I hate those guys," Storem said, when he took off his helmet.

"You're not mad at me?" I asked sheepishly.

I felt bad for putting Storem's life in danger. He could never go back to his old life and it was all because of me.

"No I'm not mad. I've never felt better!" Storem said.

"So what's your plan? How many men do they have?" I asked.

"They're probably calling in reinforcements right now. If news of you and the illegal fights leak out, the VD is finished. He's going to do everything in his power to get to us, but he has to do it without drawing too much attention. We're going to need help. There's no way that just the two of us can walk in there and get your girl."

"I know some guys over there." I pointed towards the prison.

Storem smiled.

"You know, I heard a rumor that they stopped the fights over there," Storem said, nodding in the direction of the prison.

"I heard that the inmates won't kill the newbies anymore. When the newbies ask why, they say 'don't thank me, thank Zehn Mortalix.' So yeah, you've got quite the following over there."

I was shocked.

"Really? Is that true?"

"You know me. I don't lie and I don't tell shewa stories," Storem said.

"What do we do about the Warden?" I asked.

"You leave that up to me," Storem said, tapping his gun.

I told Storem about the hanger before we headed over to the prison; Storem didn't seem very surprised. We decided to go there and look for weapons or anything that we could find that might help us.

The hanger was pretty big so we decided to walk in opposite directions around the perimeter, looking for an armory or anything that looked useful. After searching for just a few minutes, I found a door to a room that I hadn't noticed before. Inside the room it looked like there were some kind of armored suits standing in place just waiting to be used. I called for Storem.

"Looks like you found some old AFI Units," Storem said when he got to me.

"Armored Flying Infantry Units," Storem said, after seeing the confused expression on my face.

"It's ancient technology. We don't want to mess with this junk. They stopped using AFIs a long time ago when they completely replaced the men in the infantry with mechanized units," Storem said.

"Couldn't we use these AFIs to fly the men over to Grindolstin?" I asked.

"No, flying AFIs would take a lot of training and we don't have time for it."

"Look, I found something else, what do you think it is?" I said, holding up a small backpack with shoulder straps and a belt. I opened a small pocket and I found a controller inside.

"I don't know what that is. It looks old! I'd just leave it, it's junk! We don't have a lot of time to mess around," Storem said.

I'd been so impressed with the technology that went into the hover bike and everything else I'd seen that was made by the Tyrols, I decided to investigate further.

I pulled out the controller from the small pocket and put the back pack on. I buckled the belt around my waist. The small power indicator light on the controller turned on. I pushed a button that looked like a menu button and a small holodisplay opened up just above the controller.

"It's an AG pack! I wonder how fast and high it goes. It even has a stealth mode," I said, after reading the display.

"We don't have time to find out how high it goes. I doubt it even works," Storem said, sounding more like his angry old-self.

I decided to bring the AG pack with me even if we didn't have time to test it.

Storem decided we should hide the halo jump device and suits in the library. He believed that his access level to use the device would be taken away at any time. He also didn't want the tech to be confiscated by the guards.

We didn't find anything else so we made our way towards the prison. I was actually excited to see my friends Charlie and Sargas. I didn't think I'd ever see them again. I wished I knew how we were going to rescue Char. I hoped that she was okay. I was glad that I had Storem on my side.

When we entered the main building, the sun was just starting to set. We saw a few inmates but nobody paid us much attention at first. A man finally recognized me and came running with his hands up in the air yelling my name. Before long we were completely surrounded by inmates. The inmates were asking questions so fast it was impossible to answer them. The men were so excited that their energy brought more inmates to see what all the commotion was about.

They wanted to know how I'd survived being banished from the prison. I answered the men's questions as fast as I could. By the time I was finished answering their questions, a new group of inmates would show up asking the same questions all over again. In the middle of explaining things I lost track of Storem.

I looked and found that Storem had made his way to the rear of the crowd. He was talking to my friend Charlie.

Storem must have sensed my gaze because he looked up at me. When our eyes met he nodded his head. Charlie saw me and waved at me. I could see that he was smiling. He was happy to see me. I walked over to Charlie.

"This saved my life, but it belongs with you. You saved my life Charlie," I said, handing him the little heater that had helped save my life.

Charlie smiled and his eyes looked moist, he was getting emotional.

"I didn't know synthetics could be so emotional," I said, with a smile.

The excitement from the newness of my arrival finally died down enough that I was able to explain to the men that I needed their help to rescue Char. A few of the weaker types indicated that they didn't want any part of the rescue and left. I felt hopeful when the vast majority of the men said they were in on the rescue.

"Everyone STAY where you are!" a loud voice said. The loud voice belonged to one of the prison guards and he was carrying a gun.

"STAND BACK! I have orders to shoot this man," another voice said coming from behind me.

I turned around to face a guard who was pointing his weapon in my direction.

I couldn't believe it! I'd made it this far only to be shot

by the guards! I didn't know what to say or do. I was hoping that Storem would do something. It's a horrible feeling knowing that you may die and there's absolutely nothing you can do about it. I wished I had my own gun.

"I wouldn't do that if I were you!" Storem said in a menacing voice. The expression on the guard's face changed from looking like he was in charge, to surprise, and then to fear.

Storem was standing just a few talens away from the guard with his weapon pointed directly at the man. The guard lowered his weapon and set it on the ground. The inmates started cheering!

"We weren't going to shoot him. We're just messing around," the guard said.

A few of the meaner looking inmates started to approach the guard, it looked like they wanted to do the man some harm.

"Stop right there!" Storem yelled at the inmates, pointing his gun in their direction.

From the sound of Storem's voice I could tell he was getting a little irritated.

The inmates immediately stopped walking towards the guard, obeying Storem's command.

"Where's the warden?" Storem asked the guards.

"The warden's gone. He left me in charge. We know why you're here. We want to help rescue the girl," the guard said with a grin.

"How do we know that we can trust you?" I asked the guard.

I wasn't sure that we could trust the guards.

The other guard that was still holding his gun pointed in Storem's direction, walked over and handed me his weapon, "What do you think now?" he asked.

I smiled, "I think we're good!"

"Good! Now that it's settled, I've got a plan!" Storem said, almost sounding excited.

Storem's plan was to have the prison guards report to the Vice Director's men that they had us in custody. When the Vice Director's men came over in their transporter from Grindolstin to pick us up, we'd take control of the transporter and use it to launch a surprise attack. According to Storem, most of the guards in Grindolstin were armed only with stun guns but there were also some heavily armed mechanized troops. Once we were in Grindolstin the inmates would create a diversion while me and Storem would go after Char.

"I'll take you over to the transporter hanger. With the guards' weapons we should be able to take control of it. Just in case we need a pilot, I know how to fly transporters. I used to be a pilot before they put me in here," Sargas said.

I didn't know that Sargas was a pilot but I was glad that he was coming because I knew that I could trust him.

It felt like many hours had passed until the transporter finally arrived. I hid behind the service modules waiting for the guards to take over the transporter. The transporter was one of the larger varieties. I wondered how many men were on board. I was pretty sure that it could hold several hundred men.

"There are three men, one pilot and two guards on board the transporter model 7Z2D. The transporter model 7Z2D has the capacity for 100 mechanized infantry units and supplies," the Grid replied in my mind.

I must be passing visual data from my E-chip to the Grid. I didn't have to tell the Grid what type of transporter I was looking at.

"Correct, the Programming AI access interface with your E-chip has been completed," the Grid responded.

I hadn't realized that an interface was being programmed but I guess it meant faster communication with the Grid.

The doors of the transporter opened and two armed men came down the ramp. I watched the prison guards raise their weapons and they persuaded the armed men to put down their weapons. The pilot came down the ramp a minute later with his arms up. We had control of the transporter.

The flight over to Grindolstin took longer than I thought it would. It took us several hours to arrive at the hanger. The prison inmates had been very effective in persuading the pilot to fly us over and act as if everything was normal in all his communications with the people at Grindolstin.

Massive hanger doors in the side of the Grindol mountains opened up to let us in. There were several transporters sitting on the ground inside the hanger. The hanger was much larger than I expected. I wondered how many men would be waiting for us when we landed.

"There are 100 men waiting. The Vice Director and his men are expecting trouble," the Grid responded to my questions.

"What would they do if they knew we were coming?" I asked Storem.

"They'd probably hang back and wait til everyone was off the transporter, then surround us when we're in the tunnel that leads to the city," Storem said.

"They know we're coming," I said to Storem, quietly so nobody else could hear.

Storem squinted his eyes and with a confused look on his face he asked, "How would you know that?"

"The Grid," I replied.

"What can we do if they know we're here?" I asked.

"First, we'd need to clear the hanger. Then we'd have to fight our way into the city and hope they don't use your girl as a hostage. They'd probably threaten to kill her unless we give ourselves up. If we gave ourselves up they'd kill us all, including the girl. If they know we're coming we should fly out of here now or all of us will end up dead," Storem said, quietly, not wanting the men to hear what he was saying.

"I think it's a trap. They know we're coming," I said, loud enough for all the men to hear.

"Is that right?" one of the inmates said, sticking a knife into the ribs of the pilot. The pilot squirmed in his chair interrupting the landing process. The engines suddenly lost power and we hit the ground hard.

The men that were standing lost their footing and fell to the ground. The transporter was not sitting flat on the ground; we were sitting on an angle.

"If they didn't know something was up, they do now!" I heard somebody yell. Some of the men started arguing. I could barely make out a few curse words.

"The landing gear is broken!" The pilot yelled, over the noise.

"The doors won't open, how do we get out?" somebody yelled.

"There's a small hatch on the top of the cargo hold. You can get out that way," the pilot yelled.

"They've got us surrounded," Storem said, pointing towards the cockpit window.

Storem was right. I could see armed men running into the hanger.

"Do not exit the transporter with a weapon or you'll be shot! We have you surrounded," a voice said, coming over the transporter's audio system.

Everyone in the transporter went quiet.

"I'm not going out without a fight," Sargas said, determined.

"They'll shoot you. We can only go out one at a time. It won't be a fight. You'll just die," Storem said, sounding irritated.

It must be hard for a man of Storem's experience to be stuck working with amateurs.

I felt responsible for all these men. It was all my fault. I didn't want them to die.

"I'll go out first, it's me they want," I said.

"Nobody's going out! Fly us out of here!" Storem said to Sargas.

Sargas chucked the pilot out of his chair and took over the controls. The transporter's engines roared to life. We lifted off the ground. The men outside on the ground started shooting at the transporter, but it wasn't having any effect. The explosive rounds bounced harmlessly off the ship's hull thanks to the transporter's deflector shields. The hanger doors were closing. It didn't look like we were going to make it out.

The men in the hanger scattered, looking for cover as the cannons on the transporter began firing back at them.

The hanger was filling up with smoke. I could see some of the men lying on the ground of the hanger, they were dead or injured shot by the transporter's cannons.

"They're bringing out the big guns!" Storem said pointing in the direction of some large mechanized artillery units. The artillery units were pointing their massive canons our way.

"Those guns are big enough to take us out!" Storem yelled.

"I see'em!" Sargas yelled.

The transporter rocked hard to one side and then back again in the opposite direction as it crashed hard against the hanger wall. We'd taken a hit from one of the artillery units.

I saw several trails of smoke heading towards the mechanized artillery units and then there was a massive explosion. Flames and smoke filled the hanger. Sargas must have fired some missiles at the artillery units.

The transporter slammed hard into the ground! The engines were screaming. I couldn't see anything through all the smoke that was blocking the view from the cockpit window.

"I think the ceiling has completely collapsed on top of us. I CAN'T get the transporter OFF the ground!" Sargas yelled, over the noise of the engines.

"I'm surprised we're still alive. I can't believe you fired those missiles inside the hanger! That was a bold move!"

Storem yelled.

"The engines won't SHUT OFF!" Sargas yelled.

The transporter was filling up with smoke. I could hear men coughing and cursing. There was a terrible smell of burnt metal.

"There's a maintenance hatch right under us! Maybe we can use it to get out!" Sargas yelled.

Sargus pushed a button on the control panel and the floor behind his seat opened up to a small passageway with a ladder inside. I hated small spaces but I decided I wanted to get off this transporter more than I hated small spaces. I grabbed my bag and my gun and started down the ladder before anyone could stop me. Once I got to the bottom of the ladder there was barely enough room to move. The transporter was leaning just a little bit to one side. I decided to take the tunnel that led away from the lean of the craft.

I crawled through the tunnel dragging my gear behind me until I was able to pull myself outside of the ship. The transporter was leaning just enough to leave space for a man to crawl out from underneath it. I stuck my head back inside the hatch and yelled, letting the men know that I was out. I wasn't sure if anyone could hear me over the noise coming from the engines. I crawled to the edge of the ship. I wanted to make sure the area was clear before I left the cover of the ship. The hanger was full of dust and smoke and had gone mostly dark. I could barely see anything. The main source of light was coming from the transporter's engines. The engine light was deflecting off the piles of debris that had fallen from the ceiling, making it extremely difficult to see. I wanted to see if there were any men out there waiting for us to leave the ship.

I waited a few minutes... I didn't hear or see anything out of the ordinary. I decided to risk it. I crawled out from under the transporter. Sargas was right, a large portion of the ceiling had collapsed on top of the transporter; it wasn't going anywhere.

There was a large pile of rocks and debris where the tunnel to the city used to be. We were trapped inside the hanger. The missiles had completely destroyed the mechanized artillery units but the force of the explosions had blocked our way into the city. Red emergency lights turned on in sections of the hanger that hadn't collapsed.

"Sorry about the mess!" It was Sargas. The men were coming out from the transporter.

"I think we'd be worse off if it hadn't been for you," I heard someone say from behind Sargas.

I wondered if there was another way out of the hanger.

"There is a walkway attached to the ceiling with several access points to tunnels that lead to the main tunnel to the city," the Grid responded to my question.

I could see a map of the hanger in my mind. The ceiling was very high. It would be next to impossible to get to the walkway.

I pulled out the AG Pack from my bag and put it on.

Maybe I could make it to the walkway with the AG Pack. I could tell that Storem was skeptical by the expression on his face.

I pulled up the menu on the controller and selected stealth mode. I heard someone gasp for air.

"Whoa, where did Zehn go?" one of the men asked.

"I'm right here. I'm using stealth mode," I replied, waving my arms in the direction of the man.

He looked towards me but I could tell from the empty look in his eyes that he couldn't see me.

"They'll be able to pick up your heat signature. You might as well turn the stealth mode off," Storem said, impatiently.

I could see my hands, arms and my weapon, they looked normal but everything else I looked at was distorted and blurry. With stealth mode on it was as if I were looking at the world from under water. My normal field of view was much less and everything on the edges was black and blurry.

I turned off the stealth mode and my vision returned to normal. I decided to head towards the hanger where the walkway was.

A large explosion knocked me to the ground. My ears were ringing and my body felt like it had been crushed in a vice. An incoming explosive round had landed just a few talens from where I'd been standing. I hoped that none of the men had been hit. Looking towards the men,

I couldn't see much because of all the dust and lack of light.

"Put down your weapons and surrender. You are surrounded. There is no possibility of escape," the almost human, yet robotic voice of a mechanized troop commander said.

I decided it was by design that the voices of the mechs were so menacing and not quite human sounding.

The mechs' fearsome red eyes pierced the darkness as they closed in on us. The mechs were too powerful. They were military mechs. We didn't have enough weapons to defeat them. We might get lucky and take out a few units if we tried to fight them. The mechs walked upright and were shaped to look like human soldiers. The mechs' heads were made to almost look like human skulls. They didn't wear clothing over their shiny metallic exoskeletons. They were killing machines, and unlike humans they didn't have any fear and wouldn't show any mercy.

"Obey our commands or you will die," the mechanized troop commander said.

The mechs moved much faster than humans. It would be impossible to outrun them. Their visual sensors allowed them to see in the dark and they could even see through smoke. Our only options were surrender or die. The men put down their weapons. I turned on stealth mode.

The mechs began scanning the men's ID-chips and organizing them into a line and putting restraints on their hands. I decided to stand where I was instead of forming up in the line. I would know really quick if the mechs' vision sensors could detect me...

Several of the mechs came within a few talens of me but made no indication that they'd detected me. I didn't dare move my feet with all the dust and debris on the floor of the hanger. I was afraid since I hadn't obeyed the mech commander's initial orders, the mechs would shoot to kill if I was detected. I didn't want to die like this. I was so close to getting home. I could feel my heart racing.

"Grid, change my access to Programmer AI. Restore all blocked memories on all E-chips. Disable the ability for memories to be blocked on all E-chips. Change all climate and geo-engineering system settings to be optimal-for-life on Tyrol and any other world where they are in place," I said to the Grid, in my mind.

If I was going to die today, I wanted to fix as many things as I could.

I wished that Nebs would know how much I loved her. I wanted her to know that I hadn't given up. I wished everyone could see how corrupt the Vice Director and the SGC were.

"*Access Granted. Your commands are being executed,*" the Grid replied to my mind.

"Grid, give me control over all mechanized troops on Tyrol."

I wasn't sure if I could get access to military units but it was worth a try.

"Access Granted. All Mechanized Troops and Commanders are waiting for your command," the Grid replied.

"Troop Commanders, order your troops to not kill any humans," I said to the Grid.

"All Mechanized Troops have been set to non-lethal," the Grid responded.

"Troop Commanders, take the Vice Directer and his men into custody and put them in the detention facility," I said to the Grid.

"Your commands are being executed," the Grid responded.

"They're just leaving... The mechs are leaving." It was Sargas.

Despite the blurry vision caused by stealth mode, I could see confused and relieved looks on the men's faces as they watched the mechs walking away.

I walked over next to Storem and turned off stealth mode.

"They didn't even take our weapons," I heard one of the men saying in the middle of a conversation.

"I'm going to follow them and see if I can find a way in to the city," I said to Storem, who was looking at me, shaking his head in disbelief.

"I can't believe those bots didn't detect you. They had to have their heat sensors on in the dark," Storem said, still shaking his head.

"We don't have time. I'm going to follow them! I'll let you know what I find," I said to Storem.

Storem nodded his head and before he could say anything, I turned stealth mode back on and started after the mechs.

The mechs went to the debris filled entrance and they started removing the debris. There were other maintenance robots also working to clear the debris.

"Grid, can you give me an estimated time of when the main entrance to the city will be available?" I asked, hoping that it wouldn't take days.

"Estimated time to clear the debris is two days," the Grid responded.

We didn't have two days to wait.

"Grid, has the Vice Director and his men been taken into custody?" I asked, hoping there were other mechs inside the city. I was worried about Char and the people in the city.

"The Vice Director has evacuated the city and ordered all his men to follow. The city is on lock-down, anti-personnel measures will initiate in 30 minutes," the Grid responded.

Why would the Vice Director evacuate the city I wondered.

"The Vice Director is a fugitive of the law. All law enforcement measures have been put in place for his capture.

The Vice Director is wanted for illegal human trafficking, illegal gambling rings, illegal treatment of inmates, murder of inmates, corruption, bribing public officials, taking bribes..."

"How is this possible?" I asked the Grid, interrupting the long list of crimes committed by the Vice Director.

"An official investigation into the corruption of the Vice Director was initiated by the Law Enforcement AI," the Grid responded.

I couldn't believe it. When I wished that everyone could see how corrupt the Vice Director was, my Programmer AI access must have initiated the investigation. I didn't have time to enjoy the news.

I wanted to know what the anti-personnel measures were and how to turn them off.

"The anti-personnel measures are mechanized troops that will destroy all living persons in the city," The Grid responded to my question even though I hadn't asked the Grid specifically.

"Grid, stop all anti-personnel measures immediately!" I heard myself say out loud.

"Access Denied! The anti-personnel measures can only be stopped manually in the city command center," the Grid responded.

My mind was racing. I didn't know what to do. I didn't know if it would be possible to get to the command center in 30 minutes. I could see a map of the hanger and the city in my mind. The grid was showing me how to get to the command center. I needed to get to the walkway that was on the ceiling of the hanger. It led to some tunnels that come out above the President's Mansion. The command center was in the basement of the mansion.

I decided to see if I could fly the AG Pack back to the men. I wanted Storem to know what I knew. I pushed the controls up and I left the ground a lot faster than I expected. I was sure that I was going to crash into the ceiling. The acceleration upwards was insane, just before I hit the ceiling I stopped moving upwards and found myself floating a few talens away from the ceiling. I couldn't believe my luck! The AG Pack had collision avoidance. I wasn't surprised by the collision avoidance. The same people of Tyrol who'd made the amazing hover bike and lights that never needed to be replaced had also made this AG Pack.

Without the fear of running into anything I pushed the controls in the direction of the men. I don't think it would ever be possible to get used to the insane acceleration of this AG Pack. Flying this AG Pack would never get boring.

I landed next to Storem who was sitting on some debris.

"They're evacuating the city and they've started anti-personnel measures. We've got less than 30 minutes to shut them off!"

"TURN OFF THE STEALTH MODE!" Storem yelled at me.

I'd startled Storem so much he'd nearly fallen off his seat. I'd forgotten that stealth mode was on and I turned it off.

After talking to Storem we quickly decided that I should use the AG Pack to try and enter the city. Storem said he would do what he could to find a way to follow me. Storem was hopeful that there would be a maintenance vehicle with a lift that he could use to reach the walkway.

"Before you go, take this with you," Storem said, handing me his gun.

"I've got it set on a rotation of armor piercing, and exploding rounds, it should be able to take out pretty much anything you encounter," Storem said, looking directly at me with a serious look on his face.

"Thanks," I said, feeling thankful that Storem was on my side.

CHAPTER XX
ANTI-PERSONNEL MEASURES

I activated the stealth mode on the AG pack and took off following the directions of the map that the Grid had shown me. I found the walkway. It was long and narrow with just enough room for a person to walk on it. Looking down to the end of the walkway I could see a blast door.

When I made it to the door I found out that it was locked.

"Grid, open this blast door!"

"*Access denied,*" the Grid responded.

"What do you mean, DENIED!" I yelled at the Grid.

"*The anti-personnel measures don't allow you permission to open the door,*" the Grid responded.

I didn't have time for this. A lot of people were going to die. The thought, '*go to the main tunnel*' came to my mind.

It didn't make any sense, why would I go to the main tunnel. It was going to take over two days to clear it... The thought, '*go to the main tunnel*' came again.

I didn't have a better idea so I took off for the main tunnel. I quickly saw the reason why. Some of the maintenance bots were using laser torches to cut up the debris. I grabbed a torch and it took me less than a minute to cut my way through the blast door.

I flew through the tunnels following the map that the Grid showed me. When I finally came out of the tunnels, I was high up on the rocks above the President's Mansion. I turned off stealth mode so I could see better. I didn't see anyone. The normal line of people waiting at the gates was gone.

A message was playing over the city's broadcast system. "Attention citizens there has been a cave-in caused by a small earthquake. Please return to your homes and make sure all your family members are accounted for. Please return to your homes to avoid being in violation of the emergency curfew."

The normal appearance of a blue sky above the city was now red, most likely to indicate there was an emergency.

I wondered how much time I had left before the mechs would start killing everyone in the city.

"The anti-personnel measures will start in 15 minutes and 35 seconds," the Grid responded to my question.

I turned on stealth mode, pushed the AG Pack controls, and headed for the detention center. I came in fast, trusting that the AG Pack wouldn't let me crash into the ground. The AG Pack performed perfectly. I landed without crashing. I got my gun ready and entered into the detention center. I didn't meet any resistance. None of the guards were there. I went to the control room and found Char's cell number. I could see her through the camera. She was laying on the bed in her cell. She was on her back staring up a the ceiling. I opened the door to Char's cell remotely. She didn't move. I felt fear raising inside of me. If something bad had happened to her, I didn't know if I'd ever be able to get over it.

I made my way as fast as I could to Char's cell worrying that she was gone. I'd never get to hear her cheerful voice and make her laugh. The thought of Char being dead was making me emotional and angry. I was sad that it had taken me so long to realize how much I loved her, and I was angry at the Vice Director

Char was lying motionless on the bed when I entered her cell.

"Char, are you okay?" I asked, nervous that I wouldn't get a response.

"Zehn, is that you? You can't be here because you're immortal," Char said quietly as she sat up looking in my direction. There was a sad and blank expression on her face. I could tell that she'd been crying because her eyes were red.

"I can't see you probably because I'm dead and you're not. I can hear you..." Char said, before I had a chance to respond.

I'd forgotten to turn off stealth mode.

"I'm right here!" I said, turning off stealth mode.

Char smiled ran to me and hugged me tight.

"How can you be here? You can't die, you're immortal," Char asked.

"I came to get you as soon as I could... The Vice Director, I mean the President has evacuated the city and anyone that stays here is going to die! We've got to get to the control center to stop it," I said, grabbing Char's hand and pulling her towards the exit.

"I'm already dead!" Char said, tugging on my hand stopping my momentum. I turned around to look at her.

"You're not dead!" I said, confused at why she would say and think she was dead.

"The guard told me that I was going to go to sleep and I'd never wake up again. When I heard your voice, I remembered when you had to leave for Ethos and how sad I was when I thought I'd never see you again. I remember things that I didn't know I'd forgotten. I remember things about my dad. I remember everything," Char said, squeezing my hand.

Char was remembering everything because I'd used the programmer AI access to unblocked her E-chip!

I hugged her tightly and gave her a kiss.

"If you were dead do you think you would have felt that?" I asked her with a smile.

Char's face was turning red and she smiled at me. Her

eyes were shining and all the redness was gone.

"We're not dead!" Char said, hugging me tight again.

"We'll be dead if we don't get to the control center!" I grabbed Char's hand and headed for the exit.

We headed across the lawn towards the President's Mansion once we were outside of the detention center.

As we were approaching the mansion a loud siren sounded and then a recorded voice said, "WARNING! Lethal security measures have been activated. DO NOT enter the building, or you may be injured or killed."

'I've got to go in there," I said looking down at Char.

She had a frightened look on her face.

"I know you think you're immortal but I don't want you to go in there," Char said, quietly in a pleading voice that I'd never heard before.

"If I don't go in there, everyone will die," I said.

"No matter what happens, I want you to know that I love you. Promise me you won't follow me in there," I said to Char before she had time to respond.

Char nodded, "I love you. Please come back!" she said.

I hugged her and said, "I'll be back in a few minutes. You find a place to hide. If I don't come out in 10 minutes, you need to get out of here. The city will be crawling with mechs with orders to kill everyone."

"Grid, order all the mechanized troops to stand down!" I said to the Grid in my mind.

It was worth a try.

"Access Denied, the Mechanized Troops can only accept authorized orders from the control room," the Grid responded.

After Char left and I believed she was at a safe distance, I turned on stealth mode and headed for the main entrance with my gun ready.

I could see from the Grid that each entrance to the mansion was guarded by mechanized soldiers. The Grid was showing me the security features of the building. I was glad that Storem had let me use his gun.

The door to the main entrance didn't open when I approached it. The door must be secured or it didn't detect me with stealth mode turned on. I stepped back to what I thought was a safe distance and opened fire.

I felt a blast of super heated air as I watched the door explode. The blast of hot air pushed me backwards and probably would've knocked me to the ground if it wasn't for the AG pack's compensation.

I could see red eyes peering through the smoke left over from the explosion from behind where the door used to be. There were maybe a half a dozen mechs coming towards me.

An explosion knocked me backwards. An exploding shell hit into the ground were I'd been just seconds before. My ears were ringing from the noise of both explosions.

I decided to use the AG pack to get some elevation. I went high above the mansion. Looking down I could see the mechs exiting the building. The mechs were not looking in my direction. The AG pack's stealth mode was blocking any heat signature. The mechs hadn't detected me.

I looked to see if I could see Char anywhere. I didn't see her.

I decided to stay in the air. My thinking was that as soon as I fired my weapon the mechs would be able to detect me and they'd fire on my location. If I was constantly moving they'd have less chance of hitting me. I'd have to take one shot at a time, otherwise they might be able to guess my future positions and take me out.

The mechs had formed into a line protecting the entrance to the mansion. I decided to risk a pass at the mechs to see if my plan would work. I fired my gun aiming at the line of mechs. My first shot was a direct hit. I hit one of the mechs directly in the chest, it felt good to watch it explode. I felt a blast of air pushing me forward and heard multiple explosions. The mechs had fired almost in unison at the position where I'd taken my shot. I was far enough away that the AG Pack's deflector shields were able to stop any shrapnel that came from the explosions.

Suddenly there was an extremely loud explosion. I was pretty sure that my hearing had suffered irreversible damage. I looked down at the line of mechs and instead of seeing the mechanized soldiers, I saw a small crater filled with smoke and melted scrap metal. I could feel the intense heat on my face. The heat was rising from the melted metal in the crater. The smell of burnt metal and residue of the exploded shells was not a pleasant one.

I heard men cheering. It was Storem! Somehow he and the men had made it into the city. Storem was holding a rocket launcher. It must have been him that took out the line of mechs. Storem and the men had taken cover behind the building that was adjacent to the President's Mansion. I turned off stealth mode and landed next to Storem.

"How did you know you wouldn't take me out with that shot? Where did you get that rocket launcher?" I asked Storem before he had time to answer my first question.

"I didn't," Storem said with a smile.

"I saw where your last shot came from. It looked like you were far enough away," Storem said, after seeing the disbelief on my face.

"I found this rocket launcher in the hanger," Storem said.

"What's your plan? I asked Storem after getting over my initial shock.

I wondered how much time we had left.

"*The anti-personnel measures will activate in 4 minutes and 22 seconds,*" the Grid informed me.

"The mechs are on auto mode so their tactics are predictable. They'll send overwhelming force to our location. We'll keep them occupied while you get into the command center from the top," Storem said, pointing up towards the roof of the mansion.

"Be safe!" It was Char. She was holding a weapon.

"You look great, by the way," Char said in a cheerful voice, winking at me.

I was worried. I didn't want anything to happen to her.

"I want to help. It's my home," Char said, after seeing the look of disapproval on my face.

I didn't have time to argue. I hugged Char, "You be safe," I said.

I turned on stealth mode and headed for the roof of the mansion. The door on top of the mansion was locked. I decided that I was really going to enjoy blowing up that door. I moved to a safe distance and opened up on the door. I didn't see any red eyes piercing through the smoke. I entered the mansion following the map in my head. I was heading for the control center which was located in the basement.

The décor of the mansion was very fine. Everywhere I looked, I saw impressive paintings, vases and sculptures. The hallways were wide enough for large groups of guests to pass through without feeling crowded. The stone floors had intricate designs built into them.

A large section of the wall exploded as I turned the

corner of the hallway that led towards one of the many sitting rooms. I dropped to the ground trying to see where the shot came from. I wondered how the mechs had detected me... I didn't have time to find out. I heard fast, heavy foot steps of mechs coming from behind me. Looking forward into the large sitting room I saw that it was filling up with mechs. I was trapped! I decided the shot came from behind me. I hoped that there were less mechs coming down the hallway than there were in the sitting room. I decided to go back the way I'd came.

I opened fire with Storem's gun as I turned the corner and entered into the hallway. The explosions from the rounds hitting the mechs knocked me backwards. I felt extreme heat on my face coming from the melting metal of the mechs that I'd hit. The burning debris was filling the hallway with smoke causing me to cough. The smell from the burning metal was not helping the situation. I used the AG Pack and flew through the smoke with my gun ready, hoping that there weren't any more troops in the hallway. I didn't see any troops when I made it through the smoke. I needed to find another way to the basement. I couldn't see any other way when I checked the map that the Grid was showing me in my mind.

I heard fast, heavy foot steps coming from behind me. The mechs I'd seen in the sitting room were coming for me! I didn't have much time! It would be impossible for me to take them all out even with Storem's gun.

I suddenly knew what to do. Using the AG pack I flew up as close as I could to the top of the ceiling in the hallway hoping the troops would pass under me. I was counting on them not being able to detect me in stealth mode. The mechs are much taller than average people and thankfully the hallway was high enough that the mechs didn't detect me.

I didn't see any more mechs on my way to the basement. The door to the control room was at the end of a narrow hallway. A loud explosion of hot air knocked me into the wall hard as I stepped into the narrow hallway. I felt a sharp pain in my shoulder which had taken the worst part of the collision with the wall. The security system must have detected me somehow. I thought the stealth mode on the AG Pack would've kept me hidden.

"The floor sensors can detect intruders by the change in weight," the Grid informed me.

"What other sensors are there?" I asked the Grid.

The hallway only had floor sensors, the Grid showed me in my mind.

I decided to use my AG pack to fly to the door at the end of the hallway. I could hear the heavy footsteps of mechs. The footsteps were loud and fast. The mechs were coming for me. I was having a hard time breathing. I think most of the oxygen had been burned off by the explosion, or it was a feature of the security system. My mind wasn't thinking clearly. I remembered I needed to open the door. I turned to look back when I reached the door. I could see mechs entering the hallway...

A massive explosion knocked me off my feet. The AG pack wasn't able to compensate for the blast because I felt a sharp pain in my head which had hit the ground hard. I dropped the gun when I hit the ground. I couldn't breathe. No matter how hard I tried I couldn't breathe in any air. The air had been knocked out of my lungs by the explosion. I began to panic, wondering if I'd ever be able to breathe again. My lungs were finally able to gasp for air after what felt like an extremely long amount of time had passed. The hallway was filled with smoke and burning debris. I wasn't getting enough air..

"DON'T JUST LAY THERE! GET OUT OF THE WAY SO WE CAN OPEN THE DOOR!"

Storem was looking down at me and shaking his head with a disgusted look on his face. He pulled me to my feet and pushed me away from the door. I heard another explosion and felt someone pulling me.

"The door's not opening!" I heard someone say.

I felt myself sitting down... I could finally breathe again. I looked into Char's pretty face. I was surprised to see her. I wondered how she could see me and realized that the explosions must have damaged the AG Pack.

"Are you okay?" Char asked, kneeling down and taking a good look at me.

"How did you get here?" I asked her.

"He told us we had to get in here because it was too quiet. He was afraid that you'd be in trouble because none of the bots were attacking us," Char said pointing at Storem.

I felt the blast and heard a loud explosion. Storem had fired at more of the mechs entering the hallway.

"We're all going to be dead if we don't get that door opened!" Storem yelled.

"Try this!" I stood up and pulled out the laser torch that I'd used on the blast door.

"Well aren't you full of surprises!" Storem said, taking the torch with a big grin on his face.

"Cover us!" Storem said, handing me his gun.

I didn't wait for any mechs to enter the hallway. I held down the trigger sending a steady flow of rounds towards the entrance. The noise from the rounds made me sure that I was going to need to see an ear doctor if we made it out alive.

Storem cut open the door and yelled something that sounded like give me a few seconds as he ran into the control room. I couldn't understand what he was trying to tell us over the exploding shells...

Someone from behind me grabbed my arm. Storem must have finished deactivating the anti-personnel measures.

"We're good you can stop shooting," the man yelled in my ear.

I stop firing the gun and looked over at Char. She was smiling at me. I felt myself smiling back at her.

Storem came out of the control room and walked over.

"Sorry, kid. I had to take out those bots. Otherwise we'd never've made it!"

The blast from Storem's rocket launcher must have been the one that nearly took me out and disabled my AG Pack.

"How did you know you wouldn't kill me with that shot?" I asked.

"I didn't," Storem smiled.

"It just felt like the right thing to do," Storem said, mimicking my voice and sounding very sarcastic.

I could feel my ears turning red.

"So are you finally ready to defend your title?" I asked Storem.

"Sure kid. You did good!" Storem said, ignoring my defend-your-title question.

"What are we going to do now?" Char asked.

"After I recover, we're going to find my daughter Nebs!"

I could hardly believe those words were coming out of my mouth. If I had my halo device on me, I would've left for Zendreo at that very moment.

"You have to take me with you! Remember? You promised to take me with you," Char said, making a face that was impossible to say no to.

I felt happy. My insides were ready to explode. I was

more happy then I knew was possible. Leena was right. I was feeling better than I ever imagined possible especially after how low I'd been on Ethos. I hoped to find Leena again one day so I could tell her she was right and thank her.

"I can't wait for you to see Zendreo it's going to blow your mind!" I said, hugging Char.

Char's eyes opened wide, "I just remembered I need to find my mom and Nanna they don't know where I'm at."

I looked at Storem; he nodded in Char's direction indicating that I should go with her.

"Let's meet up back here tomorrow. We've got some planning to do. We need to get these men back over to the prison, they can't stay here... Take this with you just in case you run into any stray bots," Storem said handing me his gun.

"Don't worry, I've got a few spares laying around," Storem said, when he saw the look on my face.

"You should come with us," Char said to Storem before I had a chance to thank him.

Storem's eyes widened just a little and he frowned. I could tell that he was surprised at Char's invitation.

"No, you go without me, besides don't you two want some alone time?"

"Please... I think you should come for dinner," Char

persisted, turning her head to one side and smiling at Storem.

Storem looked at me and I was pretty sure without talking he was asking me if it was okay to say no.

"Come with us it'll be fun," I said, nodding my head.

It was obvious to me that Storem didn't want to come but he was having a hard time saying no to the face that Char was making.

"If I come it doesn't mean we're going to be friends and start making this a regular thing," Storem said, frowning and squinting his eyes.

I could tell that he was still thinking and maybe trying to come up with some reason why he couldn't come with us.

"I am getting hungry... Let me talk with some of the men first and then we can go," Storem said, after he'd finished thinking about it.

"I want him to meet my mom," Char whispered, when Storem was out of earshot.

"Okay but I don't think he's the dating type," I whispered back.

When we arrived at Char's home I could see the relief in her Mom's eyes. The home was newer than her Nanna's but not nearly as nice. You had to walk up several levels of stairs just to get to the front door of the small apartment. The apartment complex was made out of bricks. It wasn't carved out of the rock like her Nanna's house. There were identical apartment buildings on both sides of a narrow street facing each other. The windows were so tiny, they seemed useless. The designer of these apartment buildings was probably suffering from depression.

Char's mom must have seen us coming through one of the semi-useless windows because she came out to meet us before we got to the door. Her mom was a little taller than Char and she had blonde hair like her daughter. I think it's obvious to anyone with eyes where Char got her beauty.

"Where have you been? It's been more than a day..." Char's mom asked her daughter ignoring me and Storem.

"These two rescued me from the detention center and we had to fight some mechs..."

"What? Why would you need to be rescued?" her mom interrupted Char mid-sentence.

Me and Storem waited quietly while Char tried to explain what had happened to her. We responded with a nod or quick yes whenever her mom would look at us with questioning eyes.

"I'm sorry. I'm being rude it sounds like this discussion could take awhile and now is not the right time for it. Come inside," Char's mom said after listening a few minutes to her daughter's explaining.

The inside of the apartment was small but it was a lot less depressing than the outside. The walls were painted with bright colors and it was well lit. There were paintings on the walls and one of them was of a little girl with blonde hair. I knew the little girl had to be Char when I saw it.

"My husband was an artist, it's a painting of Chara when she was a little girl," Char's mom said, confirming my belief when she saw me staring at the painting.

"He's a great artist. I wish I could've met him."

"Chara's told me a lot about you, I'm glad we've finally met."

"I've invited them to stay for dinner if that's okay," Char informed her mother.

"It is getting about that time, why don't you go get your Grandma and bring her to dinner, she's been worried sick about you."

"I'll go with you," I said looking over at Storem.

His eyes narrowed, he frowned, and he glared at me for just a split second telling me that he didn't appreciate being left alone with Char's mom. His glaring look was fast and he was facing away from Char's mom so I don't think she noticed.

I couldn't have planned it better. Char was a natural at match making. She was smiling at me when I grabbed her hand. We headed out for her Nanna's house before Storem could say anything.

...

Storem took a deep breath and seemed to relax a little when we returned with Nanna. It was obvious to everyone he felt out of place being left alone with an attractive woman that he didn't know.

"Storem has been telling me all about you while you were gone," Char's mom said to me as we sat down at the table.

"He said there isn't a better man than you for my daughter."

I could feel myself smiling.

It felt good to hear those words because I knew that Storem never says anything nice about anyone. Char's face was turning red. I guessed that she was probably embarrassed to have her love life being discussed by her mom in front of everyone.

"He told me about the mechs and how you went all by yourself to rescue Char. He said he's never seen true greatness until he met you. He told me what you did on Ethos..."

I was surprised by her words. When I looked over at Storem, he nodded and said, "This doesn't mean I like you and you don't get your title back."

I could feel myself smiling.

"I wouldn't be here without him. He's one of the best men I've ever known. I'm lucky to have him as a friend." I said.

Char's Mom was smiling back at me. Storem had a rare smile. I'm not sure what had changed in him but he was no longer the man that I'd met in the detention center. He had a light about him that I'd never noticed before.

"What's this title-thing you two keep talking about?" Char asked.

After I explained the story with a little help from Storem, everyone laughed but me. I was still mad about Storem fighting dirty.

When dinner was over Storem left for the President's Mansion. I said goodbye to Char and took Nanna home.

After saying goodbye to Nanna I started out for my little campsite. With the pain in my head and shoulder, I knew the only way I was going to get any sleep was in my AG bed. When I finally made it back to my camp site and saw my bed I remembered something I wanted to do for the people of Grindolstin.

"Grid change my access level to Programmer AI. Grid halo jump to the hanger of the city of Grindolstin on Tyrol, food replicators one per family and AG beds enough for everyone in the city covertly."

I wasn't so sure about the covertly-part but I decided it was worth a try.

"Access granted, executing your commands estimated duration will be two or three weeks, shipments will arrive at different intervals to maintain the covert request," the Grid responded to my mind.

I couldn't wait the see the faces and hear what the people would say when they didn't have to wait in food lines and were sleeping in real beds. I was so excited that I wasn't sure if I'd be able to get any sleep. I laid down in my AG bed and the pain in my shoulder started to go away. Maybe tomorrow I'd finally be able to plan my trip home to find Nebs...

...

"Wake up! You're not going to believe this!" It was Char.

My body was telling me that I needed more sleep but I knew that would be impossible now that Char was here. My shoulder was feeling a lot better thanks to a good night's sleep in the AG bed.

Char dragged me to my feet and started pulling me down one of the tunnels.

"You've got to come see the sky! It's blue! I've never seen it look like this before ever! There are clouds!"

Char took me to some of the vents that she had opened. "Look at how light it is out there, it's brighter than I've ever seen it. Did you do something to the mirrors? Did you turn them off somehow?"

The sky was a beautiful light blue and it was full of white fluffy clouds.

I told Char about when I was in the hanger and I thought

the mechs might kill me, I asked the Grid to change the mirrors.

I wondered what season it was supposed to be.

"The mirrors settings have been changed by the Programmer AI to optimal-for-life which means Tyrol will slowly warm up to avoid flooding which would be devastating to life. Tyrol is entering into the spring season," the Grid informed me.

"It's spring time," I let Char know.

I was surprised at how fast the climate could be affected by the system of mirrors. I'd expected that the sky would be lighter but I didn't anticipate seeing clouds this soon.

"I don't even know what that means but it's amazing we've got to tell everyone!" Char said, jumping up and down.

She took off running back towards the city. My body was still tired from the day before so I didn't try to keep up with her. I took my time walking and thinking about how amazing it was going to be for the people to see a blue sky something I'd taken for granted my entire life.

When I reached Grindolstin the streets were full of people talking about the possibilities of a blue sky with clouds and warmer temperatures. The procession of people was on it's way to the main doors of the city to see if the rumors were true. The hum of excited voices reminded me of fans lining up to go to a playoff game at the academy

"The old stories are true! The sky is blue! The sky is

blue!"

It was an older woman who was going against the flow of people. The woman was practically running. She must have recognized me because she came over and hugged me. I was going with the flow of people so nobody had seen my face and noticed me until now.

"Thank you, I have no words! This is the best day of my life and I'm old. Thank you so much, words cannot express how amazing this day is," the woman said with tears in her eyes.

I wondered what she'd say after she finally slept in a real bed, it just might be the best night of her life...

It was a humbling experience to see people so excited over something as simple as a blue sky and a few clouds.

After the woman finally stopped thanking me and let me go, I noticed that the procession of people had stopped moving forward because there were too many people in the streets. I decided to take one of the almost empty side streets that led away from the crowds of people and head over to the President's Mansion to meet with Storem.

"Have you seen the blue sky that everyone's talking about?" Storem asked, when I found him near the President's Mansion.

"Yes I've seen it."

"You wouldn't have anything to do with it would you? I've been meaning to ask you why the VD was suddenly under investigation and how you knew that they were waiting for us."

I decided that I could trust Storem so I explained to him how he'd given me the Programmer AI access to the Grid.

"You realize having the Programmer AI access makes you the most powerful man in the galaxy?" Storem asked, shaking his head in disbelief after I'd finished explaining everything.

I knew Storem was right. I hadn't given it much thought until that moment.

"This explains why we've been getting a lot of strange messages in the COMM center. The News AIs have been broadcasting incriminating videos of government officials. People are rioting all over across the galaxy. The SGC has declared military law and has been sending out messages that a coup is taking place. They are deploying mechs everywhere."

I explained to Storem how, when I was in the hanger and I thought the mechs might kill me, I wished that everyone could see how corrupt the Director and the SGC were.

"You're definitely not subtle. This has you written all over it," Storem replied, when I was done explaining.

"What do you think I should do?"

"I think for now, we just have to wait and see what happens. I'd try to get rid of that Programmer AI access if I were you because that kind of power changes a man for good."

I suddenly knew that I needed to get to Zendreo, and fast, before things got out of control. I needed to find Nebs.

CHAPTER XXI
THE RESISTANCE

It was a cold and rainy morning. The summer had come and gone. Winter was arriving. Nebia woke up in her tent feeling cold. She couldn't remember the last time she had eaten a good meal and felt happy and content. The cold rain seemed to tell her to give up because only the dark days of winter were ahead.

Nebia had joined the resistance which at first had seemed like a brave and smart thing to do, but now she wasn't sure anymore. The mechs sent by the SGC to put down the resistance had been extremely effective. Most of the people in the resistance that she knew had been captured or killed. Living on the fringes of society for years out in the woods and sleeping on the ground in a tent in the cold, didn't help bolster her decision to join the resistance.

She had as good a reason as anyone to join the resistance. The SGC had killed her mother, killed her grandparents and framed her father for the murders. The SGC had sent her father off world to the prison on Tyrol. He might as well be dead because she knew she'd never see him again.

Nebia was no longer a little, fragile girl. She'd grown up fast living in foster care. Nebia hadn't done well in foster care. She wouldn't allow herself to bond with the foster families. She was never going to let anyone hurt her again. She wouldn't let anyone in.

When Nebia had joined the resistance she believed that her father and grandmother would approve. She didn't know why but she still wanted to make her father proud even though he wasn't around to see it. Nebia wanted to prove to herself and to everyone that she wasn't a quitter.

The resistance was formed by people who believed that the SGC was responsible for the death of Senator Mortalix, Nebia's grandmother. The people believed the SGC had killed the Senator because she was in the process of exposing corruption at the highest levels of government. The SGC had been caught messing around with people's E-chips.

The first wave of mechs had killed men, women and children indiscriminately. The SGC had sent a message of their absolute power. They'd made one mistake. The SGC had miscalculated the resolve of the Zendreon people and instead of having the desired effect of ending the resistance quickly, the resistance grew.

Nebia was well-known in the resistance because of her grandmother. Many people looked to her for strength and leadership...

"She has to see this! Where's Nebia?" Nebia heard someone say in the middle of a conversation.

"I have to see what?" Nebia said, crawling out of her tent into the rain.

A man handed her a display device.

"This is playing everywhere, on every channel, on every billboard. It's playing everywhere. You're not going to believe it!" the man said.

Nebia wasn't listening to the man. She was looking at the screen in complete disbelief. She saw a man that looked exactly like her dad sitting in a cage talking to a beautiful woman. The man was wearing strange clothes that barely covered him. The man had huge muscles much bigger than she remembered her father having.

When she heard the man's voice, even though he was speaking in a strange language, she knew it was her dad! Her father's face looked exactly the same as she remembered him, he hadn't aged a day. Nebia wished that she could understand what he was saying...

"What's he saying?" Nebia asked the man who gave her the device.

The man took the display device from Nebia, changed the language setting, and handed the device back to her.

"I'm fighting for justice and my daughter because she needs me. I'm fighting for my friend, Char, who I promised I'd come back to after this is all done. I'm fighting for the old man that gave me the Eroken armor... I'm probably fighting for my daughter and justice the most..." Nebia heard her father saying to the woman in the video.

Nebia could feel tears coming to her eyes. She quickly wiped them away, hoping nobody noticed.

The scene on the device changed. Two men were fighting in an arena full of people. Nebia recognized almost immediately that one of the men was her father. Her father looked small and almost out of place compared to the man he was fighting. The large man was fighting with a mace on a chain. It looked like the larger man was winning. Nebia watched in horror and disbelief as the mace hit her father in the head, knocking his lifeless body to the ground. The crowd in the arena went silent for a few seconds and then they were cheering!

Nebia had seen her mother die, and now seeing her father die was causing her to relive the grief of that terrible day all over again. She didn't want to watch anymore, and she was about to throw the device into a nearby tree when someone grabbed her arm.

"Keep watching this next part!" the man said.

Nebia saw her father's lifeless body moving slowly... he was getting up. He wasn't dead! Her father got up on his knees and then onto his feet. He stumbled around looking for his sword and when he found it, he held his sword ready to defend himself. The huge man that he was fighting against was gone. He'd already left the arena. The noise from the crowd was the loudest she'd heard it, even coming from the display device it was loud. The crowd began yelling her father's name over and over again. The half-full arena was filling up as people came rushing in to see what the cheering was about.

The scene changed to a close up of her father's face which was covered in blood.

"How are you still alive? You should be dead," a man said to Nebia's father in the video.

"I can't die. I have a daughter and she needs me... Nebia needs me." Her father said slowly in Pythar.

"Does anyone know what he's saying?" a man's voice asked in the video.

"I think he's speaking in Zendreon. He's got a serious head injury. He's not making any sense," another man said.

"I'm making perfect sense. You promised I could go home to my daughter. Take me home!" Nebia's father said slowly, on the verge of losing consciousness.

Nebia could no longer control her feelings, she sat down on the ground sobbing in the rain. She missed her dad now more than ever before.

The scene on the device changed. Nebia couldn't take her eyes off of the screen and through her sobs, continued watching.

A man was talking to her father.

"You didn't think I was going to leave you here forever did you?" the man asked her father.

Nebia watched her father struggling with his emotions. She felt more love for her father than she could ever remember. Watching her father struggle for words, she realized how much he loved her.

"I did, I did..." her father said after a long pause.

"Nobody wanted to leave you. It was the President. He made us leave without you. He doesn't know that I'm here."

"I can't believe you're here..." Nebia's father replied.

"How can you be here? Won't the President notice that you're gone?" Nebia's father asked.

"I'm on vacation," the man said with a smile.

"You're on vacation! I can't believe you're on vacation and here!" her father blurted out.

"I can't believe I'm here either. The smell of this place isn't exactly up to my vacation standards," the man said with a smile.

"I thought you didn't like me?" Nebia's father asked.

"I don't like you. I don't like anyone. In my line of work, I can't afford to like people. I made you a promise and I intend to keep my promise," the man said, looking sincere.

"I recognize this man! Has he come to take you home?" said a happy female voice.

It was the beautiful woman that Nebia had seen talking

to her father in the cage.

"Yes, he can take me home..." her father paused in the middle of his sentence looking at the woman.

"I promised the Sar that I wouldn't leave..." Nebia's father said slowly.

"Don't worry about him. The Sar will understand. Promise me that you will bring your daughter back to meet me," the woman said.

The woman took off a ring and handed it to Nebia's father.

Nebia realized that a Sar must be someone important, maybe someone like a king, and the woman talking was a princess.

"Give this to your daughter to wear. I'm loaning it to her. When she comes to meet me, she can return it..." the woman said, hugging her father.

Her father looked over at the man who nodded.

"I promise. I will bring her to meet you," Nebia's father said.

Nebia stopped sobbing and for the first time in a very long time she felt at peace. She wasn't sure how, but she knew she was going to see her father again and it was going to be soon.

"My dad is coming home!" Nebia said, looking up at the circle of people who had gathered to see her reaction to the video.

Nebia noticed writing on the screen of the device.

Attention:

Nebia Mortalix of *Zendreo* this *emergency broadcast* is on a loop and coming directly from your father **Zehn Mortalix**. The E-chip videos in this broadcast have been verified as authentic by the SGC Official News AI.

This broadcast will continue on all SGC channels please continue watching for more details...

DICTIONARY

Andros Mountains [an-drose]
A rugged coastal mountain range that is home to the Great Zelecon Wildlife Refuge. The mountain range is also famous for the zelecon pine trees which are the tallest trees in the known galaxy. The coastal climate makes these mountains some of the greenest in the galaxy.

AG
Anti-gravity technology

BR scanner
A bone repairs scanner is a medical device that is used to repair bone fractures in a matter of minutes.

Deklious Space Port [deck-lee-us]
The space port is a large abandoned city floating on one of the oceans of Tyrol. The city has a space elevator that allows people and materials to be moved into orbit and transferred to waiting space ships.

E-chip
Enhancement chip. The chip is implanted at birth. The chip has a connection to the optic and auditory nerves and records all life events which can be accessed by the person like normal memories. Most people are so used to accessing the chip they can't tell the difference

between the chip and memories stored in the brain. The memories can be transferred from the chip storage system and shared with others.

Ethos
Ethos is the second planet from it's sun which is a red dwarf in the Eotheena [ee-oh-th-eena] solar system. The civilizations on Ethos are primitive. Ethos has a large moon that is almost one quarter the size of the planet it orbits.

Edum Teramus [ee-duhm ter-ah-mus]
The capital city of the Teramus civilization on the planet Ethos. Edum Teramus is a coastal city with a primitive population.

Erok Civilization [ee-rauk]
The Erok Civilization comes from the planet Ethos. The Erokens were conquered by the Termus after many terrible wars. The Erokens are a very religious people, they believe in one God that rules the universe.

FodHopper
Insects with long powerful hind legs which are great for jumping. Ancient civilizations on Zendreo ground up the insects and made them in to a drink.

H36
The element used to power reactors, with small amounts of H36 space ships can fold space and travel large distances at speeds faster than light.

Life support containment shields
Invisible to the naked eye these shields maintain a comfortable environment for humans capable of sustaining life in very harsh environments including ones without breathable air.

Perthasol[pirth-ah-saul]
A Zendreon coastal city that is world famous for it's pastries. Perthasol is located between the coast and the Andros Mountains.

Sar [Sahr]
A title given to royalty similar to a king on the planet Ethos by the Teramus civilization.

Sara [Sahrah]
A title given to the daughter of a Sar on the planet Ethos by the Teramus civilization. A sara is also known as a princess.

SGC
Supreme Galactic Council is the governing body of more than 50 planets from more than 50 different star systems. Only worlds with a certain level of technology are allowed to join the SGC as full-fledged members. Primus is the most technologically advanced world in the known galaxy and home to the SGC.

Talen
Zendreon unit of measurement defining length or displacement. 1 talen is equivalent to 15 inches or 38 centimeters.

Tyderius
An ancient language on the planet Tyrol that is no longer spoken.

Tyrol
The second planet in the Tyrolia solar system with more h36 than any other known world.

VD
Vice Director: The Vice Director to the Director of the Supreme Galactic Council is the second most powerful leader in the SGC.

Voratar [voor-ah-tar]
Top predator cat like animal. The animal has large claws and large teeth.

Zefer
Zendreon unit of measurement defining weight 1 zefer is equivalent to 1.3 lbs or just over ½ a kilogram.

Zendreo [zen-dreey-oh]
Zendreo is the world made famous by Zehn Mortalix and is the third planet of seven in the Zertzies [zerht-zees] solar system.

Zorok
A large predator animal similar to a bear.

Printed by Amazon Italia Logistica S.r.l.
Torrazza Piemonte (TO), Italy

12829841R00244